喚醒你的英文語感！

Get a Feel for English !

從死背到活用自如的單字學習奇蹟！

職場單字
進化術

作者：商英教父 Quentin Brand

100個
關鍵字

Vocabulary
Upgrade
Biz
Your
English

貝塔語言出版
Beta Multimedia Publishing

IRT 語言測驗中心
Language Testing Center

Introduction 前言

The aims of this book are to give you the meaning of the most frequently used and important key words in business English; to show you how to use these words in sentences; and to show you how to combine the words you're learning with other words to improve your English as quickly and as easily as possible.

Each key word has its own entry in the dictionary, giving important grammar and pronunciation information, information about synonyms, information about the other words which are most frequently used with the key word, and lots of examples. There are also language development tasks in each entry to help you consolidate your understanding of how to use the key word and its partners.

You can use this book as a reference tool, to check the meaning and use of new words, to find out what verbs and what adjectives are most frequently used with words you already know and to help you develop your vocabulary in an active way.

I hope you find the book useful!

本書的目的是要針對商業英文中最常用到與最重要的關鍵字來呈現它們的「意義」，說明這些字在句子中要「如何使用」，並告訴各位所學到的字跟其他的字要「如何搭配使用」，使各位能以最快與最輕鬆的方式來強化英文實力。

每個關鍵字首先會呈現重要的文法和發音資料、同義字的資料、最常跟關鍵字搭配使用的搭配詞表格，然後是豐富又實用的例句。最後則是填空練習題，以協助各位更加了解要怎麼使用關鍵字和它的搭配詞。

各位可以把本書當作參考工具，以查閱新字的意義與用法，找出你已經認識的單字最常搭配哪些動詞和形容詞，並積極幫助自己增進字彙。

希望各位覺得這本書有用！

Contents 目録

★ 100 個關鍵字

本書使用說明

本書使用起來非常簡便，先呈現一個關鍵字的相關資料，繼而說明關鍵字的使用方法，最後再讓讀者透過練習，更熟悉關鍵字。

各位可以將本書當成參考工具，以快速查閱所用到的字，也可以依照下列五個簡單的步驟來累積自己的字彙。

Step 1

先看頁面最上方的關鍵字相關資訊，包括音標、中譯、同義字。

Step 2

看搭配詞表。熟悉搭配在關鍵字前後的動詞、形容詞以及介系詞有哪些。

Step 3

接著看例句，這時即可充分了解它們跟搭配詞表有什麼關係。並請特別注意觀察句子中的粗體字要如何使用。

Step 4

完成填空題。

Step 5

最後請對照載於本書最後的解答。對答案時，再次思考自己答錯的地方，能更加深學習印象。每次複習這本書，都可以重複練習唷！

❶ 搭配在前面的動詞	❷ 搭配的形容詞		❸ 關鍵字	❹ 搭配在後面的動詞
do perform undertake carry out conduct	careful detailed in-depth thorough extensive preliminary brief further more	statistical cost-benefit economic financial strategic market	**analysis (of sth.)**	show n.p./v.p. suggest n.p./v.p. reveal n.p./v.p. demonstrate n.p./v.p. provide n.p. confirm n.p./v.p. indicate n.p. indicate that v.p.

❶ 本欄呈現最常和關鍵字搭配使用、而且放在關鍵字「前面」的動詞。意思相似的動詞編成一組。每組中,最常用的動詞擺在最前面,最少用的動詞擺在最後面。

❷ 本欄呈現最常與關鍵字搭配使用的形容詞。意義相似的字列在一組。

❸ 本欄呈現關鍵字本身、搭配的介系詞。此外,有些關鍵字的後面並不是接動詞,而是接本欄下半部的複合名詞。

❹ 本欄呈現最常和關鍵字搭配使用、而且放在關鍵字「後面」的動詞。意思相似的動詞編成一組。每組中,最常用的動詞擺在最前面,最少用的動詞擺在最後面。

★ 兩種句型

你可以用搭配詞表非常迅速而簡單地造出理想又道地的英文句子。有時候你會有兩個句型可以使用。

■ 句型1:

直接以左邊的第一欄為起點,並從左到右:主詞＋搭配在前面的動詞＋形容詞(有需要的話)＋關鍵字等等。

例如:We **did more** analysis and found the problem.。

■ 句型2：

以左邊的第二欄為起點，形容詞＋關鍵字＋搭配在後面的動詞等等。

例如：A **detailed financial** analysis will **show** more results.。

　　句型2通常比句型1高級，在寫作時也比較有用。有些關鍵字則只有一種句型。

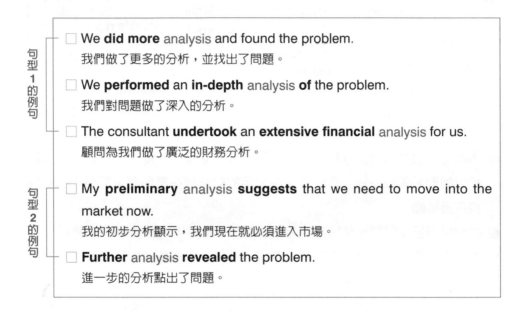

句型1的例句

　☐ We **did more** analysis and found the problem.
　　我們做了更多的分析，並找出了問題。

　☐ We **performed** an **in-depth** analysis **of** the problem.
　　我們對問題做了深入的分析。

　☐ The consultant **undertook** an **extensive financial** analysis for us.
　　顧問為我們做了廣泛的財務分析。

句型2的例句

　☐ My **preliminary** analysis **suggests** that we need to move into the market now.
　　我的初步分析顯示，我們現在就必須進入市場。

　☐ **Further** analysis **revealed** the problem.
　　進一步的分析點出了問題。

★ 注意形容詞用法

　　有些搭配詞表會有不只一個形容詞欄位。在正常情況下，每個形容詞欄位只能用一個形容詞。例如你可以說 an in-depth financial analysis，但不能說 a thorough preliminary analysis，或是 a economic financial analysis。這聽起來很奇怪！

　　假如從每個欄位中各取一個形容詞，你就可以在名詞前面使用連串的形容詞：an in-depth financial analysis。像這樣使用連串的形容詞會讓你的意思更準確，也更專業：more thorough cost-benefit analysis 就優於 more analysis of the cost-benefits which is very thorough。

填填看

請從「搭配詞表」中選出適當的字,完成下面句子。例解請見第333~353頁。

☐ We (1)_____ a (2)_____ analysis. We looked at all the numbers in detail.

☐ We (3)_____ a (4)_____ analysis. We didn't have much time so we just did it very quickly.

☐ If we have more time, we can (5)_____ (6)_____ analysis. Maybe we can find the result.

❺ 填填看練習題:一面作習題,一面思考句子的意義,並小心動詞的時態。全部完成再對答案。常常好幾個答案都有可能可以填入,因為有很多字的意思是類似的。

　　如果想進一步練習使用不同商業領域的關鍵名詞,以及談論不同的商業話題,各位可能會想參考以同樣100個專業名詞所寫成的姊妹作:《商英教父的單字勝經》。

| 1 | **advertisement**
[ˌædvɚˈtaɪzmənt] | 可數名詞 廣告 |

搭配在前面 的動詞	搭配的形容詞		關鍵字	搭配在後面 的動詞
place put take out run show make produce	full-page half-page good new misleading a series of + ★ +s	TV television radio newspaper magazine print Internet viral	**advertisement/ ad/advert (for sth.)**	go out run show n.p. feature n.p.

★為關鍵字

小叮嚀 英式英語常會將advertisement縮簡為advert。

好搭例句

◎ **MP3-01**

☐ We will **place full-page** ads in all the major newspapers.
我們將在各大報上刊登全版廣告。

☐ The client wants to **put** an advert in the newspaper.
客戶想在報紙上打廣告。

☐ Let's **take out** an ad in all the national newspapers.
我們在所有的全國性報紙上買廣告吧。

☐ We **ran** the advert for three weeks on national television.
我們在全國性電視上播了三週廣告。

☐ They **showed** a **misleading** ad and were told to remove it.
他們播了一則誤導廣告，被下令停播。

☐ They are really good at **making funny radio** adverts.
他們十分擅長做搞笑的電台廣告。

☐ We are **producing** a **new series of TV** ads.
我們在製作一系列新的電視廣告。

☐ The **TV** advert will **go out** on Tuesday nights at 9:00 p.m.
這則電視廣告將在星期二晚上九點播出。

☐ The **radio** ad will **run** for one week.
這則電台廣告會播一星期。

☐ The **print** advert **shows** a car on a mountain road.
這則平面廣告所呈現的是車子在山路上跑。

☐ This **series of viral** ads will **feature** our product being used by
famous actresses.
這個系列的病毒式廣告將主打知名女演員使用我們的產品。

✎ 填填看

請從「搭配詞表」中選出適當的字，完成下面句子。例解請見第333~353頁。

☐ Let's **(1)**_____ a **(2)**_____ advertisement in the
newspaper. Then most readers will surely notice it.

☐ I think **(3)**_____ ads are more effective than **(4)**_____
adverts. People can read them more slowly and get more information
about the product.

☐ It will be very expensive to **(5)**_____ a **(6)**_____ ad for
two weeks. Air time is very expensive.

☐ It will be very expensive to **(7)**_____ a whole **(8)**_____
of TV adverts. Why don't we just **(9)**_____ one?

☐ The **(10)**_____ ad **(11)**_____ last Sunday night and will
(12)_____ for one week every night.

□ We want the (13)_____ advert to (14)_____ the product very clearly.

□ The (15)_____ ad will (16)_____ our product being used by Tiger Woods.

□ Some people said the (17)_____ advert was (18)_____ －they liked it, others said it was (19)_____, they didn't think the product was so good, but they all agreed it was the first time they had seen the product depicted in that way.

進階造句

請嘗試利用「搭配詞表」中的字彙，造出想要表達的句子。

_____

_____

_____

_____

_____

_____

_____

| 2 | **advertising**
[ˈædvɚˌtaɪzɪŋ] | 不可數名詞 廣告 |

2 advertising [ˈædvɚˌtaɪzɪŋ] 不可數名詞 廣告

搭配在前面的動詞	搭配的形容詞		關鍵字
use	television/TV	national	
get	Internet	local	
create	media	great	**advertising**
	free		
increase	direct		

 好搭例句　　　　　　　　　　　　　　 **MP3-02**

☐ We have decided to **use local** advertising only, as **national** advertising is too expensive.
我們決定只推地方廣告，因為全國廣告太貴了。

☐ We are tying to **get** some **free** advertising with the local TV station.
我們正設法向地方電視台爭取一些免費廣告。

☐ We used an ad agency and they **created** some **great** advertising for us.
我們找了一家廣告公司，他們幫我們做了一些很棒的廣告。

☐ We need to **increase** our **media** advertising. Our **direct** advertising is not working well enough.
我們需要增加我們的媒體廣告。我們的直接廣告成效不夠好。

填填看

請從「搭配詞表」中選出適當的字，完成下面句子。例解請見第333~353頁。

☐ If we (1)＿＿＿＿＿ (2)＿＿＿＿＿ advertising, using TV and radio together, will we get a better result?

☐ The product is old, and people don't like it any more, so we need to (3)_____ some really (4)_____ advertising to change the image of the product.

☐ We already have enough (5)_____ advertising targeting our current customers. We need to (6)_____ our (7)_____ advertising so that more people know about the product.

☐ Obviously (8)_____ advertising, you know, just in this city, is cheaper than (9)_____ advertising.

☐ Can we (10)_____ some (11)_____ advertising from our clients? Ask them to tell their customers about how good our product is?

進階造句

請嘗試利用「搭配詞表」中的字彙，造出想要表達的句子。

_____

_____

_____

_____

_____

_____

_____

_____

| 3 | **agenda**
[ə`dʒɛndə] | 可數名詞 議程 |

搭配在前面的動詞	搭配的形容詞	關鍵字
have approve draft draw up include sth. on put sth. on remove sth. from go through turn to the next item on stick to	meeting conference	**agenda (for sth.)**

 好搭例句　　　　　　　　　　　　◉ MP3-03

☐ Do we **have** an agenda **for** this meeting?
我們這場會議有議程嗎？

☐ I'm still waiting for my boss to **approve** the agenda. When he's done that, I'll send it over to you.
我還在等我老闆核准議程。等他一完成，我就把它寄給你。

☐ I'm **drafting** the agenda at the moment. Is there anything you would like me to **put on** it?
我目前正在草擬議程。你有沒有要我把什麼東西給列進去？

☐ Can you please **draw up** a **conference** agenda and let me have it by next week?
能不能麻煩你擬一份會議議程，並在下星期前交給我？

☐ Please **include** this item **on** the next **meeting** agenda.

麻煩把這點納入下次的開會議程中。

☐ I've been looking at the **conference** agenda. I think we will need to **remove this item from** the agenda.

我看了會議議程。我想我們需要把這點從議程中剔除。

☐ I'd like to **go through** the agenda as quickly as possible.

我想要盡快把議程討論完。

☐ I'd like to **turn to the next item on** the agenda now.

我想要現在就進入下一項議程。

☐ Can you please **stick to** the agenda, otherwise we will run out of time.

能不能麻煩你照著議程走？否則我們會把時間給耗光。

填填看

請從「搭配詞表」中選出適當的字，完成下面句子。例解請見第333~353頁。

☐ I'll ask Tracy to **(1)**_____ an agenda **(2)**_____ the meeting next week. Please send me a list of the items you want to **(3)**_____ the agenda.

☐ Let's **(4)**_____ the agenda. If we have time at the end of the meeting we can discuss any other business.

☐ We **(5)**_____ that item from the **(6)**_____ agenda because it's already too long. Remember, the conference only lasts two days, so we can't include everything.

☐ Have they **(7)**_____ the **(8)**_____ agenda? I need to know what we are going to discuss so that I can prepare myself for the meeting.

☐ Do we (9)_____ an agenda? No? Why not? Tracy, I thought I asked you to (10)_____ one?

進階造句

請嘗試利用「搭配詞表」中的字彙，造出想要表達的句子。

_____

_____

_____

_____

_____

_____

_____

_____

4	**alliance** [ə`laɪəns]	可數名詞 聯盟

搭配在前面的動詞	搭配的形容詞	關鍵字
form make forge create establish seek break off	strategic strong mutually beneficial	**alliance (with sb.)**

 好搭例句 ◎ **MP3-04**

☐ We are going to **form** a **strategic** alliance **with** our supplier to see if we can develop the market.
我們要跟我們的供應商組成策略聯盟，以看看我們能不能打開市場。

☐ We need to study the advantages and disadvantages of **making** an alliance **with** them.
我們需要研究一下跟他們結盟的優缺點。

☐ It's important to **forge strong** alliances **with** partners and customers.
跟夥伴及顧客構成堅強的同盟很重要。

☐ We try to **create mutually beneficial** alliances **with** all our customers. It helps to bring in repeat business.
我們試圖跟所有的顧客形成互惠的同盟。這有助於招攬回頭生意。

☐ We are in the process of **establishing** an alliance **with** one of the other companies in the market. This will help us to increase market share.
我們正在跟市場上的另一家公司建立同盟。這將有助於我們提高市占率。

☐ We are **seeking** an alliance **with** an overseas company.
我們在跟一家海外公司尋求結盟。

☐ We found them to be very unreliable, so we had to **break off** the alliance.

我們發現他們非常不可靠，所以我們不得不中止結盟。

填填看

請從「搭配詞表」中選出適當的字，完成下面句子。例解請見第333~353頁。

☐ I spent a long time trying to (1)_____ an alliance with them, and then they (2)_____ the alliance with no explanation!

☐ We are (3)_____ an alliance with an overseas company. We hope they will agree.

☐ We hope that this arrangement will lead to a (4)_____ alliance between our companies, and that together we can develop the market.

☐ A (5)_____ alliance will help us to develop into other markets.

進階造句

請嘗試利用「搭配詞表」中的字彙，造出想要表達的句子。

_____

_____

_____

_____

_____

5	**analysis** [ə`næləsɪs]	可數名詞 分析 同義字：research、assessment

搭配在前面 的動詞	搭配的形容詞		關鍵字	搭配在後面的動詞
do perform undertake carry out conduct	careful detailed in-depth thorough extensive preliminary brief further more	statistical cost-benefit economic financial strategic market	**analysis (of sth.)**	show n.p./v.p. suggest n.p./v.p. reveal n.p./v.p. demonstrate n.p./v.p. provide n.p. confirm n.p./v.p. indicate n.p. indicate that v.p.

 好搭例句   ◎ **MP3-05**

☐ We **did more** analysis and found the problem.
我們做了更多的分析，並找出了問題。

☐ We **performed** an **in-depth** analysis **of** the problem.
我們對問題做了深入的分析。

☐ The consultant **undertook** an **extensive financial** analysis for us.
顧問為我們做了廣泛的財務分析。

☐ We **carried out** a **brief market** analysis and found some interesting
results. 我們做了簡略的市場分析，並發現了一些有趣的結果。

☐ We need to **conduct further strategic** analysis before we reach a
decision. 在形成決議前，我們需要做進一步的策略分析。

☐ A **detailed financial** analysis will **show** more results.
詳細的財務分析會透露出更多的結果。

☐ My **preliminary** analysis **suggests** that we need to move into the market now.

我的初步分析顯示，我們現在就必須進入市場。

☐ **Further** analysis **revealed** the problem.

進一步的分析點出了問題。

☐ The **cost-benefit** analysis **provided** some interesting data.

成本效益分析提供了一些有趣的資料。

☐ **Economic** analysis **confirmed** our hunch that the market is shrinking.

經濟分析證實了我們對於市場正在萎縮的預判。

☐ The **market** analysis we have carried out **demonstrates** that there is growing demand for our product.

我們所做的市場分析證明，外界對我們產品的需求正在提高。

☐ The analysis **indicates that** we are on the right track.

分析指出，我們走對了方向。

☐ Our analysis **indicates** a problem in sector 4.

我們的分析指出，第四區有問題。

填填看

請從「搭配詞表」中選出適當的字，完成下面句子。例解請見第333~353頁。

☐ We (1)_____ a (2)_____ analysis. We looked at all the numbers in detail.

☐ We (3)_____ a (4)_____ analysis. We didn't have much time so we just did it very quickly.

☐ If we have more time, we can (5)_____ (6)_____ analysis. Maybe we can find the result.

☐ Before investing my money in this company, I need to (7)_____ (8)_____ (9)_____ analysis.

- (10)_____ analysis (11)_____ that the market conditions are pretty good for us.

- (12)_____ (13)_____ analysis (14)_____ that although the production costs are high, profits will also be high.

- We need to (15)_____ some (16)_____ analysis before we make a decision about how to deal with our competitors.

- Let's (17)_____ some more analysis (18)_____ the situation before we make a decision.

進階造句

請嘗試利用「搭配詞表」中的字彙，造出想要表達的句子。

_____

_____

_____

_____

_____

_____

_____

	6	**appointment** [əˋpɔɪntmənt]	可數名詞 約定

搭配在前面的動詞		搭配的形容詞	關鍵字
have have got make arrange change confirm	keep cancel fail to keep fail to turn up for miss	important pressing urgent	**appointment** **(to V)** **(with sb.)**

 好搭例句

◉ **MP3-06**

☐ Hello. I **have** an **important** appointment **with** Mr. Braddock. Can you let him know I've arrived?

哈囉，我跟布拉多克先生有個重要的約會。你能不能通知他說我到了？

☐ Sorry, I have to go. I**'ve got** an **urgent** appointment **with** Kate.

抱歉，我必須走了。我跟凱特有個緊急約會。

☐ I'd like to **make** an appointment **with** Colin **to** talk about the new project.

我想跟柯林約一下，以談談新案子。

☐ We **arranged** the appointment last week, but they **cancelled** it at the last moment.

我們上星期安排了約會，但他們在最後一刻取消了。

☐ It's very difficult to find time to meet with him. He's always **missing** our appointments.

要找時間跟他見面非常困難。他總是錯過我們的約會。

☐ I'm calling to **confirm** my appointment. Is it still on?

我打電話來是要確認我的約會。還是不變嗎？

☐ Look, I know you are very busy next week. Will you still be able to **keep** our appointment? Or do you want to **change** it to some other time?

聽好，我知道你下星期非常忙。你還是有辦法赴約嗎？或者你想要改成別的時間？

☐ She **failed to keep** our **pressing** appointment! She simply did not turn up! How rude is that!

她沒來赴我們的急約！她竟然沒出現！真是太失禮了！

☐ I must apologize for **failing to turn up for** our appointment. My little boy was suddenly taken sick at school, and I had no time to contact you.

我必須為了沒能赴約而道歉。我兒子在上學時突然生病了，所以我沒時間跟你聯絡。

填填看

請從「搭配詞表」中選出適當的字，完成下面句子。例解請見第333~353頁。

☐ We (1)_____ the appointment last week. I'm just calling to (2)_____. Is it still happening?

☐ Hi, I'm calling to (3)_____ our appointment next week. Can we (4)_____ it to the following week? It's not (5)_____.

☐ No, that time is not convenient for me, I already (6)_____ an appointment at that time.

☐ I've (7)_____ an (8)_____ appointment with my director this week to talk about the proposal I presented to him last Friday.

☐ I must **(9)**_____ my doctor's appointment today. I keep
(10)_____ it.

☐ She **(11)**_____ our appointment this morning, and she is not at
her desk. Can you call her home and see if everything is okay with her?

☐ I have an appointment **(12)**_____ Mr. Greed **(13)**_____
talk about the new development.

進階造句

請嘗試利用「搭配詞表」中的字彙，造出想要表達的句子。

7	**assessment** [əˋsɛsmənt]	可數名詞 評估 同義字：analysis、research

搭配在前面 的動詞	搭配的形容詞		關鍵字	搭配在後面 的動詞
do carry out make undertake provide	accurate general initial rough comprehensive detailed careful annual monthly	environmental impact risk self tax	**assessment (of sth.)**	suggest n.p./v.p. show n.p./v.p. be

 好搭例句 　　　　　　　　　　　　　　◎ MP3-07

☐ We've **made** a **detailed** assessment **of** the market and come up with a strategy.

我們對市場做了詳細的評估，並提出了一套策略。

☐ Before we decide to build the new factory we need to **carry out** a **comprehensive environmental** assessment.

在決定蓋新廠前，我們要先做好廣泛的環境評估。

☐ Can you **provide** me with a **rough** assessment **of** how long the project will take?

你能不能替我大約估一下，這個案子要做多久？

☐ In your **initial tax** assessment you stated revenue of 3.5 million. Is that an **accurate** assessment?

在初步的稅務評估中，你說營收會有350萬。那是準確的評估嗎？

☐ Before the interview with the HR manager, you need to **do** a **self** assessment **of** your performance this past year.

在跟人力資源經理面談前，你要先對自己過去這一年來的表現做一番自我評估。

☐ We need to **undertake** a very **careful risk** assessment before investing in those markets.

在投資這些市場前，我們要先做非常仔細的風險評估。

☐ My **initial impact** assessment **suggested** that the factory would have a very bad influence on the surrounding neighborhood.

我的初步影響評估顯示，這座工廠會嚴重危害到周邊的鄰近地區。

☐ My **general** assessment **of** the situation **is** not good.

我對於局勢的整體評估是不太有利。

☐ Our **annual tax** assessment **shows** we made a loss last year. Is that right?

我們的年度稅務評估顯示，我們去年是虧錢的，對嗎？

填填看

請從「搭配詞表」中選出適當的字，完成下面句子。例解請見第333~353頁。

☐ We need to (1)_____ a (2)_____ (3)_____ assessment before we think about building a bigger factory. We must know what the impact on the environment will be.

☐ My (4)_____ assessment of the project timeline (5)_____ about three months. But that's just a guess.

☐ You need to (6)_____ me with a (7)_____ assessment of your performance. Then we can talk about your bonus.

☐ We are in the process of (8)＿＿＿＿＿＿ our (9)＿＿＿＿＿＿

(10)＿＿＿＿＿＿ assessment. Thank goodness you only have to pay

taxes once a year because it's really a big job!

☐ We have (11)＿＿＿＿＿＿ a (12)＿＿＿＿＿＿ (13)＿＿＿＿＿＿

assessment. We looked carefully at all the variables, and we believe the

bond market is not a good place to invest right now.

☐ We need an (14)＿＿＿＿＿＿ assessment of the situation. Please

don't make any mistakes.

☐ Our (15)＿＿＿＿＿＿ assessment (16)＿＿＿＿＿＿ the market

(17)＿＿＿＿＿＿ that the profit will be huge. We are still doing more

analysis, however, and can let you know the results next week.

進階造句

請嘗試利用「搭配詞表」中的字彙，造出想要表達的句子。

＿＿＿＿＿＿＿＿＿＿＿＿＿＿＿＿＿＿＿＿＿＿＿＿＿＿＿＿＿＿＿＿＿＿

＿＿＿＿＿＿＿＿＿＿＿＿＿＿＿＿＿＿＿＿＿＿＿＿＿＿＿＿＿＿＿＿＿＿

＿＿＿＿＿＿＿＿＿＿＿＿＿＿＿＿＿＿＿＿＿＿＿＿＿＿＿＿＿＿＿＿＿＿

＿＿＿＿＿＿＿＿＿＿＿＿＿＿＿＿＿＿＿＿＿＿＿＿＿＿＿＿＿＿＿＿＿＿

＿＿＿＿＿＿＿＿＿＿＿＿＿＿＿＿＿＿＿＿＿＿＿＿＿＿＿＿＿＿＿＿＿＿

＿＿＿＿＿＿＿＿＿＿＿＿＿＿＿＿＿＿＿＿＿＿＿＿＿＿＿＿＿＿＿＿＿＿

＿＿＿＿＿＿＿＿＿＿＿＿＿＿＿＿＿＿＿＿＿＿＿＿＿＿＿＿＿＿＿＿＿＿

| 8 | **bank**
[bæŋk] | | 可數名詞 銀行 | |

搭配在前面 的動詞	搭配的形容詞		關鍵字	搭配在後面 的動詞
instruct ★ to V authorize ★ to V borrow sth. from go to negotiate with	big large major private foreign overseas international	investment clearing issuing savings commercial	**bank** bank account bank balance bank card bank charges bank loan bank statement bank transfer	lend sth. underwrite sth.

★為關鍵字

 好搭例句 ◎ MP3-08

☐ I need to **go to** the bank today **to** withdraw some cash.
我今天要去銀行提領一些現款。

☐ I have already **instructed** our bank **to** send the money to your account by bank transfer. I will also **authorize** the bank **to** make this a regular monthly payment,
我已經要我們的銀行透過銀行轉帳把錢匯到你們的帳戶。我也會授權銀行把它變成每月固定付款。

☐ Our bank balance is looking pretty good at the moment. We are getting good interest in our bank accounts.
我們的銀行存款餘額目前看起來相當不錯。我們的銀行帳戶滾了不少利息。

☐ I'm going to **negotiate with** the bank to reduce their bank charges.
我要跟銀行協商調降他們的銀行手續費。

☐ The **clearing** bank is holding the money for three days.
清算銀行會把這筆錢保留三天。

☐ The **issuing** bank **is underwriting** the bank loan.
發行銀行在承作銀行貸款。

☐ He works for a **major investment** bank. His salary is very high.
他服務於一家大型投資銀行。他的薪水非常高。

☐ One of my major clients is a **large international savings** bank. They have a lot of wealthy customers.
我有一家大客戶是大型的國際儲蓄銀行。他們有很多有錢的客戶。

☐ **Commercial** banks are feeling the effects of the credit crunch. The issuing of new bank cards has been suspended.
商業銀行感受到信用緊縮的衝擊。新的銀行卡已中止發行。

☐ I'm going to **borrow** a couple of million **from** the bank.
我要去跟銀行借個幾百萬。

☐ The bank has agreed to **lend** us 10 million. This bank loan will take us three years to clear, and will put quite a strain on our finances.
銀行同意借給我們 1,000 萬。我們要花費三年才能還清這筆銀行貸款，而且我們的財務狀況會相當吃緊。

☐ I spent the morning reading through our bank statements.
我早上把我們的銀行對帳單仔細看了一遍。

✦ ✎ 填填看

請從「搭配詞表」中選出適當的字，完成下面句子。例解請見第 333~353 頁。

☐ I have (1)_____ the bank to make regular payments to your (2)_____. Please check your (3)_____ every month to make sure you have received payment.

☐ We (4)_____ a large sum of money (5)_____ the bank, and now we are paying interest on the (6)_____.

☐ My cousin works for a small local (7)_____ bank as a bank clerk, while his wife works as a fund manager in a (8)_____ (9)_____ bank. Who do you think makes the most money?

☐ I am trying to (10)_____ the (11)_____ bank to reduce their (12)_____ charges. They are simply too expensive.

☐ Our (13)_____ is too low. We do not have enough money to meet our expenses.

☐ The bank has refused to (14)_____ the loan. It seems the bank cannot (15)_____ us any more money.

☐ Have you seen my new (16)_____? It's really cool!

☐ Have you seen the (17)_____? They are ridiculously expensive now!

進階造句

請嘗試利用「搭配詞表」中的字彙，造出想要表達的句子。

_____

_____

_____

_____

_____

brand
[brænd]

可數名詞 品牌

搭配在前面的動詞	搭配的形容詞		關鍵字
sell			**brand**
buy			
own	particular	luxury	brand name
create	leading	up-market	brand loyalty
develop	major	mass-market	brand image
produce			brand awareness
launch	well-known	proprietary	
establish	popular		
promote			

 好搭例句

◎ **MP3-09**

☐ We **sell** many different **proprietary** brands.
我們有販售許多不同的獨家品牌。

☐ Our customers like to **buy** our brands because they trust the brand name
我們的顧客喜歡買我們的品牌，是因為他們相信這個招牌。

☐ We **own** the **major** car brands in the market.
我們擁有市場上主要的汽車品牌。

☐ If we **create** a **mass-market** brand, we will increase our profits and keep our costs low.
假如我們創造大眾市場品牌，我們就能增加獲利並壓低成本。

☐ We need to **develop** brand loyalty and encourage our existing customers to buy more of the product.

我們需要培養品牌忠誠度，並鼓勵老顧客購買更多的產品。

☐ We **produce** some of the most **popular up-market** brands on the market.

我們有生產一些市面上最受歡迎的高檔品牌。

☐ We are **launching** a new **luxury** brand this month, so I am very busy.

我們這個月要推出新的精品品牌，所以我忙得不可開交。

☐ We **established** this **particular well-known** brand a few years ago and it's performing very well.

我們在幾年前建立了這個知名的特定品牌，而且它表現得非常好。

☐ We need to **promote** brand awareness so that it's easier to sell the product.

我們需要提升品牌知名度，好讓產品更容易賣出去。

☐ We must be careful not to damage the brand image.

我們必須小心避免損及品牌形象。

填填看

請從「搭配詞表」中選出適當的字，完成下面句子。例解請見第333~353頁。

☐ This company (1)_____ many of the world's (2)_____ (3)_____ (4)_____: Gucci, Chanel, and Yves Saint Laurent.

☐ I never (5)_____ (6)_____ brands — they are usually overpriced, and I don't want to pay for the image.

☐ We (7)_____ this (8)_____ brand last year. Do you like it?

☐ We (9)_____ this (10)_____ brand in order to try to increase our sales. Up-market brands don't sell so much.

☐ It's very important to (11)_____ the (12)_____, that way people will be happy to pay more for the product.

☐ We (13)_____ many (14)_____ brands on the market. Other companies follow our ideas.

☐ We must (15)_____ more (16)_____ so that our existing customers don't buy other brands in the future.

☐ If we (17)_____ (18)_____ it will be easier to sell more products when people recognize the brand.

進階造句

請嘗試利用「搭配詞表」中的字彙，造出想要表達的句子。

_____

_____

_____

_____

_____

_____

_____

10 budget
[ˈbʌdʒɪt]

可數名詞 預算

搭配在前面的動詞		搭配的形容詞		關鍵字	搭配在後面的動詞
have be on cut reduce increase set prepare approve	manage control allocate go over overspend exceed run out of spend keep within	annual quarterly half-yearly total tight shoestring limited big	departmental advertising marketing training entertainment production R&D IT	**budget (for sth.)**	run out run into #

為數字

 好搭例句

◎ MP3-10

☐ We **have** a **tight entertainment** budget this year.
我們今年的娛樂預算很緊。

☐ We **are on** a **limited production** budget.
我們的生產預算有限。

☐ They **cut departmental** budgets in an effort to control spending.
他們削減了部門預算,以藉此控制開銷。

☐ We need to **reduce** budgets for the second half of the year.
我們需要縮減今年下半年的預算。

☐ My boss **increased** my **half-yearly** budget!
我老闆調高了我的半年度預算!

☐ We usually **set annual** budgets at the end of the previous year.
我們通常是在前一年的年底編列年度預算。

☐ I'm **preparing** my budget for next year now.
我目前正在編訂我明年的預算。

☐ My boss didn't **approve** my budget. I have to **prepare** it again.
我老闆沒有核准我的預算。我必須重編一次。

☐ I need to learn how to **manage** a budget if I want to get promoted next year.
假如我明年想升官，我就得學會該怎麼管理預算才行。

☐ I find it difficult to **control** my budget because it's so **tight**.
我覺得我的預算很難控制，因為它緊得不得了。

☐ As finance manager I have to **allocate** budgets to different departments.
身為財務經理，我必須把預算撥給不同的部門。

☐ We **overspent** our **production** budget last year. My boss was not happy.
我們去年透支了我們的生產預算。我老闆不太開心。

☐ We must not **go over** budget.
我們不可以超支預算。

☐ If you **exceed** your **R&D** budget this year, you will **have** less budget next year.
假如你們超出了今年的研發預算，明年的預算就會減少。

☐ We can't do any more training — we have **exceeded** our **training** budget this year.
我們不能再辦任何訓練了——我們已經超出了今年的訓練預算。

☐ I can't finish the marketing campaign — I have **run** out **of marketing** budget.
我沒辦法把行銷活動給做完——我把行銷預算給花光了。

☐ If we don't **spend** all the **advertising** budget, we won't get one next year.
假如我們沒有把廣告預算全部花完，明年就拿不到了。

☐ It's so difficult to **keep within** the **IT** budget when all the equipment is so old and keeps breaking down.

當所有的設備都這麼老舊又頻頻故障時，要維持在資訊科技預算的範圍內便難如登天。

☐ My **production** budget has **run out**. I can't spend any more on this project.

我的生產預算用完了。我在這個案子上再也沒錢可花了。

☐ The **IT** budget **for** this company **runs into** millions of dollars.

這家公司的資訊科技預算有好幾百萬美元。

✏ 填填看

請從「搭配詞表」中選出適當的字，完成下面句子。例解請見第333~353頁。

☐ I (1)_____ a (2)_____ (3)_____ budget this year, so I can't take any English classes!

☐ Since my boss (4)_____ my (5)_____ budget, I can't stay in any nice hotels when I go on business trips next year.

☐ I am currently (6)_____ my (7)_____ budget for the whole of next year.

☐ I hope my boss will (8)_____ my budget. It took me a long time to (9)_____ it.

☐ I find it quite difficult to (10)_____ my budget. It always seems to be too small for my needs.

☐ We are (11)_____ (12)_____ budgets for the next year to the different departments now.

☐ Last year I **(13)**_____ my budget, so this year my boss

   (14)_____ it.

☐ My budget **(15)**_____ millions of dollars. Controlling such a lot

   of money is a big responsibility.

☐ I can't have any more training as my budget has **(16)**_____.

進階造句

請嘗試利用「搭配詞表」中的字彙，造出想要表達的句子。

_____

_____

_____

_____

_____

_____

_____

| 11 | **business** ① [ˋbɪznɪs] | | 不可數名詞 事業 |

搭配在前面的動詞	搭配的形容詞	關鍵字
do conduct		**business**
attract affect discuss be good for be bad for	good day-to-day	business cycle business confidence business associate business administration business strategy

 好搭例句　　　　　　　　　　◎ **MP3-11**

☐ We **do good** business in Japan. It's our major market.
我們在日本經營得不錯。那是我們的主要市場。

☐ I am responsible for the business strategy of the company, but leave my vice president to **conduct day-to-day** business. He has a degree in business administration from Oxford.
我負責公司的經營策略，但讓我的副總裁來處理日常業務。他有牛津的企管學位。

☐ Revenue is down because it's a low point in the business cycle. Business is always bad at this time of year. However, we need to **attract** more business.
營收下滑，因為遇到了景氣循環的低點。在一年的這個時候，生意總是不好。不過，我們需要招攬更多的生意。

☐ The fall in interest rates will **affect** business. It will probably **be bad for** business as it will damage business confidence.
利率降低會影響生意。它八成會對生意不利，因為它會打擊到商業信心。

☐ A good reputation **is good for** business. We must work hard to establish this.

好的名聲有利於生意。我們必須努力把它建立起來。

☐ I usually have lunch with my main business associates to **discuss** business.

我通常會跟主要的生意夥伴共進午餐，以討論生意。

填填看

請從「搭配詞表」中選出適當的字，完成下面句子。例解請見第333~353頁。

☐ It's a pleasure **(1)**_____ business with such nice **(2)**_____. Most of them are very good people.

☐ We must **(3)**_____ business in an ethical way.

☐ In order to stimulate revenue growth we need to **(4)**_____ more business.

☐ If the government wants to stimulate **(5)**_____, they will need to do something about the economy so that business people feel more confident about investing.

☐ There are several economic factors **(6)**_____ business this year.

☐ I met John the other day and we **(7)**_____ business. He agrees that the economy is slow, but he told me not to worry, it's just this point in the **(8)**_____. It will improve soon.

☐ A slow economy **(9)**_____ business. People don't want to spend money.

☐ Sponsoring local charities **(10)**_____ business. It helps more people know about your company. PR is an important part of my

(11)_____.

☐ You don't need a degree in (12)_____ to (13)_____ the

(14)_____ business of a small company.

進階造句

請嘗試利用「搭配詞表」中的字彙，造出想要表達的句子。

_____

_____

_____

_____

_____

_____

_____

12	**business** ② [ˈbɪznɪs]	可數名詞 企業 同義字：company

搭配在前面的動詞		搭配的形容詞	關鍵字
run	start	good	**business**
manage	establish	thriving	
operate	form	profitable	business plan
	found	lucrative	business enterprise
develop			business unit
expand	affect	large	business community
build	impact	medium-sized	business manager
		small	

 好搭例句　　　　◎ **MP3-12**

☐ I **run** a **medium-sized** business. We export lenses to China.
我經營了一家中型企業。我們外銷鏡片到中國。

☐ I got my experience by **managing** a number of **small** businesses before I got this job.
在應徵上這份工作前，我所累積的經驗是來自管理一些小企業。

☐ Although we **operate** this business as a separate business unit, we are actually part of a larger group.
雖然我們把這家企業當成獨立的事業單位來經營，但我們其實是更大集團的一份子。

☐ We need to **develop** the business over the next five years. My business plan is to **expand** the business 20%.
未來五年，我們要把事業發展起來才行。我的營業計畫是要把事業擴展兩成。

☐ This is a very **profitable** business enterprise.
這是一家非常賺錢的工商企業。

☐ He **started** the business 10 years ago in his dining room and **built** the business into a thriving multi-billion dollar company. He's an excellent business manager.

他10年前在自家飯廳裡創業，並把這項事業打造成了一家數十億美元的興盛公司。他是一位傑出的企業經理人。

☐ When I **established** the business 10 years ago, I had no idea it would become such a **lucrative** business.

我在10年前建立事業時，沒想到它會變成這麼賺錢的事業。

☐ It's a **good** business, even though its not **large**.

這是一家不錯的企業，即使它並不大。

☐ He is a well-known figure in the local business community.

他在當地的商界可是個知名人物。

☐ I don't think the new regulations will **affect** the business too much.

我認為新規定不致於對企業造成太大的影響。

☐ He **formed** the business 10 years ago, then he **founded** another business a few years later. He's an amazing guy.

他在10年前成立了這家企業，幾年後又創立了另一家企業。他是個了不起的傢伙。

🖊 填填看

請從「搭配詞表」中選出適當的字，完成下面句子。例解請見第333~353頁。

☐ I (1)＿＿＿＿＿ a (2)＿＿＿＿＿ business. Revenue and profits are very high.

☐ I am the (3)＿＿＿＿＿ of a (4)＿＿＿＿＿ business, not too small, and not too big. It's good for me that way because I am still learning how to (5)＿＿＿＿＿ a business.

☐ I think my (6)_____ is solid. I intend to (7)_____ the business to 30 million in terms of revenue within the next 3 years.

☐ He (8)_____ the business 10 years ago, and now he is a respected figure in the local (9)_____.

☐ This is just a (10)_____ (11)_____ in the company. The company is very big, but our department is quite small.

☐ In this country the government gives grants to (12)_____ (13)_____, but you have to be very big to qualify.

☐ If they change the regulations regarding small businesses, that will definitely (14)_____ the business. We will have to make changes.

進階造句

請嘗試利用「搭配詞表」中的字彙，造出想要表達的句子。

_____

_____

_____

_____

_____

_____

_____

| 13 | **campaign**
[kæm`pen] | | 可數名詞 宣傳活動 | |

搭配在前面 的動詞	搭配的形容詞		關鍵字	搭配在後面 的動詞
plan organize coordinate launch begin start initiate	national nationwide local successful new	direct mail advertising sales public relations marketing promotional media	**campaign**	last/ran n.p. target n.p. focus on

 好搭例句

◎ **MP3-13**

☐ We are **planning** our **new marketing** campaign at the moment.
我們目前正在規劃新的行銷活動。

☐ You did a great job of **organizing** such a **successful public relations** campaign!
你表現得很好，籌辦了這麼成功的公關活動！

☐ This year we are going to **launch** three **new advertising** campaigns.
今年我們要推出三場新的廣告活動。

☐ We will **begin** the **new promotional** campaign at the start of Q3.
我們在第三季的季初會展開新的宣傳活動。

☐ I think we will be ready to **start** the **national sales** campaign at the end of the month.
我想等到月底時，我們就可以展開全國性的促銷活動。

☐ We **initiated** a **local direct mail** campaign to try to increase our profile in the neighborhood.
我們舉辦了地方性的直寄郵件活動，以設法提高我們在鄰近地區的知名度。

☐ Mary is **coordinating** our **local** and **national sales** campaigns.
瑪莉正在協調我們地方性與全國性的促銷活動。

☐ The **promotional** campaign will **last** for three months.
宣傳活動會持續三個月。

☐ The **new marketing** campaign will **target** the 35 to 40 (year-old) female segment.
新的行銷活動是鎖定35到40歲的女性階層。

☐ This **public relations** campaign must **focus on** repairing the damage to our reputation caused by the faulty products.
這場公關活動必須著重於彌補瑕疵品對我們的名聲所造成的傷害。

✎ 填填看

請從「搭配詞表」中選出適當的字，完成下面句子。例解請見第333~353頁。

☐ I'm (1)_____ a great (2)_____ (3)_____ campaign for our new product! We are going to show the product on TV and in the newspaper for the first time in our company history!

☐ In order to increase market share we need to (4)_____ a (5)_____ (6)_____ campaign, not just focus on one city.

☐ We are going to (7)_____ the (8)_____ campaign with a party for the sales team to give them some incentive.

☐ This (9)_____ campaign will (10)_____ certain existing customers only. We want to encourage them to increase their spending.

☐ The (11)_____ campaign (12)_____ our company's

contribution to the local community.

☐ The (13)_____ campaign (14)_____ for two months

and increased market share by 3%. A great success in my view!

進階造句

請嘗試利用「搭配詞表」中的字彙，造出想要表達的句子。

_____

_____

_____

_____

_____

_____

_____

_____

14	**capital** [ˈkæpət]]	不可數名詞 資金 同義字：investment

搭配在前面的動詞	搭配的形容詞		關鍵字
have			**capital (of #)**
raise		working	
attract		share	capital appreciation
invest	additional further		capital expenditure
		venture	capital gains
borrow		private	capital inflow/outflow
repay			capital investment
need			capital markets

 好搭例句　　　　　　　　　◎ **MP3-14**

☐ We are required by law to **have** a **working** capital **of** 1 million.
依法我們必須有100萬的流動資本。

☐ We need to **raise additional** capital. Shall we go to the bank, or issue some shares and try to attract some **share** capital?
我們需要擴大增資。我們是要去找銀行，還是發行一些股份，並設法招攬一些股本？

☐ We hope this new project will **attract venture** capital.
我們希望這件新案子能吸引到創投資金。

☐ We need to **invest further** capital in overseas expansion.
我們需要對海外擴張投入更多的資金。

☐ We have had an excellent year, so we are able to **repay** some of the capital we **borrowed** from the bank.
我們有個出色的一年，所以我們有辦法償還一些向銀行借來的資金。

☐ He started the company with **private** capital. I think it was family money.

他是靠私人資本開了這家公司。我想那是家裡的錢。

☐ Our share offering produced capital gains of around 8 billion. Not as much as we were hoping for.

我們靠出售持股獲得了 80 億左右的資本利得。沒有我們所期望的多。

☐ The government has regulations in place to restrict capital inflow and outflow.

政府有既定的規範來限制資金的流入與流出。

☐ We intend to use the money we get from the share offering on capital expenditure. For example, we need to build a new factory in China.

我們打算把出售持股所賺的錢用在資本支出上。比方說，我們需要在中國建一座新廠。

☐ We will need to make a huge capital investment to bring our machinery up to date.

我們需要從事龐大的資本投資，以引進最新的機具。

☐ Although we issued the shares at $8.00 each, the current value of the shares on the capital market has increased, which means there has been a capital appreciation.

雖然我們發行的股票是每股八美元，但股票在資本市場上的現值已經上漲，這表示出現了資本增值。

☐ We **need** more **working** capital.

我們需要更多的流動資本。

✦ ✐ 填填看

請從「搭配詞表」中選出適當的字，完成下面句子。例解請見第 333~353 頁。

☐ If we sell some shares, that will help us to (1)_____ capital.

☐ We don't (2)_____ enough (3)_____ capital to meet our everyday expenses. That's bad.

☐ Let's see if we can (4)_____ some (5)_____ capital. Let me ask some of my wealthy friends and see if they are willing to (6)_____ capital in this idea.

☐ There are two ways of (7)_____ (8)_____ capital. We can either (9)_____ it from the bank, or sell some shares.

☐ The benefit of having (10)_____ capital is that you don't need to (11)_____ it. If you (12)_____ capital, you do need to repay it.

☐ Our factory and plant are very outdated. We need more (13)_____ in the factory, and we need more (14)_____ for the plant.

☐ Our shares are selling very well on the (15)_____. This is because our previous share offering was so successful. Shareholders had some (16)_____.

☐ We are prevented from moving money out of the country because of government restrictions on (17)_____. However, we can bring in (18)_____ from outside the country because there are no restrictions on (19)_____.

☐ If we want to go ahead with this project, we will (20)_____ more capital.

 進階造句

請嘗試利用「搭配詞表」中的字彙，造出想要表達的句子。

15	**cash** [kæʃ]		不可數名詞 現金

搭配在前面的動詞	搭配的形容詞	關鍵字	
pay		**cash**	
take	petty		
withdraw	spare	cash cow	cash injection
get	extra	cash discount	cash limit
use	surplus	cash dispenser (ATM)	cash outflow
raise	operating	cash flow	cash reserve
generate		cash inflow	cash card

 好搭例句

◎ MP3-15

☐ I always ask my customers to **pay** cash for small amounts, and I usually give them a cash discount.
我總是請顧客在小額上付現，而且我通常會給他們現金折扣。

☐ Do you **take** cash? Or must I **use** a cash card for this purchase?
你們收現嗎？還是我這筆採購必須用現金卡？

☐ I need to **withdraw** some **extra** cash from my account before my trip tomorrow.
在明天啓程前，我需要先從戶頭裡提領一些額外的現金。

☐ I need to **get** some more **petty** cash from my manager. My cash reserve has run out.
我需要向經理申請多一點的零用錢。我的現款準備金用完了。

☐ If we ask all our sales to **use** cash for their expenses, it will help us to manage our cash flow.
假如我們要求所有的業務員用現金來支應開銷，這將有助於我們掌管現金流量。

☐ This kind of product is a cash cow for the company: it **generates** most of our cash inflow.

這種產品是公司的搖錢樹：我們大部分的現金流入都是由它所帶來。

☐ We need to **generate** some **operating** cash fast, as we have reached our cash limit, and we don't have enough to meet our operating costs.

我們要趕緊籌措一些營運現款，因為我們達到了現金限額，沒有足夠的錢來支付我們的營運費用。

☐ Our company needs an urgent cash injection to meet this unexpected cash outflow.

我們公司需要緊急挹注現金，以應付這筆突如其來的現金流出。

☐ The cash dispenser at the bank is broken and I can't **withdraw** any cash. Is there another ATM nearby?

銀行的提款機壞了，我沒辦法提領任何現款。附近有沒有別的自動櫃員機？

☐ Please **use** any **surplus** cash from your budgets before the end of the month.

預算中如有任何盈餘現金，請在月底前用掉。

填填看

請從「搭配詞表」中選出適當的字，完成下面句子。例解請見第333~353頁。

☐ If you (1)＿＿＿＿＿＿ cash for this sale, I can give you a

(2)＿＿＿＿＿＿. It will cost you 10% less!

☐ We never (3)＿＿＿＿＿＿ cash for large amounts — our company rules don't allow us to accept it.

☐ I went to the bank to (4)＿＿＿＿＿＿ some cash, but the

(5)＿＿＿＿＿＿ was broken. Can you lend me some?

☐ I need to (6)_____ some (7)_____ cash from my manager. I had quite a lot of expenses last month that I need to claim.

☐ I have some (8)_____ cash from my budget this month. I didn't spend it all. What shall I do with it?

☐ My job is to manage the department (9)_____. I have to make sure the (10)_____ and (11)_____ balance at the end of each quarter.

☐ Because the cash outflow is usually more than the cash inflow, it's very difficult to manage the (12)_____.

☐ We need to (13)_____ some cash. We don't have a lot of money in our current account and our (14)_____ is a bit low.

☐ If the R&D department can develop a product that will really sell fast, that will give us a lot of money quickly, and then the product may become a (15)_____ and give us a (16)_____. That's the only way out of our financial problems.

☐ I have set a new (17)_____ on your (18)_____. You need to control your spending.

進階造句

請嘗試利用「搭配詞表」中的字彙，造出想要表達的句子。

_____

_____

_____

_____

16 challenge
[ˈtʃælɪndʒ]

可數名詞 挑戰

搭配在前面的動詞	搭配的形容詞	關鍵字
face	greatest	
meet	biggest	
pose	serious	
present	major	
	real	**challenge (to sth.)**
resist	considerable	
overcome		
	exciting	
relish		
welcome	new	

 好搭例句

◉ MP3-16

☐ We are currently **facing** a **serious** challenge from our main competitor.
我們目前面臨到主要競爭對手的嚴厲挑戰。

☐ We **met** many **major** challenges along the way, but **overcame** them together and are now successful.
我們一路上遇到了許多重大的挑戰，但都能一起克服，才有了現在的成功。

☐ The price of oil **poses** the **greatest** challenge **to** our business. We are dependent on shipments of raw materials.
油價對我們的生意構成了最大的挑戰。我們是靠運送原料為生。

☐ The short lead time **presents** a **real** challenge **to** this project.
前置時間短暫為這個案子帶來了真正的挑戰。

☐ I **relish** an **exciting** challenge. It brings out the best in me.
我偏好刺激的挑戰。它能充分激發出我的潛力。

The **biggest** challenge we need to **resist** is our competitors stealing all our key employees. This is a **considerable** challenge, as they are able to offer better salaries than we can.

我們需要抵擋的最大挑戰就是，競爭對手把我們的重要員工全部挖走了。這是個很大的挑戰，因為他們給得起比我們更好的薪水。

We **face new** challenges all the time.

我們一直在面臨新的挑戰。

填填看

請從「搭配詞表」中選出適當的字，完成下面句子。例解請見第333~353頁。

Our (1)_____ challenge is getting the price right. I find that the most difficult part.

We (2)_____ a (3)_____ challenge from the government at the moment. They want to impose stricter working regulations, which will add considerably to our costs.

The availability of cheaper labor in Vietnam (4)_____ a (5)_____ challenge (6)_____ us, because many of our competitors can take advantage of that.

We need to (7)_____ this challenge if we are going to meet the project deadline for this year.

A good business manager should not be afraid of challenges, but should (8)_____ them!

It's an (9)_____ challenge, and I look forward to it!

In the future we will (10)_____ many (11)_____ challenges. We must be ready to expect anything.

進階造句

請嘗試利用「搭配詞表」中的字彙，造出想要表達的句子。

change
[tʃendʒ]

可數名詞 改變

搭配在前面的動詞	搭配的形容詞		關鍵字
make implement introduce see bring about cause resist deal with manage	major necessary slow gradual fundamental significant sweeping profound possible	rapid sudden drastic radical proposed recent organizational structural	**change (to sth.)**

 好搭例句

◎ MP3-17

☐ We need to **make** some **fundamental** changes **to** our systems so that we can work more efficiently.
我們需要在制度上做一些根本的改變，好讓我們能運作得更有效率。

☐ I hope to **implement** these **proposed** changes over the next few months.
我希望在未來幾個月能落實這些所提議的變革。

☐ In my first month on the job I **introduced sweeping organizational** changes. The company operates much more smoothly now.
在任職的第一個月，我推行了全面性的組織變革。如今公司運作起來順利多了。

☐ Over the last year we **have seen significant** changes **to** the way people pay for their purchases.
去年我們看到，民眾在購物的付款方式上出現了重大的變化。

☐ We need to **make** some **major structural** changes **to** the design of the product.

我們需要在產品的設計上做一些重大的結構調整。

☐ These **necessary** changes will take some time to **implement**.

這些必要的調整要花點時間來落實。

☐ We **have seen** a **slow** but **profound** change to the public's attitude towards business ethics.

我們看到民眾對於企業倫理的態度出現了緩慢但深刻的變化。

☐ It is human nature to **resist** any **rapid** change. However, with good planning, **sudden** change can be managed.

抗拒任何急速的改變是人的天性。但只要規劃得宜，突然改變也有辦法管理。

☐ They keep **making drastic** changes **to** the design specs. How can we complete the project on time?

他們一而再、再而三地大幅修改設計規格。我們怎麼有辦法把案子準時完成？

☐ Please keep me informed of any **possible** changes **to** the specs.

如果規格出現任何可能的變化，請通知我一聲。

☐ The rise in oil prices will **cause gradual** changes **to** the way people do business, especially in terms of logistics.

油價上漲會逐漸改變大家做生意的方式，尤其是在物流方面。

☐ **Recent** changes include a restructuring of the project team.

近來的變革包括重組專案團隊。

☐ I want to **bring about** a **radical** change **to** the way we work as a team. We are not efficient.

我想要把團隊的運作方式徹底改變。我們很沒效率。

☐ How you **deal with** change is the true test of a manager.

如何因應變化是對經理人的真正考驗。

 填填看

請從「搭配詞表」中選出適當的字，完成下面句子。例解請見第333~353頁。

☐ I want to (1)_____ some (2)_____ changes to our working practice. We don't have to do this quickly, but everything must be changed.

☐ I have studied your (3)_____ changes and I agree we need to (4)_____ them as soon as possible.

☐ We have (5)_____ too many (6)_____ changes in the company recently. What we need now is some stability.

☐ My goal is to (7)_____ some (8)_____ changes (9)_____ the company. I think the structure of the organization is inefficient. However, I am still thinking about how to best (10)_____ these changes.

☐ The (11)_____ changes to the project team were (12)_____ by the fact that one of our colleagues left to have a baby.

☐ It's more difficult to (13)_____ (14)_____ change than it is to manage (15)_____ change.

☐ I don't know what do to. The client has been (16)_____ these changes. He doesn't seem to understand that these changes are (17)_____ if the product is going to work smoothly.

☐ We will (18)_____ many (19)_____ changes once the new boss comes on board. You wait and see. One (20)_____ change I reckon will happen is that a lot of people will lose their jobs.

 進階造句

請嘗試利用「搭配詞表」中的字彙，造出想要表達的句子。

18	**client** [`klaɪənt]	可數名詞 客戶 同義字：customer

搭配在前面的動詞		搭配的形容詞		關鍵字
				client
have get advise ★ to V help ★ to V assist ★ to V	tell inform notify visit meet	existing potential prospective new	corporate private regular major	client base client list client profile client relationship client service client report

★爲關鍵字

 好搭例句　　　　　　　　　◎ MP3-18

☐ We **have** two kinds of clients: **corporate** clients, which are big companies who use our services, and **private** clients, who are individuals. Our client base is an even mix of these two kinds.
我們有兩種客戶：企業客戶，也就是採用我們服務的大公司；以及私人客戶，也就是個人。我們的客群是由這兩種平均組成。

☐ Our client list is usually wealthy individuals who need financial advice. We offer excellent client service.
我們的客戶名單通常是需要財務諮詢的有錢人。我們提供了一流的客戶服務。

☐ I managed to **get** two **new** clients last week! They both meet our client profile.
我上星期好不容易拉到了兩家新客戶！他們都符合我們的客戶條件。

☐ We always **advise** our **new** clients to think carefully before making any decisions based on our recommendations. It helps to build trust and make the client relationship firmer.
我們總是勸告新客戶，在根據我們的建議下任何決定前，要先經過深思熟慮。這有助於建立信任以及強化顧客關係。

☐ We **help** our **regular** clients to achieve their financial goals.

我們幫助常客達到他們的財務目標。

☐ We **assist** our **major** clients with all their travel needs. That's part of our VIP service.

我們協助主顧滿足一切的差旅需求。那是我們貴賓服務的一部分。

☐ I **told** our **existing** clients that I was leaving the company.

我告訴老客戶說，我要離開公司了。

☐ Can you **inform** the client that we no longer offer that service? Don't forget to put it in the client report.

你能不能去通知客戶說，我們不再提供這項服務了？別忘了把它寫在客戶報告裡。

☐ I already **notified** the client about the changes to our service.

我已經把變更服務的事告知了客戶。

☐ I am **visiting** a **prospective** client next week. I hope I get them!

我下星期要去拜訪一家預期客戶。我希望我能爭取到他們！

☐ I **met** a **potential** client last week. I am going to follow up now and see if I can get them onto our client list.

我上星期去拜會了一家潛在客戶。我現在要追蹤下去，看看能不能把他們拉進我們的客戶名單裡。

填填看

請從「搭配詞表」中選出適當的字，完成下面句子。例解請見第333~353頁。

☐ Our (1)_____ is a mix of business customers, (2)_____, wealthy individuals, and (3)_____.

☐ My target this month is to (4)_____ three (5)_____ clients. I already (6)_____ some (7)_____ clients, but I need to get more.

☐ We (8)_____ our clients to manage their wealth. We (9)_____ them to make careful decisions.

☐ Tomorrow I have a busy day. I am (10)_____ a (11)_____ client. I hope I can persuade him to purchase our services.

☐ This company is one of our (12)_____ clients. He gets a VIP card from us and excellent (13)_____.

☐ Most of our (14)_____ clients have the same (15)_____. They are remarkably similar. It's the VIP clients who have different needs.

☐ I have to (16)_____ this client that we no longer offer this kind of service.

☐ I am taking over your clients when you leave. Can you let me read their (17)_____?

☐ I'm trying to build up a good (18)_____ with the names on this (19)_____.

進階造句

請嘗試利用「搭配詞表」中的字彙，造出想要表達的句子。

_____

_____

_____

_____

_____

19	**company** [ˈkʌmpənɪ]	可數名詞 公司 同義字：business

搭配在前面的動詞	搭配的形容詞		關鍵字	搭配在後面的動詞
form found own run manage start establish control join privatize buy acquire	local listed public private family state owned subsidiary sister huge medium sized small multinational international	insurance financial manufacturing consultancy pharmaceutical oil energy shipping IT trading	**company** company director company car company spokes-person company policy company head-quarters company logo	operate employ manufacture produce supply sell

 好搭例句　　　◎ MP3-19

☐ He **formed** the company in 1965. Two years later he **founded** its **sister** company. Now there are ten **subsidiary** companies. Since they all have different company logos, many people don't know they are the same company.

他在 1965 年成立了這家公司。兩年後，他創辦了它的姊妹公司，現在則有十家子公司。由於它們各有不同的公司商標，因此有許多人並不曉得它們是同一家公司。

☐ A Frenchman **started** the company in the early days of the 19th century. He **established** the company first in China, then it moved here.

有一位法國人在 19 世紀初創立了這家公司。他先是在中國開公司，後來才搬到這裡來。

☐ He **owns** a **huge family trading** company. It's a totally **private** company and is not **listed** on any exchange. The company headquarters is in Taipei.

他擁有一家龐大的家族貿易公司。它是完全私有的公司，而沒有在任何交易所掛牌。該公司的總部在台北。

☐ It's currently a **state owned energy** company. However, the company spokesperson announced that they are going to **privatize** the company. Shares will be listed in Shanghai.

它目前是一家國有的能源公司。但該公司的發言人宣布說，他們要把公司私有化。股票將在上海掛牌。

☐ I got most of my experience **managing small local IT** companies, so this job is a real challenge for me.

我的經驗大部分都是來自管理小型的地方資訊科技公司，所以這項職務對我來說是一項真正的挑戰。

☐ The group CFO **controls** the **insurance** and **financial** companies which form part of the group. He also makes company policy.

集團的財務長是在控管集團旗下的保險和財務公司。他還要制訂公司的政策。

☐ In 1999 I joined a **medium sized consultancy** company. After three years, I was made the company director and given a company car. I was **running** the company!

1999 年時，我加入了一家中型顧問公司。三年後，我當上了公司的董事，並獲得了公司配車。我掌管了這家公司！

☐ We are planning to **buy** a **multinational shipping** company. If we **acquire** this company, it will help to reduce our shipping costs in the long term.

我們打算買一家跨國運輸公司。假如我們買下這家公司，這將有助於降低我們的長期運輸成本。

☐ The company **operates** in several markets and **employs** several hundred thousand people worldwide.
該公司跨足好幾個市場，並在世界各地雇用了幾十萬人。

☐ Most **pharmaceutical** companies **manufacture** their own products under license.
大部分的製藥公司都是生產獲得核可的自有產品。

☐ This **international manufacturing** company **produces** clothing for the American market.
這家國際製造公司所生產的衣服是銷售到美國市場。

☐ This **oil** company **supplies** most of East Asia with its energy needs.
這家石油公司供應了東亞大多數地區的能源需求。

☐ The company **sells** soybeans on the world market.
這家公司是把大豆賣到全世界的市場上。

☐ This **public** company issued shares on the London exchange last week.
這家公開發行公司上星期在倫敦交易所發行了股票。

填填看

請從「搭配詞表」中選出適當的字，完成下面句子。例解請見第333~353頁。

☐ He (1)_____ the company a few years ago, but he doesn't (2)_____ it. His sister (3)_____ it now.

☐ I (4)_____ a (5)_____ (6)_____ company. We only have five employees, and we have only one customer. The company (7)_____ shower curtains to a local supermarket chain.

☐ It's a (8)_____ company, so it's (9)_____ by the shareholders.

☐ This company (10)_____ cars to the local market. Our (11)_____ company — a (12)_____ company — provides finance for customers wishing to purchase the cars.

☐ The group is huge. There are several (13)_____ companies, including an (14)_____ company, to provide insurance coverage, a (15)_____ company which (16)_____ engine parts, a (17)_____ company, which delivers the parts we produce to our overseas customers, and a (18)_____ company, which provides expertise and advice to other companies in the same industry.

☐ The (19)_____ issued a press release announcing that the (20)_____ was changing. They hope to become more ethical. She also announced that the (21)_____ would change to reflect this new policy direction.

☐ It's a (22)_____ (23)_____ (24)_____ company. Because it's so big, and is owned by the government, they have to be very open and honest about how they deal with environmental issues. Actually, I heard a rumour that the government plans to (25)_____ it.

☐ I (26)_____ a (27)_____ (28)_____ (29)_____ company when I left college. They produced software for the hotel industry. They were very good to me, they gave me a (30)_____, and made me (31)_____!

☐ Although it's a (32)_____ company with branches all over the world, its (33)_____ are in Taiwan.

☐ It started as a (34)_____ company, but now the family members have decided to make it a (35)_____ company.

☐ It's a huge (36)_____ company. It (37)_____ in many different markets, because people all over the world need drugs, and it (38)_____ thousands of people.

☐ We are going to (39)_____ this small company. It will add to our portfolio of companies which we own.

進階造句

請嘗試利用「搭配詞表」中的字彙，造出想要表達的句子。

20	**concern** [kənˋsɜn]		可數名詞 顧慮	

搭配在前面的動詞	搭配的形容詞		關鍵字	搭配在後面的動詞
be be of have express share address raise	serious vital primary central important key main	initial greatest legitimate principle	**concern (about sth.)**	be

 好搭例句　　　　　　　　　　◎ **MP3-20**

☐ This **is** a **central** concern that I shall be looking at in my presentation.
這是我在提報時會去看的一個主要疑慮。

☐ It**'s of vital** concern that we solve this problem immediately.
有個重大的關注在於，我們要立刻解決這個問題。

☐ I **have** a number of **initial** concerns I'd like to discuss with you.
我有一些初步的疑慮想跟你討論一下。

☐ I'd like to **express** my concern **about** your lack of progress on this issue.
對於你們在這個問題上沒有進展，我想表達我的疑慮。

☐ Please be assured that we **share** your concerns.
請放心，我們對你們的疑慮感同身受。

☐ I'd now like to **address** a **primary** concern.
我現在想說明一下主要的疑慮。

☐ You've **raised** a **legitimate** concern.
你指出了一個合理的疑慮。

☐ The **greatest** concern we have at this point is cost.
我們目前最大的顧慮在於成本。

☐ One of our **key** concerns **is** employee welfare.
我們的一個關鍵疑慮在於員工的福利。

☐ An **important** concern here **is** shipping times.
此處的重要疑慮在於運送時間。

☐ The **principle** concern **is** the availability of raw materials.
最主要的疑慮在於有沒有原料。

☐ My **main** concern at this point **is** time. How much time do we have?
我目前的主要疑慮是時間。我們有多少時間？

填填看

請從「搭配詞表」中選出適當的字，完成下面句子。例解請見第333～353頁。

☐ This **(1)**_____ one of our **(2)**_____ concerns. If you can **(3)**_____ this concern, then we will be totally confident in the whole project.

☐ You've **(4)**_____ a **(5)**_____ concern. You are completely right to be worried about this. Let me try to explain this to you.

☐ Let me stress that the company **(6)**_____ your concerns **(7)**_____ workers' conditions. We also think it's a very important issue.

☐ We **(8)**_____ a number of **(9)**_____ concerns. We must be confident about these before we continue.

☐ I (10)_____ my (11)_____ concern about this in my previous email, but you did not respond. How could you ignore such a serious issue?

☐ An (12)_____ concern here (13)_____ cost. You haven't mentioned that in your presentation.

☐ My (14)_____ concern as CEO (15)_____ to make a profit. Frankly, I care only about the bottom line.

進階造句

請嘗試利用「搭配詞表」中的字彙,造出想要表達的句子。

_____

_____

_____

_____

_____

_____

_____

_____

21 **consignment** [kən`saɪnmənt]		可數名詞 運送的貨品

搭配在前面的動詞	搭配的形容詞	關鍵字
deliver dispatch send ship receive collect accompany track delay	large huge small valuable whole entire particular single	**consignment (of sth.)**

 好搭例句　　　◎ MP3-21

☐ We're going to **deliver** the **whole** consignment next week.
我們下星期會把整批託運品交寄出去。

☐ We usually **ship** the **large** consignments by ocean freight and **send** the **small** consignments by air. Is that okay with you?
我們通常是船運大型託運品，空運小型託運品。這樣你們可以嗎？

☐ We have already **dispatched** the consignment **of** raw materials. You should **receive** it next week.
我們已經把原料的託運品快遞出去了。你們應該下週就會收到。

☐ You need to take the documentation with you to the warehouse when you **collect** the consignment.
你去領託運品時，需要帶證明文件去倉庫。

The transfer note will **accompany** this **particular** consignment.
出貨單會跟著這件託運品一起過去。

We **ship valuable** consignments separately in case anything happens to them.
我們會把貴重的託運品分開運送，以防發生任何意外。

The **whole** consignment is rotten. It was not packed properly.
整個託運品都爛了。它沒有裝好。

With our new computer system we can **track** the consignment. This will help us to ensure that consignments don't get lost or **delayed** in transit.
有了新的電腦系統後，我們就能追蹤託運品。這將有助於我們確保託運品不致遺失或延誤運送。

The **entire** consignment was lost. The container it was in fell overboard.
整批託運品都不見了。裝它的貨櫃落水了。

✎ 填填看

請從「搭配詞表」中選出適當的字，完成下面句子。例解請見第333~353頁。

When can you (1)＿＿＿＿＿＿ the consignment. It's very urgent and we need it as soon as possible.

Will the transfer note (2)＿＿＿＿＿＿ the consignment, or will you fax that separately to me?

You need to (3)＿＿＿＿＿＿ the consignment from customs. The collection fee is not included.

The (4)＿＿＿＿＿＿ consignment (5)＿＿＿＿＿＿ fruit was rotten. We are not paying for it.

☐ This is a very (6)_____ consignment. Can you please make sure it is insured and that you (7)_____ the consignment for every stage of the journey. We don't want to lose it.

☐ Why did you (8)_____ the goods we ordered in (9)_____ consignments? We have to make many trips to the warehouse to (10)_____ them. Next time, please send the (11)_____ consignment as one (12)_____ consignment, rather than lots of (13)_____ ones.

☐ They have (14)_____ a (15)_____ consignment (16)_____ tomatoes! What are we going to do with them all? Where are we going to store them?

☐ The typhoon will probably (17)_____ this (18)_____ consignment by a few days.

進階造句

請嘗試利用「搭配詞表」中的字彙，造出想要表達的句子。

_____

_____

_____

_____

_____

_____

contract
[ˈkɑntrækt]

可數名詞 合約

搭配在前面的動詞		搭配的形容詞	關鍵字	搭配在後面的動詞
negotiate draw up sign win secure award ★ to n.p. renew	fulfill honor follow enforce break terminate cancel	terms of the fixed term open ended short term long term # year new written	**contract**	run expire run out specify n.p./v.p. state n.p./v.p. stipulate n.p./v.p. cover n.p.

★爲關鍵字，＃爲數字

 ## 好搭例句

◎ **MP3-22**

☐ When we have successfully **negotiated** the **terms of the** contract, we can **draw up** the contract and then **sign** it.
等我們順利談成合約條款，我們就能擬訂合約，然後簽署。

☐ We have **won** a **new** contract to supply Yoyodyne with our products for three years.
我們拿到了新合約，可以把我們的產品供應給 Yoyodyne 三年。

☐ We have **secured** a **three year** contract with the biggest company in the market.
我們從市場上最大的公司那裡得到了一紙三年的合約。

☐ We have decided to **award** the contract to you. You will be our exclusive supplier.
我們決定把合約給你們。你們將成為我們的獨家供應商。

☐ Do you think they will **renew** our contract when it **runs out**?

你認為他們在期滿時會延長我們的合約嗎？

☐ It's an **open ended** contract, which means that we can **terminate** it at any time we want.

它是無期限合約，這表示我們可以隨時在想要的時候把它終止。

☐ If you do not **fulfill** the **written** contract, then we shall be forced to **cancel** it.

假如你們沒有履行書面合約，那我們就會被迫把它中止。

☐ We shall seek legal advice to **enforce** the contract if you do not **follow** it.

假如你們不依約行事，我們就會尋求法律諮詢，以強制執行合約。

☐ They didn't **honor** the contract, so we **cancelled** it.

他們沒有照合約走，所以我們把它中止了。

☐ Please **follow (the terms of)** the contract.

請遵守合約（的條款）。

☐ The contract **expires** next month.

下個月合約就到期了。

☐ The contract **runs** until the end of the year.

合約到年底為止有效。

☐ It's a **fixed term** contract so it will **run out** soon.

它是固定期限合約，所以很快就會到期了。

☐ The **written** contract **specifies** that you should supply us with high grade raw materials.

書面合約規定，你們應該供應高級的原料給我們。

☐ The **new** contract **states** the delivery periods. Please refer to it.

新合約註明了交付期間。請參閱。

☐ The contract **stipulates** that you may not supply any of our competitors.

合約明訂，你們不能供貨給任何我們的競爭對手。

☐ The contract **covers** everything.

合約涵蓋了一切。

📝 填填看

請從「搭配詞表」中選出適當的字，完成下面句子。例解請見第333~353頁。

☐ I'm a sales person. My job is to (1)_____ the contracts with customers and then (2)_____ the contract. After that, my boss (3)_____ it. That's the process.

☐ The (4)_____ contract (5)_____ the payment period. Please follow it.

☐ Because you did not (6)_____ the contract, we are (7)_____ it. Sorry things didn't work out.

☐ If you (8)_____ the contract, we shall have no choice but to (9)_____ it.

☐ We have been (10)_____ a one (11)_____ (12)_____ contract to supply Yoyodyne with our products.

☐ Because I managed to (13)_____ the contract, I got a big bonus!

☐ The contract (14)_____ all the terms of our agreement. Study it carefully. If you feel it's okay, then you can (15)_____ it.

☐ The current contract (16)_____ at the end of the year. Do you think we should (17)_____ it?

☐ It's an (18)_____ contract, so it (19)_____ until either party (20)_____ it.

☐ I don't like the (21)_____ contract. They are too strict.

進階造句

請嘗試利用「搭配詞表」中的字彙，造出想要表達的句子。

_____

_____

_____

_____

_____

_____

_____

	23	**control** [kən`trol]	可數名詞 控管

搭配在前面的動詞	搭配的形容詞		關鍵字
have implement put in place exercise maintain	tight strict effective	security production quality financial budgetary cost	**control(s)**

 好搭例句

☐ We **have** very **tight security** controls on the premises. You need to show your badge at all times.
我們的廠房有非常嚴密的安全控管。你要隨時佩戴證件。

☐ If we **implement** tighter **quality** controls, then such mistakes won't happen again.
假如我們實施更嚴格的品管,那就不會再發生這種錯誤了。

☐ Lots of our projects are running over budget. Please ask your team members to **exercise budgetary** control.
我們有很多案子都超出了預算。請要求你的組員做好預算控管。

☐ Last month we **put in place strict financial** controls to prevent money from being lost.
上個月我們實施了嚴格的財務控管,以防止虧錢。

☐ We **maintain** very **effective production** controls over the whole manufacturing process to ensure quality is high and costs are low.
我們對整個製造流程採取了非常有效的生產管制,以確保高品質與低成本。

☐ We **have** very **strict cost** controls to limit unnecessary spending.
我們做了非常嚴格的成本控管,以限制不必要的花費。

填填看

請從「搭配詞表」中選出適當的字，完成下面句子。例解請見第333~353頁。

☐ I cannot go over budget on this product. We have very (1)_____

(2)_____ controls in this company.

☐ Our products are of the highest standard because we (3)_____

such (4)_____ (5)_____ control.

☐ Our production line is not very efficient. Projects are often late, over

budget, and of poor quality. We need to (6)_____ some more

(7)_____ (8)_____ controls.

☐ I left my badge at home and, because of the (9)_____ controls,

I couldn't get into the factory. So I took the day off.

進階造句

請嘗試利用「搭配詞表」中的字彙，造出想要表達的句子。

_____

_____

_____

_____

_____

_____

24	**cost** [kɔst]		可數名詞 成本

搭配在前面的動詞	搭配的形容詞		關鍵字	搭配在後面的動詞
have incur bear		running fixed	**cost**	
reduce cut minimize estimate calculate meet recover cover	high low heavy increased	total extra additional administrative labor operating development production	cost efficiency cost reduction cost cutting	rise go up fall go down include n.p.

 好搭例句

◎ MP3-24

☐ We **have** quite **high running** costs in this factory. It would be good if we could **reduce** them.

我們在這座工廠花了相當高的營業成本。如果我們能把它降低就好了。

☐ We **incurred heavy labor** costs because of the increase in national insurance payouts.

我們負擔了高額的勞務成本,因為國內的保險支出增加了。

☐ We have to find ways to **bear** the **increased operating** costs due to the rise in the price of oil.

我們必須想辦法負擔因為油價上漲而增加的營運成本。

☐ If we can **cut** our **administrative** costs, we'll have more money to spend on marketing. We will have to do some cost cutting.

假如我們能降低行政成本，我們就有更多的錢可以用在行銷上。我們必須把成本降低一點。

☐ It's impossible to **minimize** our **fixed** costs. However, we could try to **reduce** our **additional** costs.

把固定成本降到最低是不可能的事。但我們不妨試著降低附加成本。

☐ I **estimate** our **operating** costs at 5 million. I **calculate** our **production** costs at 3 million. I'm sure we can do some cost reduction here.

我估計我們的營運成本是500萬。我算出我們的生產成本是300萬。我相信我們可以在這方面把成本減少一點。

☐ Can we **meet** the costs of this project at our current level of production?

以我們目前的生產水準，我們能不能支應這個案子的成本？

☐ We only need to sell 100 units to **recover** our **development** costs. Our cost efficiency levels are very high.

我們只需要賣100件就能賺回我們的開發成本。我們的成本效益水準非常高。

☐ **Administrative** costs are **falling** and **labor** costs are also **going down**, but **operating** costs are **rising** and **fixed** costs are also **going up**.

行政成本在減少，勞務成本也在下滑，但營運成本卻在增加，固定成本也在上漲。

☐ Do these costs **include** transport?

這些成本含不含運送？

填填看

請從「搭配詞表」中選出適當的字，完成下面句子。例解請見第333~353頁。

☐ Last month we (1)_____ quite (2)_____

(3)_____ costs due to the increase in the price of oil. We didn't expect that.

☐ We need to (4)_____ (5)_____ costs. It simply costs too much to keep the factory running. We need to increase our (6)_____, or do some (7)_____.

☐ We (8)_____ our (9)_____ costs will (10)_____ due to the oil price increase, but that our (11)_____ and (12)_____ costs will stay the same.

☐ We are going to have to sell a lot of units to (13)_____ our (14)_____ costs on this new project.

☐ How much is the (15)_____ cost for everything? And what does that (16)_____ exactly?

進階造句

請嘗試利用「搭配詞表」中的字彙，造出想要表達的句子。

_____

_____

_____

_____

_____

_____

_____

25	**credit** [`krɛdɪt]	可數名詞 信用貸款

搭配在前面的動詞	搭配的形容詞	關鍵字
		credit
give extend get obtain refuse	interest-free unsecured	credit crunch credit rating credit card credit agreement credit limit credit risk

 好搭例句 ◎ MP3-25

☐ I'm afraid we cannot **give** you credit for this purchase — it's against our company policy.
恐怕我們沒辦法在這筆採購上給你信貸──那違反我們公司的政策。

☐ If you place a large order, we can **extend** 6 months **interest-free** credit to you.
假如你下大筆的訂單，我們就能提供你六個月的無息信貸。

☐ Because our company has a bad credit rating with the bank, it's difficult to **get** credit from them.
由於我們公司對銀行的信用評等不佳，所以很難向它們取得信貸。

☐ I have managed to **obtain unsecured** credit from the bank to finance our new factory. The credit agreement stipulates that we have to pay back the loan in 5 years.
我好不容易向銀行申請到了免擔保信貸，以便為我們的新廠融資。信貸約定書上明訂，我們必須在五年內還清貸款。

☐ Due to the credit crunch, we will have to **refuse** credit to our customers. Please explain this to them.

由於信用緊縮，我們只好拒絕對顧客提供信貸。請跟他們說明這點。

☐ The credit limit on my credit card will not allow me to make this big purchase.

我信用卡的信用額度不容許我買這麼大筆的東西。

☐ This is an acceptable level of credit risk to us.

這樣的信貸風險是我們可以接受的程度。

填填看

請從「搭配詞表」中選出適當的字，完成下面句子。例解請見第333~353頁。

☐ We never (1)_____ credit to our new customers. The (2)_____ is too high for us, as we don't know you yet. I hope you will understand.

☐ Because of the (3)_____, the banks are worried about lending money to small businesses. They will not (4)_____ us any (5)_____ credit. We have to pay a lot of interest.

☐ I spoke to the head of the credit department and managed to (6)_____ 12 months (7)_____ credit.

☐ Because we didn't pay back our last loan on time and we broke our (8)_____, our (9)_____ is now quite bad. It will be difficult to (10)_____ credit.

☐ I need to extend the (11)_____ on my (12)_____. It's not enough, and I want to use the card to make larger purchases.

☐ We do not have anything to offer as collateral, so the bank

(13)_____ (14)_____ credit to us.

進階造句

請嘗試利用「搭配詞表」中的字彙，造出想要表達的句子。

_____

_____

_____

_____

_____

_____

_____

_____

customer
[ˋkʌstəmɚ]

可數名詞 顧客
同義字：client

搭配在前面的動詞	搭配的形容詞		關鍵字
approach			**customer**
have	potential		
get	prospective	private	customer satisfaction
attract	new	corporate	customer base
keep	existing	regular	customer care
retain		major	customer complaint
lose	satisfied	overseas	customer support
satisfy	loyal		customer service
serve	valued		

 好搭例句

◎ **MP3-26**

☐ We need to **get** some **new** customers to extend our customer base, otherwise we will not be able to meet our sales targets.
我們需要招攬一些新顧客來擴大我們的客群，否則我們就會達不到銷售目標。

☐ This new brochure will help to **attract potential** customers.
這份新的宣傳冊將有助於吸引潛在顧客。

☐ If we can ensure great customer satisfaction, this will help us to **keep** our **existing** customers.
假如我們能確保理想的顧客滿意度，這將有助於我們保住老顧客。

☐ Giving great customer support helps us to **retain** our customers.
給予良好的顧客支援有助於我們留住顧客。

☐ We did not deal with this customer complaint in the right way, so we **lost** a **major** customer.
我們沒有把這件客訴處理妥當，所以損失了一位主顧。

☐ They are one of our most **valued** customers. Please give them our best customer care.

他們是我們的貴客之一。請給他們最好的顧客關懷。

☐ We lease office furniture, so our customer base consists mainly of **corporate** customers.

我們是在出租辦公家具,所以我們的客群是以企業顧客為主。

☐ Since customer care is really important to our reputation, we **have** lots of **satisfied** customers.

由於顧客關懷對我們的信譽相當重要,因此我們有很多滿意的顧客。

☐ We are offering a 20% discount to our **regular** customers on all products.

我們在所有的產品上都替常客打八折。

☐ I **serve** most of our **overseas** customers. I try to provide them with good customer service, but it's hard because they are overseas.

我服務大部分的海外客戶。我盡量為他們提供良好的顧客服務,但也很辛苦,因為他們都在海外。

☐ For our **private** customers, we can offer excellent payment terms.

對於我們的私人客戶,我們可以給予極佳的付款條件。

☐ Thank you for being such a **loyal** customer.

感謝您是這麼忠實的顧客。

☐ I **approached** the customer with this new product, but they were not interested in it.

我拿這樣新產品去找顧客,可是他們並不感興趣。

✦ ✎ 填填看

請從「搭配詞表」中選出適當的字,完成下面句子。例解請見第333~353頁。

☐ We (1)_____ many (2)_____ customers. Exports make up 30% of our revenue.

☐ We need to (3)＿＿＿＿＿＿ some (4)＿＿＿＿＿＿ customers this month. We need to expand our customer base.

☐ The best way to (5)＿＿＿＿＿＿ our (6)＿＿＿＿＿＿ customers is to give them excellent (7)＿＿＿＿＿＿. That way they will stay with us.

☐ We (8)＿＿＿＿＿＿ many (9)＿＿＿＿＿＿ customers. That's because we provide great customer support and low prices.

☐ You are our most (10)＿＿＿＿＿＿ customer. Thanks for your business over the years.

☐ My job is to (11)＿＿＿＿＿＿ our (12)＿＿＿＿＿＿ customers. Their business needs are sometimes difficult to understand.

☐ (13)＿＿＿＿＿＿ customers will be attracted by our great products and low prices.

☐ We (14)＿＿＿＿＿＿ this (15)＿＿＿＿＿＿ customer because the (16)＿＿＿＿＿＿ procedure did not work. He was not happy.

☐ Let's (17)＿＿＿＿＿＿ the customer and see if we can get them to increase their order.

☐ (18)＿＿＿＿＿＿ is one way of extending our (19)＿＿＿＿＿＿. If they like our service, they will tell their friends.

進階造句

請嘗試利用「搭配詞表」中的字彙，造出想要表達的句子。

＿＿＿＿＿＿＿＿＿＿＿＿＿＿＿＿＿＿＿＿＿＿＿＿＿＿＿＿

＿＿＿＿＿＿＿＿＿＿＿＿＿＿＿＿＿＿＿＿＿＿＿＿＿＿＿＿

＿＿＿＿＿＿＿＿＿＿＿＿＿＿＿＿＿＿＿＿＿＿＿＿＿＿＿＿

data
[ˋdetə]

不可數名詞 資訊；情報
同義字：figures 、 information

搭配在前面的動詞	搭配的形容詞	關鍵字	搭配在後面的動詞
get access retrieve collect enter process handle store record look at analyze examine	a piece of detailed precise clear accurate comprehensive supporting additional raw caller financial customer operational market	**data (on sth.)** data base data bank data collection data entry data field data gathering data processing data storage data storage capacity	show n.p./v.p. reveal n.p./v.p. suggest n.p./v.p. indicate n.p./v.p. be derived from n.p. support n.p.

 好搭例句

🔘 **MP3-27**

☐ I can't **access** the **customer** data at the moment. Can you help? The data base seems to be down.
我目前讀取不到顧客資料，你能幫個忙嗎？資料庫似乎當掉了。

☐ My computer crashed. Can you **retrieve** my **financial** data for me?
我的電腦當機了。你能不能幫我擷取我的財務資料？

☐ Can you wait while I **get** the **customer** data?
你能不能等我抓出顧客資料？

☐ You need to **enter** the **precise financial** data into the correct field to get the right results. Careful data entry is very important.
你需要在正確的欄位輸入精確的財務資料，才能得到對的結果。小心輸入資料非常重要。

☐ It will take some time to **process** the **raw** data. Data processing is usually quite slow with this amount of data.
處理原始資料要花點時間。以這樣的資料量來說，資料處理通常都很慢。

☐ Our system cannot **handle** such **detailed** data.
我們的系統無法應付這種詳細的資料。

☐ We need to keep **collecting comprehensive market** data in order to understand the market. Constant data collection is important.
我們需要持續收集廣泛的市場資料，以了解市場。不斷收集資料很重要。

☐ Where do you **store** the **caller** data? I need to call this new customer back.
你把來電資料存在哪裡？我需要回電給這位新顧客。

☐ We must make sure we **record precise operational** data so that we can track costs.
我們必須確定我們記錄了精確的營運資料，這樣才能追蹤成本。

☐ We need to **look at** the **supporting** data to get a clearer picture of the market.
我們需要看看支援資料，以便對市場有更清楚的了解。

☐ If we **analyze** the data in more detail, we'll find more information.
假如我們更仔細地分析資料，就會發現更多資訊。

☐ Let's **examine** the data carefully to see where we can make cost savings.
我們來仔細檢視資料，看看可以在哪裡節省成本。

☐ The **market** data **shows** that we already have 25% of the market share for this type of product.
市場資料顯示，我們的這種產品已經有25%的市占率。

☐ Close analysis of the **financial** data **revealed** that the company was falsifying its profits.
仔細分析財務資料就可以看出，該公司竄改了它的獲利。

☐ The data **suggests** that we need to improve efficiency and cut costs if we want to survive.
資料顯示，假如我們想生存下去的話，我們就要提升效率並降低成本。

☐ This **piece of** data **indicates** the impact of the exchange rate on our profits.
這筆資料指出了匯率對我們獲利的影響。

☐ This **supporting** data **is derived from** the **raw** data you gave me last time we met.
這筆佐證資料是來自上次我們見面時，你給我的原始資料。

☐ The **financial** data **supports** the conclusions we made last month.
財務資料印證了我們上個月所得到的結論。

☐ Data gathering consists of **collecting** data and organizing it into data fields. The size of your data bank depends on your data storage capacity, and of course the security and efficiency of your data storage.
資料蒐集指的是收集資料，並把它組織成資料檔。資料庫的大小要看你的資料儲存容量，當然還有資料儲存的安全性與效率。

填填看

請從「搭配詞表」中選出適當的字，完成下面句子。例解請見第333~353頁。

☐ We need to (1)_____ some (2)_____ data to help us make this decision. Our (3)_____ is not big enough yet.

☐ I'm finding it difficult to (4)_____ (5)_____ data I need. I can get lots of other data, but it's not exactly what I need. Is there a problem with the (6)_____?

☐ It's very important to (7)_____ (8)_____

(9)_____ data so that we always know exactly what's

happening in the factory. Accurate (10)_____ is very important.

☐ Our researchers are very good at (11)_____ (12)_____

(13)_____ data. This helps us to plan marketing strategy. The

problem is that our (14)_____ is too small.

☐ Our (15)_____ data (16)_____ exactly what kind of

consumer buys our product.

☐ The (17)_____ data in the appendix at the back

(18)_____ my proposal.

☐ Our IT department is excellent at (19)_____ (20)_____

financial data. This kind of (21)_____ helps us to manage our

financial assets in the international markets. But, of course, a lot depends

on accurate (22)_____ .

進階造句

請嘗試利用「搭配詞表」中的字彙，造出想要表達的句子。

_____

_____

_____

_____

_____

| | | 28 | **deal** [dil] | | 可數名詞 交易 |

搭配在前面的動詞		搭配的形容詞	關鍵字
make	conclude	fair	
strike	complete	good	
		great	**deal**
sign	get		**(with sb.)**
	secure		**(on sth.)**
negotiate		better	
finalize	offer	the terms of the	

 好搭例句　　　　　　　　◎ MP3-28

☐ I'll **make** a deal **with** you. You buy 10 units, I'll give you a 5% discount. How's that sound?
我跟你談個買賣。你買10單位，我給你5%的折扣。這聽起來怎麼樣？

☐ We are trying to **strike** a **better** deal **with** our distributor to reduce our distribution costs.
我們正設法跟經銷商達成更好的協議，以降低我們的經銷成本。

☐ We **signed** the **new** deal last night.
我們昨天晚上簽訂了新買賣。

☐ We are currently **negotiating** a deal **with** our suppliers to try to reduce our production costs.
我們目前在跟供應商協商買賣，以設法降低我們的生產成本。

☐ **The terms of the** deal are being **finalized** right now.
買賣條件目前正在定案。

☐ We **concluded** the deal, and both sides thought it was a **fair** deal.
我們敲定了買賣，而且雙方都認為是件公平的買賣。

☐ Unless they agree to our terms, I don't think we can **complete** this deal.
除非他們同意我們的條件，否則我並不認為我們能完成這筆買賣。

☐ I **got** a **great** deal **on** my new car!

我為我的新車做了筆划算的買賣。

☐ It's important to try to **secure** a **good** deal **on** future orders.

設法在未來的訂單上取得不錯的協議很重要。

☐ I **offered** them a **fair** deal, but they didn't accept my offer.

我提議給他們一筆公平的買賣，但他們不接受我的提議。

填填看

請從「搭配詞表」中選出適當的字，完成下面句子。例解請見第333~353頁。

☐ Can we (1)_____ a deal? We will provide our business for one year if you give us a good discount.

☐ The two negotiators are (2)_____ (3)_____ deal right now.

☐ I (4)_____ a (5)_____ deal on the new contract. I'm so proud of myself!

☐ Can you (6)_____ me a (7)_____ deal? I can't accept this one.

☐ Every time I (8)_____ them a (9)_____ deal (10)_____ the delivery terms, they want more.

☐ I (11)_____ a (12)_____ deal (13)_____ them. My boss was very pleased with me.

進階造句

請嘗試利用「搭配詞表」中的字彙，造出想要表達的句子。

29	**delay** [dɪ`le]			可數名詞 延遲	

搭配在前面的動詞	搭配的形容詞		關鍵字	搭配在後面的動詞
be experience cause avoid reduce make up (for)	long considerable slight unnecessary	production shipment	**delay** **(to n.p.)** **(in Ving)**	occur arise cost n.p. be caused by n.p.

 好搭例句 MP3-29

☐ There **was** a **considerable** delay **to** the payment. Can you explain why?
付款延誤了滿久。你能解釋一下為什麼嗎？

☐ Bad weather **caused** the delay **to** the shipment. Please accept our apologies.
天候不佳導致船運延誤。請接受我們的道歉。

☐ We would like to **avoid** any **unnecessary** delays and hope we can finish the project quickly.
我們想避免任何不必要的延誤，並希望我們很快就能把案子完成。

☐ This new system will help us to **reduce** delays **in** responding to orders.
這套新系統將有助於我們在回覆訂單時減少延誤。

☐ Should you **experience** any delay **in** receiving your order, please let us know.
萬一你在收取訂貨時遇到任何延誤，請通知我們一聲。

☐ We often **experience long** delays to the production time. We need to find out why.

我們在生產時間上經常碰到冗長的延誤。我們需要查明為什麼。

☐ It **was** just a **slight** delay; nothing serious.

只是稍有延誤，沒什麼大事。

☐ I think we can **make up (for)** the delay later in the project.

我想我們晚點可以彌補這個案子的延誤。

☐ The delay **occurred** because there was a problem with the machinery.

延誤發生是因為機械出了問題。

☐ The delay **arose** when the raw materials were not delivered on time.

當原料沒有準時送達，延誤就產生了。

☐ The **production** delay **cost** a lot of money.

生產延誤耗費了很多錢。

☐ The **shipment** delay **was caused by** the typhoon.

船運延誤是導因於颱風。

✏ 填填看

請從「搭配詞表」中選出適當的字，完成下面句子。例解請見第333~353頁。

☐ The (1)_____ delay (2)_____ bad weather.

☐ The (3)_____ delay (4)_____ because of a late delivery of raw materials.

☐ The workers went on strike, (5)_____ a long (6)_____ delay in the factory.

☐ We will need to have more people in this team if we want to

(7)_____ a delay to the project.

☐ We are (8)_____ (9)_____ delays in getting the budget approval. This will delay the project.

☐ I don't know why you are so angry. It (10)_____ just a (11)_____ delay and it didn't (12)_____ anything — we didn't lose any money.

☐ We need to (13)_____ delays (14)_____ the payment, otherwise it will be difficult to manage our cash flow.

☐ We need to think of a way to (15)_____ the delay so that we can still complete the project on time.

進階造句

請嘗試利用「搭配詞表」中的字彙，造出想要表達的句子。

_____

_____

_____

_____

_____

_____

_____

| 30 | **delivery**
[dɪˋlɪvərɪ] | 可數名詞 運送 |

搭配在前面的動詞	搭配的形容詞	關鍵字
take accept ensure guarantee expect arrange make	late early quick speedy fast next-day prompt timely special registered	**delivery (of sth.)** delivery charge delivery address delivery date delivery schedule delivery form delivery note

 好搭例句　　　　　　　　　　　◎ MP3-30

☐ When you **take** delivery, don't forget to sign the delivery note.
你在收取送件時，別忘了簽一下送貨單。

☐ I'm not authorized to **accept** delivery **of** this document. Let me get my boss.
我無權收下送來的這份文件。我去請我老闆。

☐ We **ensure timely** delivery **of** all our orders.
我們保證會及時交付我們所有的訂貨。

☐ Can you **guarantee speedy** delivery?
你們能保證迅速交件嗎？

☐ We can only **guarantee next-day** delivery if you give us a local delivery address.
假如你給我們的是地區的送件地址，我們只能保證隔日送達。

☐ If there is an extra delivery charge, we **expect quick** delivery.
假如多付送件費，我們就可望快點送到。

☐ Our delivery schedule **ensures prompt** delivery.
我們的交件時程保證準時交件。

☐ Please check the delivery date. We do not **expect** such **late** delivery.
請看看交件日期。我們沒想到會這麼晚交件。

☐ We can **make early** delivery if it's urgent.
假如很趕的話，我們可以早點交件。

☐ We recommend that you **arrange recorded** or **special** delivery.
我們建議您採用簽收或特別遞件。

填填看

請從「搭配詞表」中選出適當的字，完成下面句子。例解請見第333~353頁。

☐ I can't (1)＿＿＿＿＿＿ delivery (2)＿＿＿＿＿＿ this shipment. The
(3)＿＿＿＿＿＿ is wrong. It should be that building over there.

☐ We cannot (4)＿＿＿＿＿＿ (5)＿＿＿＿＿＿ delivery of the final
product if all the materials we need to assemble it are delayed.

☐ There is an extra (6)＿＿＿＿＿＿ for (7)＿＿＿＿＿＿ delivery, and
we will (8)＿＿＿＿＿＿ (9)＿＿＿＿＿＿ delivery so that the
shipment arrives safely.

☐ We didn't expect such (10)＿＿＿＿＿＿ delivery. Thanks for such great
service.

☐ Do you (11)＿＿＿＿＿＿ deliveries overseas?

☐ What's the (12)＿＿＿＿＿＿ for this? Will it arrive on time?

☐ I forgot to sign the (13)＿＿＿＿＿＿. Sorry about that. My bad.

 進階造句

請嘗試利用「搭配詞表」中的字彙，造出想要表達的句子。

31 **department** [dɪˋpɑrtmənt]	可數名詞 部門	

搭配在前面的動詞	搭配的形容詞	關鍵字
work in manage	advertising finance legal	**department**
work with cooperate with move to transfer (sb.) to join	marketing personnel R&D sales service IT	department manager department head department meeting

 好搭例句

◎ MP3-31

☐ John **works in** the **finance** department. He is responsible for keeping financial records for all transactions the company makes and for preparing tax reports.

約翰服務於財務部。他負責為公司所從事的一切交易做財務紀錄，以及編製稅務報告。

☐ Tracy **manages** the **advertising** and **marketing** departments. She is assistant to the department manager.

翠西管的是廣告部和行銷部。她是在協助部門經理。

☐ I **work with** the department head of the **finance** department. It's a very big department.

我和財務部的部門負責人共事。它是非常大的部門。

☐ On this project we are **cooperating with** the **R&D** department.

在這個案子上，我們是跟研發部合作。

☐ At the end of the month, I'll be **moving to** the **personnel** department.
到月底時，我就要轉往人事部了。

☐ You looking for Brad? He **transferred to** the **sales** department.
你找布雷德嗎？他調去業務部了。

☐ I just **joined** the **service** department. I'm looking forward to servicing our customers and being part of this team.
我剛加入服務部。我期待服務顧客，並融入這個團隊。

☐ The **legal** department is having a department meeting in that room.
法務部正在那個房間裡開部門會議。

☐ We often **cooperate with** the **IT** department.
我們經常跟資訊科技部合作。

填填看

請從「搭配詞表」中選出適當的字，完成下面句子。例解請見第333~353頁。

☐ I love (1)_____ the (2)_____ department. I get to be very creative and also I can use my strategic thinking skills. I especially like working with the advertising agencies we use.

☐ She does a great job of (3)_____ the (4)_____ department. It must be very challenging having to know the laws of all the countries we operate in.

☐ If the (5)_____ departments could (6)_____ the (7)_____ department, then we would be able to provide a seamless after-sales service to the customer.

☐ As (8)_____ of the (9)_____ department I get to make the decisions about who gets to work in which department.

☐ I really want to (10)_____ the (11)_____ department, where I can look after the tax affairs of the company. It would be very interesting for me.

☐ The (12)_____ is on Thursday. At that meeting I will introduce the new team members who have recently (13)_____ the department.

☐ We are (14)_____ the (15)_____ department to develop a new product.

☐ We'll need to (16)_____ the (17)_____ department. We might need some technical support on this project.

進階造句

請嘗試利用「搭配詞表」中的字彙，造出想要表達的句子。

_____

_____

_____

_____

_____

_____

_____

development
[dɪˋvɛləpmənt]

可數名詞 發展

搭配在前面的動詞	搭配的形容詞		關鍵字
encourage promote stimulate facilitate support assist await	sustainable uneven future further recent latest new rapid	industrial technological economic software business employee product	**development (of sth.)** development plan development program development project

好搭例句

◎ MP3-32

☐ One of my jobs as HR manager is to **facilitate employee** development. To do this, I have to draw up development plans.
我擔任人力資源經理的其中一個工作就是促進員工發展。為了做到這點，我必須擬訂發展計畫。

☐ It's important to **promote sustainable** development. We don't want to grow too fast. My development program ensures this.
加強永續發展很重要。我們並不想成長得太快。我的發展計畫就是在確保這點。

☐ **Uneven** and **rapid** development **of** the company may result in a weak company.
公司發展不均與急切可能會導致公司積弱不振。

☐ I increased the budget for the research and development department because I want to **stimulate new product** development.
我增加了研發部的預算，因為我想要刺激新產品的開發。

☐ The **latest software** development project is going well. We should be ready for a demonstration in a few weeks.

最新的軟體開發案進行得不錯。我們應該在幾週內就會準備發表。

☐ The government has implemented measures to **encourage technological** development. This is a good opportunity for us.

政府採取了措施來鼓勵科技發展。這是我們的好機會。

☐ I look forward to **future business** developments. Please keep me informed.

我很期待未來的業務發展。請隨時通知我一聲。

☐ Is there anything I can do to **support** the **latest** developments? Please don't hesitate to let me know.

在支持最新的發展方面，有沒有什麼我可以做的事？請儘管告訴我。

☐ **Recent economic** developments have made it easier for us to do business. Sales are up.

近來的經濟發展使我們的生意比較好做，業績也上揚了。

☐ The lifting of government restrictions will do a lot to **assist industrial** development in the region.

政府解禁在當地將大大有助於產業發展。

☐ I **await further** developments with interest.

我很有興趣等待進一步的發展。

填填看

請從「搭配詞表」中選出適當的字，完成下面句子。例解請見第333~353頁。

☐ The government is doing everything it can to (1)_____

(2)_____ development of the region, including giving tax breaks to foreign industrial manufacturers. This is a good opportunity for us and fits in with my (3)_____ for the company.

☐ It's important to (4)_____ all aspects of development in the
company, including (5)_____ development, so that new
products can be created, and (6)_____ development, so that
people feel happy working here.

☐ (7)_____ (8)_____ development is better for the
company than (9)_____ and (10)_____ development. I
want to create a business that has strong foundations for future growth.

☐ The research and development department's (11)_____
(12)_____ is very exciting. I think it will add greatly to our
revenue source.

☐ I (13)_____ (14)_____ (15)_____
developments with excitement. I'm really interested to see what exciting
new programs will be developed.

進階造句

請嘗試利用「搭配詞表」中的字彙，造出想要表達的句子。

_____

_____

_____

_____

_____

_____

director
[dəˋrɛktə]

可數名詞 董事、總監

搭配在前面的動詞	搭配的形容詞		關鍵字
be act as appoint become be promoted to get promoted to ask meet	managing non-executive assistant deputy	advertising finance HR IT legal marketing R&D sales group company	**director (of sth.)**

好搭例句

◉ MP3-33

☐ He **is** the **R&D** director.
他是研發總監。

☐ He **is acting as** the **sales** director while the **sales** director is on maternity leave.
在業務主任休產假時，就由他代理業務主任。

☐ We need to **appoint** a new **advertising** director.
我們需要任命一位新的廣告總監。

☐ He only recently **became** the **managing** director **of** the company. He's very young!
他最近才成為公司的常務董事。他非常年輕！

☐ Most **company** directors are men, and most **group** directors are old men!
大部分的公司董事都是男人，而大部分的集團董事都是老男人！

☐ As a **non-executive** director **of** the company, your role is simply to give advice when we need it.

身為公司的非執行董事，你的角色就是在需要的時候提供建議。

☐ Let's congratulate Colin, who recently **got promoted to assistant marketing** and **advertising** director!

我們來恭喜柯林，他最近升任為助理行銷廣告總監！

☐ How would you feel about **being promoted to deputy finance** director?

要是被升為副財務總監，你會有什麼感覺？

☐ Let's **ask** the **marketing** director what she thinks.

我們去問問行銷總監有什麼想法。

☐ I'm **meeting** the new **HR** director on Monday.

我星期一要去見新的人力資源總監。

☐ The new **legal** director is an old classmate of mine!

新的法務主任是我的老同學！

☐ The **IT** director is very knowledgeable about computers. Have you met him?

資訊科技總監非常懂電腦。你見過他了嗎？

填填看

請從「搭配詞表」中選出適當的字，完成下面句子。例解請見第333~353頁。

☐ I (1)_____ the (2)_____ director, so I get to make all the final decisions.

☐ I am only (3)_____ director — the actual director is on leave.

☐ The (4)_____ director has no decision making power; the post is basically a consultative job.

☐ I (5)_____ the (6)_____ director. I am responsible for planning marketing strategy with my team. I'm also (7)_____ the (8)_____ director until we can (9)_____ a director to take over the advertising department.

☐ In my company the (10)_____ and (11)_____ director are the same person, as the R&D and IT departments are linked.

☐ She used to be the (12)_____ director. She only took on this job when the department manager was on leave, but she recently (13)_____ (14)_____ director, which means she has to help the director all the time.

☐ I'm (15)_____ the (16)_____ and (17)_____ directors on Tuesday, so I'll (18)_____ them what they think of our legal and financial positions.

☐ If you (19)_____ (20)_____ director, what new products will you try to develop?

☐ If you (21)_____ (22)_____ director, you will have overall responsibility for increasing staff retention. How do you intend to do that?

☐ I'm the director (23)_____ a private company.

☐ As (24)_____ director, you will have a staff of 300 engineers and programmers.

 進階造句

請嘗試利用「搭配詞表」中的字彙，造出想要表達的句子。

discount
[ˈdɪskaʊnt]

可數名詞 折扣

搭配在前面的動詞	搭配的形容詞	關鍵字
offer give	#% generous	**discount (on sth.)** **(of #)**
get receive	substantial big	discount voucher discount card
ask for	special	discount price

＃為數字

 好搭例句　　　　　　　　　　　　　　 ◎ **MP3-34**

☐ This month we are **offering** a **special** discount **on** all imported products.
這個月我們對所有的進口產品都給予特別折扣。

☐ I can **give** you a **20%** discount **on** this purchase if you buy today.
假如你今天就買的話，我可以在這筆採購上給你20%的折扣。

☐ I **got** a **generous** discount **of** 10% from the supplier.
我從供應商那裡得到了10%的豐厚折扣。

☐ The discount price does not include delivery.
折扣價不含寄送。

☐ VIP customers and holders of the store's discount card will **receive substantial** discounts **on** many purchases.
貴賓和本店折扣卡的持有人在多項採購上可獲得高額折扣。

☐ I'm afraid we cannot **offer** you a **big** discount, but we can give you 5% off. How's that?
恐怕我們沒辦法給你多大的折扣，但我們可以給你5%的折價。怎麼樣？

☐ You need to show your discount voucher to **receive** the discount.
你要出示折扣券才能獲得折扣。

☐ If the customer **asks for** a discount, give them 5%.

假如顧客要求打折，就給他們5%。

☐ I always **ask for** a discount **on** large orders.

我對於大訂單一定會要求打折。

填填看

請從「搭配詞表」中選出適當的字，完成下面句子。例解請見第333~353頁。

☐ I (1)＿＿＿＿＿＿ my customer a 10 (2)＿＿＿＿＿＿ discount

(3)＿＿＿＿＿＿ his next purchase.

☐ If you pay cash and buy now, I can (4)＿＿＿＿＿＿ you a

(5)＿＿＿＿＿＿ discount.

☐ I forgot to take my (6)＿＿＿＿＿＿, so I did not (7)＿＿＿＿＿＿ a

discount.

☐ The (8)＿＿＿＿＿＿ includes a one year warranty on service and parts.

☐ Why do people always (9)＿＿＿＿＿＿ a discount even though the

price is already really low?

☐ I (10)＿＿＿＿＿＿ a discount (11)＿＿＿＿＿＿ 10%, but they only

(12)＿＿＿＿＿＿ me 5%.

進階造句

請嘗試利用「搭配詞表」中的字彙，造出想要表達的句子。

＿＿＿＿＿＿＿＿＿＿＿＿＿＿＿＿＿＿＿＿＿＿＿＿＿＿＿＿＿＿＿

＿＿＿＿＿＿＿＿＿＿＿＿＿＿＿＿＿＿＿＿＿＿＿＿＿＿＿＿＿＿＿

＿＿＿＿＿＿＿＿＿＿＿＿＿＿＿＿＿＿＿＿＿＿＿＿＿＿＿＿＿＿＿

| 35 | **economy** [ɪˋkɑnəmɪ] | | 可數名詞 經濟 |

搭配在前面的動詞	搭配的形容詞		關鍵字	搭配在後面的動詞
manage regulate affect transform stimulate boost strengthen revitalize damage	weak mixed domestic local regional global world shrinking sluggish unstable	stable developed growing developing	**economy**	grow (by #) expand (by #) improve become adj. remain adj. continue to V shrink (by #)

＃爲數字

 好搭例句　　　　　　　　　◎ MP3-35

☐ The government is doing a good job of trying to **manage** the **unstable** economy.
在設法穩住不穩定的經濟上，政府表現出色。

☐ They are trying to **regulate** the **local** economy, and that sometimes makes it hard for us to do business here.
他們試圖管制地方經濟，這有時候會使我們很難在這裡做生意。

☐ Changes in the **global** economy can sometimes **affect** the **domestic** economy as well.
全球經濟的變化有時候也會影響到國內經濟。

☐ The Internet has **transformed** the **global** economy.
網際網路改變了全球經濟。

☐ What can we do to **stimulate** the **sluggish** economy?
我們要怎麼做才能刺激疲軟的經濟？

☐ These new laws did not succeed in **boosting** the **shrinking** economy.
這些新法令並未成功拉抬萎縮的經濟。

☐ The new government is trying to **strengthen** the **weak** economy.
新政府試圖振興疲弱的經濟。

☐ Membership in the WTO **revitalized** the **local** economy.
加入世界貿易組織重振了地方經濟。

☐ If the government intervenes with interest rates controls, it may **damage** the **unstable** economy.
假如政府干預利率管制，可能會損害不穩的經濟。

☐ It's easier to do business in a **developed** economy, but you get better growth in a **developing** economy.
在已開發經濟體做生意比較容易，可是在開發中經濟體會有比較好的成長。

☐ The **local** economy **grew by** 3 to 4%. The **global** economy **expanded by** about the same rate.
地方經濟成長了3%到4%。全球經濟也擴張了差不多同樣的比例。

☐ The **domestic** economy has not really **improved** this year.
國內經濟今年並沒有真正改善。

☐ The Chinese economy is **becoming** more difficult to slow down.
中國的經濟變得愈來愈難放緩。

☐ The economy will probably **remain** unstable for a while until the oil price stabilizes.
經濟八成會持續不穩一段時間，直到油價穩定為止。

☐ The American economy **continues to** expand.
美國的經濟持續擴張。

☐ The economy last year **shrank by** 2%.
去年的經濟萎縮了2%。

填填看

請從「搭配詞表」中選出適當的字，完成下面句子。例解請見第333~353頁。

☐ It's getting difficult to (1)_____ the (2)_____ economy. It's (3)_____ more and more unstable and no one knows how to slow it down.

☐ The government is trying to (4)_____ the (5)_____ (6)_____ economy. The growth rate last year was only 0.5%!

☐ The growing influence of China is (7)_____ (8)_____ economies. Vietnam's economy, for example, has also been affected.

☐ The high price of oil is (9)_____ many (10)_____ economies in the region.

☐ Most (11)_____ economies (12)_____ develop at the same rate last year as they did the year before. There was not much change.

☐ Although last year the (13)_____ economy did not (14)_____ much, this year it has grown very fast.

☐ This is a (15)_____ economy. It has strong service, technology, and manufacturing sectors. We expect it to (16)_____ that way. There will probably not be much change.

☐ Last year the economy (17)_____ (18)_____ 3%! Let me tell you, that hurt business here!

 **進階造句**

請嘗試利用「搭配詞表」中的字彙，造出想要表達的句子。

| 36 | **effect** [ɪˋfɛkt] | 可數名詞 效果；影響 |

搭配在前面的動詞	搭配的形容詞		關鍵字
assess examine go into come into be in take put sth. into have produce minimize	positive beneficial desired negative devastating adverse detrimental damaging harmful cumulative knock-on opposite	significant dramatic noticeable profound immediate direct similar long-term short-term possible likely	**effect (of sth.) (on sth.)**

 好搭例句　　　　　　　　　◎ MP3-36

☐ We need to **assess** the **possible** effect **on** our business **of** the rise in oil prices.
我們需要評估油價上漲對我們生意的可能影響。

☐ We need to **examine** the **likely** effect **of** the interest rate increase on our business.
我們需要檢視利率走升對我們生意的可能影響。

☐ The new regulations will **go into immediate** effect on Monday.
新規定在星期一即刻生效。

☐ The new laws will **come into direct** effect on Tuesday.
新法令在星期二直接生效。

☐ The new system **is** already **in** effect. Go to this link to see how it works.

新系統已經開通。去這個連結看看它運作得怎麼樣。

☐ The new guidelines **took** effect yesterday. Please follow them carefully.

新準則昨天生效。請切實遵守。

☐ We need to **put** our new payment terms **into** effect as quickly as possible.

我們需要盡快實行我們的新付款條件。

☐ The price rise **had** the **opposite** effect: it stimulated demand! There was a **similar** effect in other markets.

漲價帶來了相反的效應：它刺激了需求！別的市場也有類似的效應。

☐ It's likely that the oil price rise will **have** a **long-term negative** effect **on** our business.

油價上漲可能會對我們的生意造成長期的負面影響。

☐ There was a **dramatic** effect when he announced his resignation. Everyone was completely shocked.

他宣布辭職造成了劇烈的影響。每個人都十分震驚。

☐ He **has had** a **profound** effect **on** the way people do business in this country.

他對大家在這個國家做生意的方式帶來了深遠的影響。

☐ I don't think these changes will **have** a **significant** effect. They are not bold enough.

我並不認為這些改變會造成可觀的影響。它不夠大膽。

☐ His remark **produced** a **devastating short-term** effect **on** the share price. It dropped sharply.

他的發言對股價產生了破壞性的短期影響，而使它暴跌。

☐ We need to **minimize** the **adverse knock-on** effects, otherwise things will just go out of control.

我們要把不利的連鎖效應降到最低，否則情況就會失控。

☐ The product recall **had** a **cumulative damaging** effect **on** our business. Demand for all our products started to fall.
把產品召回對我們的生意造成了累積性的有害影響。我們所有產品的需求都開始下滑了。

☐ There was a **noticeable beneficial** effect when the new salary increases were announced. Productivity increased
宣布新的薪資調漲帶來了顯著的有利影響。生產力提高了。

☐ Will there be any **harmful** effects if we implement this proposal? Or will there only be **positive** effects?
假如我們實施這個提案，會有什麼危害性的影響嗎？還是只會有正面的影響？

☐ Cold weather **has had** a **detrimental** effect **on** sales.
天冷對業績造成了不利的影響。

填填看

請從「搭配詞表」中選出適當的字，完成下面句子。例解請見第333~353頁。

☐ How can we (1)_____ the effect (2)_____ this proposal (3)_____ our business? What will happen? What do you think the (4)_____ effects will be?

☐ These new policies will (5)_____ effect tomorrow. We hope they will (6)_____ a (7)_____ effect (8)_____ the company.

☐ We must try to (9)_____ the (10)_____ effects of this price rise, otherwise the situation will get worse and worse.

☐ The change in spending habits due to the recession has (11)_____ a (12)_____ effect on our business. It's very bad indeed.

☐ Joining the WTO had a (13)_____ (14)_____ effect on our business. We hope that this effect will also be (15)_____, and not just a short-term thing.

☐ We did the same thing as our competitors, but it had the (16)_____ effect! I was expecting it to have a (17)_____ effect!

☐ Make sure you implement this proposal so that it has (18)_____ effect.

進階造句

請嘗試利用「搭配詞表」中的字彙，造出想要表達的句子。

_____

_____

_____

_____

_____

_____

_____

_____

| 37 | **employee**
[ˌɛmplɔɪˈi] | | 可數名詞 員工
同義字：staff、personnel | |

搭配在前面 的動詞	搭配的 形容詞	關鍵字	搭配在後面 的動詞
recruit inform		**employee** **(of sth.)**	
pay give dismiss lay off make ★ redundant sack fire retain motivate encourage ★ (to V) train transfer	salaried full-time part-time temporary existing new key good bad	employee turnover employee satisfaction employee training employee benefits employee management	receive earn work leave be entitled to be responsible for

★為關鍵字

 好搭例句

◎ MP3-37

☐ We need to **recruit** some **new** employees.
我們需要招募一些新員工。

☐ Please **inform** all **existing** employees that they will not receive a bonus this year.
請通知所有的現任員工，他們今年不會領到分紅。

☐ We **pay full-time** employees very well, and we're **giving** all **salaried** employees a big bonus this year.
我們給全職員工的薪酬非常優渥，而且我們今年會發高額的獎金給所有的受薪員工。

☐ We are going to have to **dismiss part-time** employees and **lay off** 5% of our **salaried** employees.
我們必須遣散兼職員工，並資遣5%的受薪員工。

☐ We **made** a lot of our employees **redundant** last year, but now we are hiring again. 我們去年裁撤了很多員工，但現在我們要重新找人了。

☐ The worst part of my job as HR manager is **sacking** and **firing bad** employees.
在我擔任人力資源經理的工作中，最難過的部分就是要開除和解雇不好的員工。

☐ If we want to **retain** our **key** employees, we will need to offer some employee training. That way we can increase employee satisfaction and reduce employee turnover.
假如我們想要留住重要員工，我們就要給予一些員工訓練。如此一來，我們就能提高員工滿意度，並降低員工異動率。

☐ Please **encourage** the employees **to** work harder.
請敦促員工更努力工作。

☐ What can we do to **motivate** employees to work harder?
我們要怎麼做才能激勵員工更努力工作？

☐ We **train new** employees so that they can work the machinery.
我們會訓練新進員工，使他們懂得操作機器。

☐ We are **transferring** some of our **good** employees to our factories in China. 我們要把一些優秀的員工調到我們的中國廠去。

☐ **Part-time** employees **receive** a generous hourly wage.
兼職員工可拿到豐厚的時薪。

☐ Most employees in this company **earn** more than the national average.
這家公司大部分的員工都賺得比全國的平均值要多。

☐ Employees have to **work** at the company for ten years before they **are entitled to** employee benefits.
員工必須在公司服務十年，才有權享受員工福利。

☐ Most of our employees **are responsible for** their own taxes.
我們大部分的員工都要負擔本身的稅金。

☐ The biggest part of my job as HR manager is employee management.
在我擔任人力資源經理的工作中，員工管理是最主要的部分。

☐ Many of our **key** employees are **leaving** to join the competition.
我們有許多重要員工都離開並加入了對手的陣營。

填填看

請從「搭配詞表」中選出適當的字，完成下面句子。例解請見第333~353頁。

☐ We are currently (1)_____ 100 (2)_____ employees. Are you interested in joining us? The pay is good and the (3)_____ are even better.

☐ Please (4)_____ all (5)_____ employees that if they can help to (6)_____ a (7)_____ employee, they will (8)_____ a bonus at the end of the month.

☐ We need to (9)_____ our (10)_____ employees more to stop them from (11)_____. Our (12)_____ is simply too high. It's a big cost for us to have so many of our most experienced employees leaving.

☐ We need to cut costs. Please (13)_____ the (14)_____ employees, those who are underperforming, and cut back all

(15)_____. They will have to teach each other how to do the job.

☐ In order to (16)_____ our employees and stop them joining our competitors, we must try to increase (17)_____ and make the company a more engaging place to work.

☐ The hardest part of (18)_____ is (19)_____ employees when they do something wrong. But, I have no choice. That's the job of the HR manager, right?

☐ We need to increase production turnover. What can we do to (20)_____ the employees?

☐ Employees who (21)_____ with us for 5 years (22)_____ much more than others in the industry.

☐ All employees (23)_____ a bonus if the company performance is good.

☐ We (24)_____ our employees in safety procedures, but employees have to (25)_____ their own safety.

☐ We are going to (26)_____ some employees to the factory in Taichung for a week. Any volunteers who want to go?

進階造句

請嘗試利用「搭配詞表」中的字彙，造出想要表達的句子。

_____

_____

_____

experience
[ɪkˋspɪrɪəns]

不可數名詞 經驗

搭配在前面的動詞	搭配的形容詞	關鍵字	搭配在後面的動詞
have	previous		show that v.p.
get	past	**experience**	suggest that v.p.
gain	valuable	**(in n.p./Ving)**	
share	relevant	**(with n.p.)**	
broaden	practical	**(of n.p./Ving)**	teach sb. wh-clause
provide	work		
offer			
lack			

 好搭例句

◎ MP3-38

☐ I already **have** quite a lot of **previous** experience **with** this kind of software.
對於這種軟體，我已經具有相當豐富的先前經驗。

☐ I **got** a lot of **valuable** experience **of** dealing with customers.
在應付顧客方面，我獲得了許多寶貴的經驗。

☐ I **gained** the **relevant** experience on my previous job.
我從前一份工作中學到了相關經驗。

☐ If employees **share** their **practical** experience **in** handling the machinery, they will learn from each other.
假如員工分享操作機器的實務經驗，他們就能互相學習。

☐ I hope I can **broaden** my **work** experience here.
我希望我能在這裡拓展我的工作經驗。

☐ We **offer** the experience **of** working in a foreign company.
我們具有在外國公司服務的經驗。

☐ Don't worry if you **lack** experience **in** this. We **provide** experience and training.
別擔心你在這方面缺乏經驗。我們會提供經驗及訓練。

☐ **Past** experience **shows that** employees who are happy stay with the company.
過去的經驗證明，滿意的員工就會留在公司。

☐ Experience **suggests that** the problems might be with the salary package.
經驗顯示，問題可能是出在薪資配套上。

☐ Experience **teaches you how** to manage a difficult boss.
經驗會教你要怎麼駕馭難搞的老闆。

填填看

請從「搭配詞表」中選出適當的字，完成下面句子。例解請見第333~353頁。

☐ I (1)_____ a lot of (2)_____ experience (3)_____ working with children in my first job as a volunteer in a school for handicapped children.

☐ (4)_____ experience (5)_____ that employees who have worked in this industry before often have better skills.

☐ I (6)_____ (7)_____ experience as I'm just out of college. But I am very willing to learn. I hope you can (8)_____ the experience I need.

☐ This is John. You will be working together. I'm sure John will be willing to (9)_____ his experience with you.

☐ I'm looking for a job that will (10)_____ my experience. I

(11)_____ much and I want to learn.

☐ Only experience (12)_____ you how to manage your time.

進階造句

請嘗試利用「搭配詞表」中的字彙，造出想要表達的句子。

_____ _____

_____

_____

_____

_____

_____

_____

_____

factor
[ˈfæktɚ]

可數名詞 因素

搭配在前面的動詞	搭配的形容詞	關鍵字	搭配在後面的動詞
be identify take into account consider examine	number of combination of various common contributory contributing key important major significant critical deciding external	**factor(s)** **(in sth.)**	be influence n.p. affect n.p. contribute to n.p. cause n.p. lead to n.p. explain n.p.

 好搭例句

◎ MP3-39

☐ There **are** a **combination of** factors **in** this situation.
這個局面綜合了各項因素。

☐ If we could always **identify** the **common** factors which **lead to** success, then we would never fail, right?
假如我們總是能找出獲致成功的共通因素，那我們就絕對不會失敗了，對吧？

☐ We need to **take into account** the most **significant** factor here: price.
我們在這裡需要考慮到最要緊的因素：價格。

☐ Let's **consider** the **critical** factors.
我們來想想關鍵因素。

☐ If we **examine** the **contributing** factors, we can see that the problem is not an easy one to solve.
假如我們去看成因，我們會發現問題並不好解決。

☐ There **are a number of various** factors we need to consider.
有一些不同的因素是我們需要考慮的。

☐ The **key** factor **is** price.
主要因素在於價格。

☐ There are many factors **influencing** the market right now.
目前有許多因素在影響市場。

☐ The **important** factor **contributing to** our success is having a really great product.
促成我們成功的重要因素是，有真正優良的產品。

☐ What factors **influenced** your decision to close the branch?
是哪些因素影響了你們決定把分店關閉？

☐ The **deciding** factor which **affected** my decision was that the branch was not performing well.
影響我決定的決定性因素在於，分店表現不佳。

☐ There are many **contributory** factors which **cause** low staff moral. The major factors **are** low pay and long hours.
有許多構成因素會導致員工士氣低落。主因則是薪水低與工時長。

☐ This is just an **external** factor which doesn't really **explain** your decision.
這只是外在因素，無法真正解釋你的決定。

✎ 填填看

請從「搭配詞表」中選出適當的字，完成下面句子。例解請見第333~353頁。

☐ Let's (1)＿＿＿＿＿＿ the factors in the market right now.

☐ Can you (2)_____ the (3)_____ factor causing the problem? What do we need to address first?

☐ Staff absenteeism (4)_____ a (5)_____ factor (6)_____ low productivity. It happens all the time.

☐ We need to (7)_____ this (8)_____ factor when we make our decision.

☐ A (9)_____ factors (10)_____ the problem.

☐ A (11)_____ factor (12)_____ the situation was the fact that we didn't have a strong team. It wasn't the most important factor, but it certainly helped to make the problems worse.

☐ His great background in IT is the (13)_____ factor which (14)_____ my decision to hire him.

☐ This is just an (15)_____ factor, and probably not very important.

☐ The (16)_____ factors which might affect us are: the economic situation, the political situation, the exchange rate, and the price of oil.

進階造句

請嘗試利用「搭配詞表」中的字彙，造出想要表達的句子。

_____

_____

_____

_____

_____

	feature [fitʃɚ]	可數名詞 特色、功能

搭配在前面的動詞	搭配的形容詞		關鍵字
be have include show	unique distinguishing distinctive standard additional	common important main key product	**feature (of sth.)**

 好搭例句　　　　　　　　🔘 **MP3-40**

☐ The product **has** many **distinguishing** features. It really stands out from other products of the same kind.
這樣產品有許多與眾不同的特色。跟其他同類型的產品比起來，它十分突出。

☐ The Fanny-G **is** a **unique** feature of this product. No other manufacturers include this feature in their products.
Fanny-G是這項產品的獨到特色。沒有別的製造商在產品中納入了這項特色。

☐ The color **is** a **distinctive** feature of the product. This dark blue looks great.
顏色是這樣產品的獨門特色。這個深藍色看起來很棒。

☐ The product **includes** all the **standard** features.
這樣產品包含了一切標準功能。

☐ There **are** a range of very interesting **additional** features for you to choose from.
有多種非常有趣的附加功能可供選擇。

☐ Going to KTV and dining together **is** a **common** feature **of** the way business is done here.
一起唱KTV和吃飯是這裡經商之道的共同特色。

☐ Relationships and family connections **are** an **important** feature **of** doing business here.

人脈和家庭關係是在這裡做生意的重要特色。

☐ One of the **main** features **of** the industry is the way R&D is located here, while manufacturing is located in China.

這項產業的一個主要特色是，如何在這裡研發，並在中國製造。

☐ A **key** feature **of** this market is its price sensitivity. People here go for a low price rather than good quality.

這個市場的主要特色在於它的價格敏感度。這裡的人偏好低價勝過良好的品質。

☐ There **are** many great **product** features. Here, let me show you some.

產品功能有很多都很棒。到這邊來，我展示一些給你看。

🖉 填填看

請從「搭配詞表」中選出適當的字，完成下面句子。例解請見第333~353頁。

☐ I like all the **(1)**_____ features. They are all great. But what **(2)**_____ features can you offer me if I want something extra?

☐ We need to think of a **(3)**_____ feature we can give the product — you know, something which will make it really special.

☐ This is a **(4)**_____ feature of this type of product. All products of this type usually **(5)**_____ this feature.

☐ A(n) **(6)**_____ feature of the product is its incredible durability. It lasts for about 10 years before you have to replace it. For many of our customers, this is its main attraction.

☐ We must (7)_____ all the (8)_____ features in the catalogue. Otherwise customers will not be able to understand the product.

☐ This is a unique feature (9)_____ the product .

進階造句

請嘗試利用「搭配詞表」中的字彙，造出想要表達的句子。

_____

_____

_____

_____

_____

_____

_____

_____

41	**figures** [ˈfɪgjəz]	可數名詞 數據 同義字：data

搭配在前面 的動詞	搭配的形容詞		關鍵字	搭配在後面 的動詞
see release calculate arrive at prepare look at adjust compare put ★ at quote	official key latest first quarter second quarter third quarter fourth quarter half-yearly year-end	trading sales performance productivity financial	**figures** **(for sth.)**	suggest n.p. suggest that v.p. show n.p. show that v.p. reveal n.p. reveal that v.p. indicate n.p. indicate that v.p. represent n.p. include n.p.

★為關鍵字

 好搭例句 ◎ **MP3-41**

☐ I just **saw** the **official half-yearly trading** figures. They aren't so good, are they?

我剛才看了正式的半年貿易數字。不怎麼好看，對吧？

☐ They have just **released** their **key productivity** figures **for** the year.

他們剛發布了年度的重要生產數字。

☐ I am currently **calculating** the **year-end sales** figures. I'll let you have them by the end of the day.

我目前正在計算年終銷售數字。我會在下班前向你報告。

☐ How did you **arrive at** these figures? Are you sure they are correct?

你是怎麼得到這些數字的？你確定正確嗎？

☐ **Preparing performance** figures is a difficult job.
編訂績效數字是件苦差事。

☐ We need to **adjust** these **sales** figures. The sales volume was not what we predicted.
我們需要調整這些銷售數字。銷售量不符合我們的預測。

☐ If we **compare first quarter** figures this year with **first quarter** figures from last year, we can see that they are not the same.
假如我們拿今年第一季的數字來跟去年第一季的數字比較，我們就會看出有所不同。

☐ I **put** the **third quarter sales** figures **at** 27%. What did you get?
我算出第三季的銷售數字是27%。你算出來是多少？

☐ Can you send me the **fourth quarter** figures **for** your department by the end of the day please?
可以麻煩你在下班前把你們部門第四季的數字寄給我嗎？

☐ He **quoted** the **latest** figures, but I know they are not correct.
他引用的是最新的數字，但我知道它並不正確。

☐ I'm **looking at** the **financial** figures now. Do you see them on page 10?
我現在正在看財務數字。你有在第10頁上看到嗎？

☐ These figures **suggest that** we are not going to meet our targets.
這些數字顯示，我們無法達到我們的目標。

☐ These figures **suggest** a 4% increase over last year.
這些數字顯示，去年增加了4%。

☐ The **second quarter** figures **show** an increase.
第二季的數字呈現出上漲。

☐ The **key** figures here **show that** business on the whole is considerably good.
這裡的重要數字顯示出，整體業績相當好。

☐ The figures **reveal** a problem.
數字透露了一個問題。

☐ The figures **reveal that** there is some difference between targets and results.
數字透露出，目標和結果有一些落差。

☐ The figures **indicate that** it won't be long before we go out of business.
數字指出，過不了多久，我們就要關門大吉了。

☐ The figures **indicate** a loss.
數字指出了虧損。

☐ These figures **represent** months of hard work by the entire finance team.
這些數字代表整個財務團隊努力工作了好幾個月。

☐ These figures do not **include** the results from last quarter.
這些數字並不包含上一季的結果。

🖉 **填填看**

請從「搭配詞表」中選出適當的字，完成下面句子。例解請見第333~353頁。

☐ I (1)_____ the figures by collecting all the data and then studying it. I'm pretty sure they are correct.

☐ Did you (2)_____ the (3)_____ (4)_____ figures? They are amazing! I'm sure everyone in the sales team will get a huge bonus this year.

☐ We need to (5)_____ these figures for inflation. It keeps going up, and that changes all the calculations.

☐ The government just (6)_____ the (7)_____ figures for the economy. They aren't looking good.

☐ Here we can (8)_____ the (9)_____ figures (10)_____ the last quarter of last year.

☐ Let's (11)_____ the (12)_____ figures for this sales team with the (13)_____ figures for the whole company. We can see that this team has contributed most of the sales to the company's trading.

☐ (14)_____ (15)_____ figures (16)_____ that the company is performing very well in all the key areas of business.

☐ I (17)_____ these figures 35% and you (18)_____ them 36%. Someone somewhere has made a mistake.

☐ The (19)_____ figures I (20)_____ earlier are not correct. Actually, the real figures (21)_____ an increase in productivity.

☐ These figures (22)_____ all performance indicators — everything is here.

☐ Let's (23)_____ the figures carefully and see if we can find the mistake.

進階造句

請嘗試利用「搭配詞表」中的字彙，造出想要表達的句子。

_____

_____

_____

_____

42	**finance** [faɪnæns]	可數名詞 財務，資金

搭配在前面的動詞	搭配的形容詞		關鍵字
raise obtain arrange provide need	additional short-term long-term	personal corporate private	**finance**

 好搭例句   **MP3-42**

☐ We need to **raise** some **additional** finance for this project. Let me ask the shareholders what they think.
我們需要為這個案子籌措一些額外的資金。我來問問股東有什麼看法。

☐ It's so difficult to **obtain** finance from the finance department for any new projects these days. They are very tight with their budgets.
近來任何新案子要向財務部取得資金都十分困難。它們的預算緊得不得了。

☐ For this project we need to **arrange** some **short-term** finance.
對於這件新案子，我們需要做一些短期融資。

☐ This bank **provides long-term** finance for companies who need extra capital.
這家銀行有提供長期融資給需要額外資金的公司。

☐ My **personal** finances are a mess. I have a big overdraft at the bank, and a huge credit card bill. I must stop shopping!
我的個人財務很糟糕。我的銀行存款大透支，還有巨額的信用卡欠款。我必須停止購物才行！

☐ I studied **corporate** finance in college, and now I am the CFO of a huge IT company. It's great!

我在大學讀的是公司財務，目前我則是一家大型資訊科技公司的財務長。真棒！

☐ We need **private** finance for this project. The bank won't lend us the money. They say the project is too high risk.

我們在這個案子上需要私人融資。銀行不會借我們錢，他們說這個案子風險太高了。

填填看

請從「搭配詞表」中選出適當的字，完成下面句子。例解請見第333~353頁。

☐ It's difficult to (1)_____ finance for construction projects. Everyone thinks the property market is going to crash.

☐ If we could (2)_____ (3)_____ (4)_____ finance, that would help us to complete the project. The bank won't lend us enough.

☐ Because the project is an international project, its very difficult to (5)_____ finance. It's very complex.

☐ The railway was built with a combination of government money and (6)_____ finance.

☐ (7)_____ finance for multinational companies is very complex. That's why it's difficult to find good financial officers these days.

☐ I specialize in (8)_____ finance — you know, helping people manage their personal income. I don't know much about (9)_____, finance, which is more about helping companies to make the best of the financial assets.

☐ When companies need to arrange some (10)_____ finance for a particular project, they usually go to a bank and borrow it. When they need to arrange (11)_____ finance it's more usual for them to issue shares.

☐ We are a private investment company. We (12)_____ finance for companies who (13)_____ finance fast.

進階造句

請嘗試利用「搭配詞表」中的字彙，造出想要表達的句子。

_____

_____

_____

_____

_____

_____

_____

43 **function** [ˈfʌŋkʃən]	可數名詞 功能

搭配在前面的動詞	搭配的形容詞		關鍵字
have perform fulfill serve exercise provide	basic primary main useful extra	search audit administrative control	**function** **(of Ving)**

 好搭例句　　　　　　　　　　　 MP3-43

☐ This machine **has** many functions. Its **basic** function is to cut the metal.
這台機器有許多功能。它的基本功能是切割金屬。

☐ The system **performs** many **useful** functions.
這套系統可執行許多有用的功能。

☐ It's not really **fulfilling** the **main** function it was designed for. I think it's badly designed.
它並沒有真正展現出它在設計上的主要功能。我想它設計得並不好。

☐ This computer **serves** the **primary** function **of** monitoring all the different processes in the factory.
這台電腦所具備的主要功能是，監控廠內所有不同的流程。

☐ We need the system to **exercise** a more specific **control** function. Can you make it do that?
我們需要這套系統行使更明確的控管功能。你能讓它做到這點嗎？

☐ Our department mainly **performs** an **administrative** function. We handle logistics paperwork.
我們部門主要是在負責行政職掌。我們要處理後勤文書作業。

☐ The finance department **performs** an **auditing** function once a year. We do this once a year.

財務部要負責一年一度的稽核職掌。我們是一年舉辦一次。

☐ The **search** function on my computer is not working efficiently.

我電腦的搜尋功能運作得不太有效率。

☐ Can you **provide** more **extra** functions in the second version of the program? Here is a list of what we need.

你能不能在第二版的程式中提供更多的額外功能？這份清單是我們所需要的項目。

✦ ✎ 填填看

請從「搭配詞表」中選出適當的字，完成下面句子。例解請見第333~353頁。

☐ I understand the main function, but I want to know how many

(1)_____ functions the software can (2)_____.

☐ The new system (3)_____ many (4)_____ functions. It will be multipurpose.

☐ The system (5)_____ mainly an (6)_____ function. It is useful for keeping records and handling transactions.

☐ The control room is the hub of the factory. These computers here

(7)_____ a (8)_____ function.

☐ We need a more powerful (9)_____ function, so that we can find our financial data more quickly.

☐ The (10)_____ function allows us to provide financial records more efficiently.

☐ Your (11)＿＿＿＿＿＿ function in this department will be to monitor quality control.

☐ What's the function (12)＿＿＿＿＿＿ this button here?

進階造句

請嘗試利用「搭配詞表」中的字彙，造出想要表達的句子。

_____

_____

_____

_____

_____

_____

_____

_____

44	**growth** [groθ]	不可數名詞 成長

搭配在前面的動詞		搭配的形容詞		關鍵字
be have achieve see experience expect	show stimulate promote sustain control	quick rapid steady sustained continued	slow sustainable long-term short-term	**growth (in sth.) (of #)** growth rate growth forecast growth target

 好搭例句 **MP3-44**

☐ There **has been** a **rapid** growth **in** demand for our products, thanks to our marketing efforts.

拜我們的行銷作業所賜，我們產品的需求出現了迅速成長。

☐ We **have had sustained** growth **in** all our markets. Our growth forecasts for next year show that this growth is set to continue.

在所有的市場上，我們都持續成長。我們明年的成長預測顯示，這樣的成長可望延續下去。

☐ It's important to try to **achieve sustainable** growth in the long term.

設法長期達到持續成長很重要。

☐ We **have seen sustained** growth **in** our share price.

我們的股價出現了持續成長。

☐ Our market share **has shown steady** growth over the last year.

我們的市占率去年呈現穩步成長。

☐ We **have experienced continued** growth **in** our overseas revenues.

我們的海外營收顯示出在不斷成長。

☐ We need to try to **stimulate** growth **in** our market share. We are falling behind the competition.

我們需要設法在市占率上刺激成長。我們落後了競爭對手。

☐ My job is to **promote** growth **in** the company's revenues.

我的工作是為公司的營收促進成長。

☐ We have grown so fast over the last two years, but I don't think we will be able to **sustain** this growth over the next two years.

過去兩年來，我們成長得非常快，但我並不認為我們在未來兩年還能持續這樣的成長。

☐ We need to try to **control** the growth, otherwise we will weaken our sustainability.

我們需要設法控制成長，否則我們就會削弱我們的持續力。

☐ I am happy with the **slow** growth rate of the company. It's more sustainable. A **rapid** growth rate can lead to problems.

我樂見公司的緩慢成長率，這樣比較持久。快速成長率會出問題。

☐ My job is to set growth targets. Yours is to meet them, okay?

我的工作是訂立成長目標，你則要達到它，明白嗎？

☐ We **saw** growth **of 3%** here last year.

我們在這方面去年成長了3%。

☐ We don't **expect much** growth over the next few months.

未來幾個月，我們並不指望會成長多少。

✎ 填填看

請從「搭配詞表」中選出適當的字，完成下面句子。例解請見第333~353頁。

☐ We (1)_____ (2)_____ growth in all our markets last year. It was very surprising that we grew so fast, but it's very good!

☐ Our revenue (3)_____ (4)_____ but (5)_____

growth over the last year. We didn't grow much, but I'm still quite happy with it.

☐ It's important to try to (6)_____ (7)_____ growth. We don't want to expand too fast and exhaust our resources.

☐ Revenue has (8)_____ (9)_____ growth. Every month we have grown just a little bit.

☐ Our revenue this month is very small. We need to urgently (10)_____ growth if we are going to meet our (11)_____.

☐ These last few months we have grown much too fast. Our (12)_____ has been too rapid. We can't sustain it. We need to (13)_____ our (14)_____ growth, otherwise in the long term we will not have the resources to supply our customers.

☐ We are trying to (15)_____ (16)_____ growth. In this kind of market, it's important to think about planning for possible future downturns.

☐ (17)_____ indicate that we will not be able to sustain this kind of growth. There (18)_____ rapid growth (19)_____ demand for our products recently.

☐ We (20)_____ growth (21)_____ 4.6% here next year. That's what all the experts are predicting.

進階造句

請嘗試利用「搭配詞表」中的字彙，造出想要表達的句子。

45 **information** [ˌɪnfɚˋmeʃən]

不可數名詞 資訊

同義字：data

搭配在前面的動詞		搭配的形容詞		關鍵字
provide give sb. divulge input enter get obtain have receive	gather collect store access retrieve require withhold	further available relevant confidential classified necessary	correct accurate detailed inside background personal useful	**information** **(about sth.)** **(on sth.)** information management information processing information service information system information technology

好搭例句

MP3-45

☐ Can you **provide** any **further** information **about** this?
你能在這方面提供任何進一步的訊息嗎？

☐ I have already **given** you all the **available** information **on** this.
我已經把這方面現有的訊息全都給你了。

☐ It's a crime to **divulge confidential** information.
洩露機密訊息是犯罪行為。

☐ Let's try to **get** some **detailed background** information **about** the company.
我們設法去針對該公司找一些詳細的背景訊息。

☐ I have managed to **obtain inside** information. Some of it is **classified** information so don't tell anyone I have it.
我好不容易獲得了內線消息。其中有些是機密消息，所以不要把我知道的事告訴任何人。

☐ I **have** lots of **useful** information **about** the product.

我有很多與產品相關的有用訊息。

☐ I have already **received** the **necessary** information.

我已經收到了必要的訊息。

☐ Information management involves **gathering**, **inputting**, **storing** and then making it easy for people to **access** the information. Modern information technology makes this much easier than it was 20 years ago.

資訊管理是在蒐集、輸入、儲存，然後使人易於讀取資訊。現代的資訊科技使它比20年前要容易得多。

☐ Our new information system makes it easier for you to **enter** and then **retrieve** the **correct** information.

我們的新資訊系統使你更容易輸入然後擷取正確的資訊。

☐ In order for us to **provide** an information service, it's essential that we **collect accurate** information.

我們如果要提供資訊服務，就非得收集精確的資訊不可。

☐ We **require** all your **personal** information. Please complete this form.

我們需要你所有的個人資料。請填寫這份表格。

☐ If you **withhold relevant** information, we will have to get a court order.

假如你隱瞞相關訊息，我們就只好訴諸法庭了。

☐ The information processing is very slow. There must be a problem with the server.

資訊處理非常慢。伺服器一定出了問題。

✐ 填填看

請從「搭配詞表」中選出適當的字，完成下面句子。例解請見第333~353頁。

☐ You will need to (1)＿＿＿＿＿＿ your (2)＿＿＿＿＿＿ information — you know, name, address, and payroll number.

☐ Make sure you (3)_____ the (4)_____ information. Otherwise, the (5)_____ doesn't work properly.

☐ Do you (6)_____ any (7)_____ information?

☐ It's going to be difficult to (8)_____ this information. Much of it is (9)_____, which means it's not publicly available.

☐ The information I'm (10)_____ you is (11)_____ , so please don't (12)_____ it to anyone.

☐ Do you (13)_____ any (14)_____ information (15)_____ the merger? I want to read more about it.

☐ (16)_____ is all about making sure the information people need is freely available. It involves (17)_____ information, (18)_____ it in a secure environment, and then helping people (19)_____ the information when they need it.

☐ I contacted their (20)_____ and I have now (21)_____ lots of really (22)_____ information. It's very helpful.

☐ I work in (23)_____. My job is to process the information I receive. It's really easy nowadays with such advanced (24)_____. The computer does all the work!

☐ I haven't got the (25)_____ information I need to make my decision.

☐ I have already sent you all the (26)_____ information. There's nothing else I can find.

☐ She (27)_____ me some (28)_____ (29)_____ information, which is completely illegal! I know exactly what is going to happen to the share price.

☐ If you know something, you should tell us. Please don't

(30) _____ information.

進階造句

請嘗試利用「搭配詞表」中的字彙，造出想要表達的句子。

_____

_____

_____

_____

_____

_____

_____

46	**investment** [ɪnˋvɛstmənt]	可數名詞 投資 同義字：capital

搭配在前面的動詞	搭配的形容詞		關鍵字
make attract encourage recoup need require protect increase	substantial massive major long-term mid-term short-term sound total additional initial	capital private minimum direct foreign	**investment (in sth.) (of #)** investment opportunity investment strategy investment fund

 好搭例句　　　　　　　　　　◎ MP3-46

☐ Over the last few years we have **made massive** investments in China.
過去幾年來，我們大舉投資了中國。

☐ We hope we can **attract** more **direct** investment **in** the project.
我們希望我們這個案子能吸引到更多的直接投資。

☐ Since the government is trying to **encourage** more **private** investment,
we see this as an **excellent long-term** investment opportunity.
自從政府試圖鼓勵更多私人投資以來，我們就把它視為絕佳的長期投資機會。

☐ We hope to **recoup** our investment within the next 5 years. It's a **mid-term** investment.
我們希望能在未來五年內回收投資。它屬於中期投資。

☐ This country **needs substantial foreign** investment before it can compete with neighboring countries.
這個國家需要大量的外國投資才能和鄰國競爭。

☐ The investment fund **requires** a **minimum** investment **of** 20 thousand. Is that okay with you?
投資基金規定，最低投資金額是兩萬。這樣你可以嗎？

☐ We have just **made** a **major capital** investment **in** a new factory in Vietnam. We think it's a **sound** investment, as all the indicators show Vietnam is safe.
我們剛對越南的新廠做了重大的資本投資。我們認為這是穩當的投資，因為所有的指標都顯示越南很安全。

☐ Our **short-term** investment strategy is to invest in high risk areas such as Vietnam.
我們的短期投資策略是投資高風險地區，比方說越南。

☐ Please remember that we can't really do anything to fully **protect** your investment.
請記住，我們無法真的做什麼來完全保障你們的投資。

☐ Our **initial** investment was 10 million, but now we need to **increase that** investment. The **total** investment will be 15 million.
我們的初步投資是 1,000 萬，但現在我們需要擴大那筆投資。總投資額將是 1,500 萬。

☐ It's a new investment fund.
它是新的投資基金。

☐ We need to **make** an **additional** investment **of** 20 million.
我們需要額外投資 2000 萬。

✎ 填填看

請從「搭配詞表」中選出適當的字，完成下面句子。例解請見第 333~353 頁。

☐ We have (1)_____ a (2)_____ investment

(3)_____ new equipment and machines.

☐ If we want to compete in this market we will (4)_____ some

investment.

☐ The project was financed with a mixture of (5)_____ and

government investment. Those private investors (6)_____ their

investment after 10 years. It was an excellent (7)_____

(8)_____ .

☐ The government there is trying to (9)_____ (10)_____

investment. The investment is (11)_____ by the government.

☐ It's a very (12)_____ (13)_____ . I'm sure we will make

good money.

☐ We need a (14)_____ (15)_____ investment

(16)_____ 20 million in order to complete the project.

☐ Our (17)_____ investment was very good. I recommend we

(18)_____ our investment now so that we can get more returns.

☐ (19)_____ (20)_____ investment last year was 30

million. That includes all companies investing directly into the local

economy.

☐ This (21)_____ tries to balance high (22)_____ returns

with (23)_____ sustainable growth. The fund manager is very

good.

☐ It's not enough. We still need (24)_____ investment if we are

going to make this work.

進階造句

請嘗試利用「搭配詞表」中的字彙，造出想要表達的句子。

47	**invoice** [ˈɪnvɔɪs]	可數名詞 發票；發貨單

搭配在前面的動詞	搭配的形容詞	關鍵字
issue give send receive get process check submit complete	tax original VAT sales	**invoice (for sth.)**

 好搭例句

◎ MP3-47

☐ We will **issue** you a **sales** invoice.
我們會開銷售發票給你。

☐ I'll **give** you a **tax** invoice in a moment.
我馬上就把稅務發票給你。

☐ I'll **send** the **VAT** invoice to you at the end of the month.
我到月底會把加值稅發票寄給你。

☐ I still haven't **received** the **tax** invoice from you.
我還是沒收到你們的稅務發票。

☐ Make sure you **get** an invoice for every purchase, and then make sure you **submit** your **original** invoices by the end of the month.
你的每筆購買一定都要拿到發票，接著在月底前一定要繳交你的原始發票。

☐ It takes me some time to **process** all the **tax** invoices from each department.
我要花點時間去處理所有來自各個部門的稅務發票。

☐ I've just **checked** this **tax** invoice and I think it's wrong. Can you check it for me as well?
我剛剛查了這張稅務發票，我想它開錯了。你能不能也幫我檢查看看？

☐ Can you show me how to **complete** this **sales** invoice? I don't know how to do it.
你能不能教我要怎麼填寫這份銷售發票？我不曉得要怎麼填。

填填看

請從「搭配詞表」中選出適當的字，完成下面句子。例解請見第333~353頁。

☐ I forgot to (1)_____ an invoice. Can you tell me your address so I can (2)_____ it to you?

☐ The (3)_____ invoice shows how much tax you paid, and the (4)_____ invoice shows how much you paid for the product.

☐ I need to (5)_____ an invoice (6)_____ this purchase.

☐ I have to (7)_____ all my (8)_____ invoices to the finance department at the end of the month. They will not accept copies.

☐ My job is to (9)_____ all the (10)_____ invoices. I have to (11)_____ them, make sure they are correct, and then (12)_____ them to the tax office.

☐ I think someone made a mistake (13)_____ the tax invoice. I hope that will not cause problems for the accounting department.

進階造句

請嘗試利用「搭配詞表」中的字彙，造出想要表達的句子。

| 48 | **issue** [ˈɪʃjʊ] | 可數名詞 議題 同義字：problem、question |

搭配在前面的動詞		搭配的形容詞	關鍵字	搭配在後面的動詞
raise identify highlight have address examine explore consider discuss	tackle confuse clarify settle decide	important major specific key fundamental complicated complex contentious controversial real underlying recurring	**issue** **(of sth.)** **(with sb.)**	be involves n.p. arise relate to n.p. be related to n.p.

 好搭例句

◎ **MP3-48**

☐ You've **raised** a **contentious** issue there.
你在那裡掀起了一個人言言殊的爭議。

☐ You **identified** several **important** issues in your presentation. How do you propose to **tackle** them?
你在提報中點出了幾個重要的爭議。你打算要怎麼處理？

☐ Do you **have** an issue **with** your manager? If so, you need to **discuss** it with him.
你跟你們經理有爭議嗎？假如有的話，你需要跟他討論一下。

☐ I will be **addressing** the **underlying** issue **of** the need for tighter project management.
我會去解決專案管理需要緊縮的根本爭議。

☐ In my report I **highlighted** several **specific** issues which we need to **settle**.
在我的報告中，我凸顯了幾個我們需要去化解的具體爭議。

☐ I'd like to **examine** the **major** issue **of** our product development process now.
我現在想查明我們產品開發流程的重大爭議。

☐ Let's **explore** some of these **complicated** issues later.
我們稍後來探討其中一些複雜的爭議。

☐ Please don't **confuse** the **real** issue. I'm talking about something else right now.
請不要弄混了真正的爭議。我現在所談的是別的事。

☐ Let's **decide** this **complex** issue later. I think we need to **clarify** it before we can **settle** it.
我們稍後來決定這個複雜的爭議。我想我們需要先加以釐清，才能把它化解。

☐ The **key** issue **is** whether we should adjust our strategy.
關鍵爭議在於，我們該不該調整策略。

☐ The **fundamental** issue we need to **consider involves** the question of prices.
我們需要考慮的基本爭議是價格的問題。

☐ The issue originally **arose** because the client changed the specs. This is a **recurring** issue with this client.
當初產生爭議是因為，客戶變更了規格。這是這家客戶一再出現的爭議。

☐ This **controversial** issue **is related to** previous attempts to regulate the market.
這個引發論戰的爭議跟之前管制市場的企圖有關。

☐ This issue **relates to** the points I made earlier.

這個爭議跟我稍早所提過的論點有關。

✏️ 填填看

請從「搭配詞表」中選出適當的字，完成下面句子。例解請見第333~353頁。

☐ Let's (1)＿＿＿＿＿＿ this (2)＿＿＿＿＿＿ issue before we go any further. Everyone certainly has his or her own opinion about it.

☐ I have (3)＿＿＿＿＿＿ two (4)＿＿＿＿＿＿ issues in my report which need to be (5)＿＿＿＿＿＿ before we make a decision about whether to go ahead with this project or not.

☐ I (6)＿＿＿＿＿＿ the issue (7)＿＿＿＿＿＿ communication at our last meeting. I pointed out then that this issue (8)＿＿＿＿＿＿ because of lack of a dedicated communication channel.

☐ I'm afraid I (9)＿＿＿＿＿＿ a (10)＿＿＿＿＿＿ issue (11)＿＿＿＿＿＿ my manager. I find her impossible to work with.

☐ Let's try to (12)＿＿＿＿＿＿ some of the issues which (13)＿＿＿＿＿＿ the project. If we understand them fully, maybe we can (14)＿＿＿＿＿＿ them a bit easier.

☐ Please don't (15)＿＿＿＿＿＿ the issue — it's already (16)＿＿＿＿＿＿ enough without you (17)＿＿＿＿＿＿ other issues which (18)＿＿＿＿＿＿ the project.

☐ This (19)＿＿＿＿＿＿ issue (20)＿＿＿＿＿＿ everybody. We all need to look at the areas of the project we are involved in and see how we can improve, so that this problem doesn't keep happening again and again.

☐ The (21)_____ issue (22)_____ cost. That is the cause

of all the problems.

進階造句

請嘗試利用「搭配詞表」中的字彙，造出想要表達的句子。

job
[dʒɑb]

可數名詞 工作

搭配在前面的動詞	搭配的形容詞	關鍵字	搭配在後面的動詞
have	good	**job**	
do	great		
look for	previous		job description
	last	job description	
get		job interview	involve n.p.
find	part-time	job opportunity	involve Ving
	full-time	job prospects	require that v.p.
quit		job satisfaction	
lose	well-paying	job security	
change	temporary	job vacancy	
offer sb.	new		

 好搭例句

◎ **MP3-49**

☐ I **have** a **great** job at the moment with good job security and job satisfaction. I couldn't be happier!
我目前有一份很棒的工作,以及良好的工作保障與工作滿意度。我夫復何求啊!

☐ You **did** a really **good** job on that report. I was very impressed.
你在那份報告上表現得相當好。我非常欣賞。

☐ I spent a long time **looking for** a **well-paying** job which also had good job prospects.
我花了很長的時間尋找工作前景也不錯的高薪工作。

☐ I need to **get** a **new** job, but there are not many job opportunities around at the moment.
我需要找新工作,可是目前周遭的工作機會並不多。

☐ I hope I can **find** a **full-time** job soon.

我希望很快就能找到全職工作。

☐ I **quit** my **last** job after they asked me to do things which were not in my job description.

我辭掉上一份工作是因為，他們要求我去做不在我工作範圍內的事。

☐ I **lost** my **previous** job when the company I was working for went bust.

我丟掉前一份工作是因為，我服務的那家公司倒了。

☐ I want to **change** jobs. Are there any job vacancies in your company?

我想要換工作。你們公司有沒有什麼職缺？

☐ I can only **offer** you a **temporary part-time** job at the moment.

我目前只能提供你臨時的兼職工作。

☐ My job **involves** dealing with customers and taking their orders.

我的工作是跟顧客打交道，以及接受他們下訂。

☐ You didn't tell me at the job interview that the job **involves** lots of travel abroad.

你在求職面談時並沒有告訴我，這份工作要常跑國外。

☐ The job **requires that** you speak good English. How is your English?

這份工作要會說流利的英語。你的英語怎麼樣？

✏️ 填填看

請從「搭配詞表」中選出適當的字，完成下面句子。例解請見第333~353頁。

☐ Are you (1)＿＿＿＿＿＿ a job? I think Yoyodyne has some (2)＿＿＿＿＿＿ at the moment. Why don't you talk to them?

☐ When I (3)＿＿＿＿＿＿ a job, I'm going to work really hard at it and always (4)＿＿＿＿＿＿ a (5)＿＿＿＿＿＿ job so that I get promoted really quickly.

☐ I love my job because it (6)_____ lots of contact with international colleagues and I love that! I have such great (7)_____.

☐ I (8)_____ a (9)_____ (10)_____ job, so although the hours are long, the pay is good. I can't complain.

☐ It's only a (11)_____ job, but I think they will make it full-time soon and then promote me, so the (12)_____ are good.

☐ My (13)_____ job (14)_____ too much paperwork. It's so boring. I preferred my (15)_____ job — it was more fun.

☐ I (16)_____ my (17)_____ job when the company closed down because the owner went to prison for fraud. I hope I can (18)_____ a job with more (19)_____ this time. I don't want to keep (20)_____ jobs.

☐ I (21)_____ my last job when the boss told me that the job (22)_____ that I collect his kids from school everyday and look after his wife. That was not in the (23)_____, and they did not tell me about it at the (24)_____. I just can't accept that kind of local business practice!

☐ We are pleased to be able to (25)_____ you a job as marketing assistant. Please let us know if you would like to accept.

進階造句

請嘗試利用「搭配詞表」中的字彙，造出想要表達的句子。

_____

_____

_____

50	**level** [ˈlɛvl]	可數名詞 層次，水準

搭配在前面的動詞		搭配的形容詞		關鍵字
reach attain achieve	reduce lower	low high	basic current	**level (of sth.)**
raise increase	determine	acceptable	present	
maintain	provide	certain	entry	

 好搭例句

 MP3-50

☐ We have now **reached** an **acceptable** level **of** revenue. Let's try to **maintain** it.
我們現在在營收上達到了可接受的水準。我們要努力維持。

☐ You have only managed to **attain** a **low** level **of** performance in your annual evaluation. You need to do better if you want to keep your job.
你只是好不容易在年度考核中達到了低水準的表現。假如你想要保住工作的話，就要更加努力才行。

☐ It's difficult to **achieve high** levels **of** quality if we don't make investments in new machinery.
假如我們不投資新機具的話，品質很難達到高水準。

☐ The **current** level **of** staff turnover is too high. We need to **raise** the level **of** staff retention.
目前的人員異動度太高了。我們需要提高人員留任度。

☐ Is there any way we can **increase** the level **of** investment in this project?
我們有沒有什麼方法可以提高這個案子的投資水準？

☐ How can we **maintain** the **present** level **of** customer satisfaction?
我們要怎麼維持現有的顧客滿意度？

☐ We need to **reduce** levels **of** spending. Costs are too high.
我們需要降低開支水準。成本太高了。

☐ Please **lower** the level **of** waste produced by your department. Remember that waste is expensive!
請減少貴部製造浪費的程度。記住，浪費可是很貴的！

☐ Your previous experience in the industry will **determine** your level **of** payment.
你在業界的過往經驗將決定你的薪資水準。

☐ My sister just got an **entry** level position at a design firm.
我妹妹剛在一家設計公司謀得了一個基層職位。

☐ We currently **provide** a **basic** level **of** customer support. I'd like to see this increased.
我們目前提供了基本程度的顧客支援。我想看到這方面有所提高。

☐ You need a **certain** level **of** experience to apply for this position.
你需要一定程度的經驗才能應徵這個職位。

🖊 填填看

請從「搭配詞表」中選出適當的字，完成下面句子。例解請見第333~353頁。

☐ We have (1)_____ an unbelievably (2)_____ level of sales revenue this quarter! You guys are fantastic! Bonuses will be huge this year!

☐ Our competitors have (3)_____ the level (4)_____ competition. We are all going to have to work harder to keep up with them.

☐ It's very difficult to (5)_____ the (6)_____ level of staffing. We need to raise salaries and reduce hours, otherwise staff turnover is going to keep increasing.

☐ Is there any way we can (7)＿＿＿＿＿＿ the level of customer complaints? There are too many of them!

☐ There is a very (8)＿＿＿＿＿＿ level of job satisfaction in this industry. No one likes it. Get used to it!

☐ There is a (9)＿＿＿＿＿＿ level of difficulty involved in managing a large company like this. Not everyone can do it.

☐ We need to (10)＿＿＿＿＿＿ the (11)＿＿＿＿＿＿ level of revenue income at which we can continue to operate.

☐ The company (12)＿＿＿＿＿＿ an (13)＿＿＿＿＿＿ level (14)＿＿＿＿＿＿ payment. Most people in the industry reckon it's quite fair.

☐ She's just an (15)＿＿＿＿＿＿ level employee. We can't ask her to take on so much responsibility.

進階造句

請嘗試利用「搭配詞表」中的字彙，造出想要表達的句子。

173

51	**loss** [lɔs]		可數名詞 損失

搭配在前面的動詞		搭配的形容詞		關鍵字
suffer make incur report announce	reduce make up cover	net pre-tax half-year quarterly annual	big heavy worse than expected estimated financial	**loss** **(of #)**

 好搭例句 ◎ **MP3-51**

☐ Last year we **suffered** a **pre-tax** loss **of** 300 million.
去年我們出現了3億的稅前虧損。

☐ We **made** an **estimated** loss **of** 2% on that deal.
在那件買賣上，我們估計損失了2%。

☐ I think we are going to **incur** a **heavy** loss on this product.
我想我們在這樣產品上會蒙受巨額的損失。

☐ They **reported** a **big annual** loss **of** 15 million
他們提報了1500萬的高額年度虧損。

☐ The company **announced** a **half-year** loss **of** 50 million
公司宣布半年虧損了5000萬。

☐ We need to try to **reduce** our **quarterly financial** losses, otherwise our final year-end figure is going to be very bad.
我們要設法降低我們的季財務虧損，否則我們的年終數字會非常難看。

☐ Our **net** loss is **worse than expected**. We had to pay back a big amount of interest, and that affected the figures.
我們的淨損比預期還糟。我們必須還一大筆利息，那會影響到數字。

☐ How can we **make up** the loss? We need to improve these figures?

我們要怎麼樣才能彌補虧損？我們需要改善這些數字嗎？

☐ I don't think we can **cover** the loss this year. We have to hope we can earn more next year.

我不認為我們今年能打平虧損。我們只好希望明年能賺更多錢了。

填填看

請從「搭配詞表」中選出適當的字，完成下面句子。例解請見第333~353頁。

☐ Due to the situation in the American sub prime market, we

(1)_____ (2)_____ losses on our investments there.

☐ I'm afraid I have to (3)_____ an (4)_____

(5)_____ loss (6)_____ 300 million. That's after tax,

and for the whole year.

☐ We managed to (7)_____ our (8)_____ loss last

quarter. This means our (9)_____ loss for the first half of the

year will not be quite as bad as we expected.

☐ I predict an (10)_____ loss (11)_____ 20%. That's just

a rough guess.

☐ Although we (12)_____ a (13)_____ loss last year, we

picked up 20% of the market share. This will allow us to

(14)_____ for the loss next year.

進階造句

請嘗試利用「搭配詞表」中的字彙，造出想要表達的句子。

_____

_____

management
[`mænɪdʒmənt`]

不可數名詞 管理

搭配在前面的動詞	搭配的形容詞		關鍵字
provide	top senior mid-level		**management (of sth.)**
improve			
delegate	day-to-day operational	financial personnel	management buy-out management consultancy
oversee		project resource	management team
simplify	effective efficient	risk	management style
require		waste strategic	management strategy management structure
inform	poor		
tell	prudent careful		
report to			
	overall		

 好搭例句

MP3-52

☐ My job is to **provide effective overall** management **of** the company. I set management strategy.
我的工作是為公司提供有效的全面管理。我要制訂管理策略。

☐ We need to **improve** the **day-to-day operational** management **of** the company. It's not **efficient** enough at the moment.
我們需要改善公司的日常營運管理，目前不夠有效率。

☐ I usually **delegate project** management. I have a great management team, who know how to get on with the job, and they like my management style.
我通常是把專案管理委派出去。我有一個很棒的管理團隊，他們知道要怎麼做好這件工作，他們也喜歡我的管理風格。

☐ If you don't **oversee mid-level** management, then you end up with **poor** management **overall**.
假如你不監督中級管理階層，那到最後你就會整個管理不善。

☐ The management consultancy recommended that we **simplify** our **senior** management structure. I hope that doesn't mean me!
管理顧問公司建議，我們應該簡化高層管理結構。我希望那不是在指我！

☐ The current situation **requires prudent financial** and **risk** management.
目前的情況需要審慎的財務與風險管理。

☐ **Careful waste** and **resource** management is the key to reducing the environmental impact of our manufacturing process.
妥善的廢棄物與資源管理是讓我們的製程減少環境衝擊的關鍵。

☐ The HR manager's job is to **provide effective personnel** management.
人力資源經理的工作是提供有效的人事管理。

☐ **Top** management is planning a management buy-out.
管理高層正在計畫管理階層收購。

☐ I will have to **inform** management about this problem. The policy is to **tell** management about all problems.
我必須把這個問題告知管理階層。原則就是要把一切的問題告訴管理階層。

☐ I am only a junior manager, so I have to **report to senior** management.
我只是個襄理，所以我必須向管理高層報告。

填填看

請從「搭配詞表」中選出適當的字，完成下面句子。例解請見第333~353頁。

☐ During the early days of the company, the (1)_____

(2)_____ very (3)_____ management

(4)_____ the company. That's why the company grew so quickly.

☐ I am too busy to (5)_____ (6)_____ management. I (7)_____ that to my team. The daily business of the company is not my job. My job is to (8)_____ (9)_____.

☐ We need to (10)_____ our (11)_____ management if we are going to get through this difficult period.

☐ (12)_____ (13)_____ management caused the environmental disaster.

☐ (14)_____ management (15)_____ the daily business of various teams in the company. (16)_____ management generally (17)_____ (18)_____ management for the whole company. The (19)_____ is like a pyramid.

☐ We brought in a (20)_____ to give us advice on how to restructure the management. They told us to (21)_____ the structure of the company. It's too top heavy at the moment.

☐ With (22)_____ (23)_____ management I think we can survive. Don't take any big risks.

☐ You need to (24)_____ your (25)_____. Many people are complaining that you are too bossy.

☐ The project is very complex. It (26)_____ very (27)_____ (28)_____ management. Also, (29)_____ management is also key — make sure you get the right people on the team.

☐ I think there will be a (30)_____ of the company soon. The management team and the main shareholders don't agree at all about anything.

☐ Junior managers (31)_____ senior management, so if there are any problems you should (32)_____ management right away.

進階造句

請嘗試利用「搭配詞表」中的字彙，造出想要表達的句子。

_____

_____

_____

_____

_____

_____

_____

_____

manager
[ˈmænɪdʒɚ]

可數名詞 經理

搭配在前面的動詞		搭配的形容詞		關鍵字
act as appoint be appointed to become be promoted to get promoted to	inform tell report to ask work with	project line assistant senior regional general personnel department	accounts advertising finance HR IT legal marketing R&D sales	**manager (of/for sth.)**

好搭例句

◎ MP3-53

☐ I am **acting as project** manager **for** this project.
我要擔任這個案子的專案經理。

☐ We need to **appoint** an **assistant IT** manager to help you with this. The workload is too heavy.
我們需要派個資訊科技副理來幫忙你處理這件事。工作負擔太重了。

☐ He **was appointed to general** manager **of** the company when he was 35 years old.
他在35歲的時候被任命為公司的總經理。

☐ She **became marketing** manager after she came back from studying marketing abroad.
她去國外讀完行銷回來後，就當上了行銷經理。

☐ Wow! I've **been promoted to senior finance** manager!
哇！我被升為資深財務經理了！

☐ My goal is to **get promoted to HR** manager in 4 years. At the moment I'm just one of a team of **personnel** managers.
我的目標是要在四年內晉升為人力資源經理。目前我只是一群人事經理中的一員。

☐ If you need to take time off over the holiday period, please remember to **inform** your managers.
假如各位需要在假日期間休假，請記得通知各位的經理。

☐ Why didn't you **tell** the **sales** manager about this problem with your customer?
你為什麼不把顧客的這個問題告訴業務經理？

☐ I usually **report to** my **line** manager, but for some projects I have to **report to** my **regional** manager.
我通常是向直屬經理報告，但在某些案子上，我則必須向區域經理報告。

☐ Let me **ask** my **department** manager about this.
我去向部門經理問問這件事。

☐ You will be **working with** the **R&D** manager very closely.
你會跟研發經理有非常密切的合作。

☐ The **legal** manager resigned! I wonder why.
法務經理辭職了！我搞不懂為什麼。

☐ I'm an **accounts** manager, but I really want to be an **advertising** manager.
我是客戶經理，但我想當的其實是廣告經理。

✏️ 填填看

請從「搭配詞表」中選出適當的字，完成下面句子。例解請見第333~353頁。

☐ He **(1)**＿＿＿＿＿＿＿ **(2)**＿＿＿＿＿＿＿ manager after only three years of working at the company. He must be really good at his job.

☐ You need to (3)_____ your manager if you think there are some problems with the project.

☐ I need to (4)_____ a (5)_____ manager for this project. Tom, can you do it?

☐ Let me (6)_____ my (7)_____ manager if I can take tomorrow off.

☐ Although I was hired as a (8)_____ manager because of my experience with customers, I am now (9)_____ (10)_____ manager as well, because I know the market very well.

☐ I want to (11)_____ (12)_____ manager in two years. Then it will be easier for me to get into top management.

☐ In this company, (13)_____ manager and (14)_____ manager are the same-looking after employees. In other bigger companies, however, they have different responsibilities.

☐ If you can't (15)_____ your manager, then we will have to let you go. You must learn to work together.

進階造句

請嘗試利用「搭配詞表」中的字彙，造出想要表達的句子。

_____

_____

_____

_____

	54	**manufacturer** [ˌmænjəˈfæktʃərə]	可數名詞 製造商

搭配在前面的動詞	搭配的形容詞	關鍵字	搭配在後面的動詞
force encourage enable	leading largest major	**manufacturer (of sth.)**	use produce make give

 好搭例句 **MP3-54**

☐ The new regulations will **force** manufacturers to use environmentally sustainable materials.
新規定將強制製造商使用環保材料。

☐ We **encourage** the manufacturers **of** the parts we use in our products to use only the best materials.
針對我們的產品所使用的零件，我們鼓勵製造商只用最好的材料。

☐ The new laws will **enable** manufacturers like us to increase our exports.
新法令將使我們這種製造商可以增加出口量。

☐ We are one of the **leading** manufacturers **of** computer components.
我們是一家電腦零組件的頂尖製造商。

☐ The **largest** manufacturer **of** laptops in the world **uses** our components.
全世界最大的筆電製造商是採用我們的零組件。

☐ We are the **major** manufacturer **of** LCD monitors. We **produce** millions of these units every year.
我們是液晶螢幕的最大製造商。我們每年要生產好幾百萬台這種裝置。

☐ The manufacturer also **makes** components for our competitors.
該製造商也替我們的競爭對手做零組件。

The manufacturer **of** these parts has **given** us a very good discount.
這些零件的製造商給了我們非常優惠的折扣。

填填看

請從「搭配詞表」中選出適當的字，完成下面句子。例解請見第333~353頁。

We are (1)_____ the manufacturers (2)_____ our components to use environmentally friendly materials.

This new design will (3)_____ the manufacturer to (4)_____ the product more cheaply.

Our partners in this venture are the (5)_____ manufacturers of cars in Japan. We are supplying them with our products.

As the manufacturer of premium ice cream, we (6)_____ only the finest ingredients.

The manufacturers of these parts usually (7)_____ a 5-year warranty for large orders.

進階造句

請嘗試利用「搭配詞表」中的字彙，造出想要表達的句子。

_____

_____

_____

_____

_____

market
[`mɑrkɪt]

可數名詞 市場

搭配在前面的動詞	搭配的形容詞		關鍵字	搭配在後面的動詞
	depressed shrinking declining		**market (for sth.)**	
enter break into	growing	labor housing	market analysis market conditions	
withdraw from	important large major	financial stock	market leader market research market share	
corner dominate flood penetrate	small insignificant	bond equity money	market segmentation	grow expand rise
create establish	competitive tough	capital		fall collapse
expand develop	foreign overseas international domestic local	export mass niche		
supply	open over-regulated saturated			

好搭例句

◎ **MP3-55**

☐ Market analysis shows that now is a good time to **enter** the **growing financial** market. Market conditions are right.

市場分析顯示，現在是進入成長中的金融市場的好時機。市場條件不錯。

- [ ] It's more difficult to **break into new** markets than it is to increase market share.

  打入新市場比擴大市占率要難。

- [ ] Our competitors have **cornered** the market with their main product and **dominate** the market **for** our other products as well.

  我們的競爭對手靠它們的主要產品壟斷了市場，並在我們其他的產品方面也掌控了市場。

- [ ] It's a very **competitive** market, and it's also a **shrinking** market, so I recommend **withdrawing from** it.

  這是個非常競爭的市場，也是個萎縮中的市場，所以我建議退出為宜。

- [ ] Cheap goods from overseas are **flooding** the market. Because of this we have not been able to **penetrate** the market.

  海外的廉價品正湧入市場。就是因為這樣，我們才沒辦法深入市場。

- [ ] The role of marketing is to **create** a market **for** the company's products. Market research is a very important part of this, and so is market segmentation

  行銷的角色是在為公司的產品創造市場。市場研究是其中非常重要的部分，市場區隔亦然。

- [ ] We need to try to **expand** our **declining overseas** market.

  我們要設法拓展我們衰退中的海外市場。

- [ ] We are aiming to **supply major foreign** markets.

  我們正致力於供應主要的外國市場。

- [ ] We are doing our best to **dominate** this **niche** market. It's an **important** market for us. We are well on the way to becoming the market leader.

  我們正竭盡全力掌控這個利基市場。它是我們的重要市場。我們即將要成為市場領導者。

- [ ] The market **for** our products has been **growing** all the time. It **expanded** by 3% last year.

  我們產品的市場一直在成長。它去年擴大了3%。

☐ I just **entered** the **bond** market when it **collapsed**.

我才剛進入債券市場，它就崩盤了。

☐ It's strange that the **domestic capital** market should be **rising** now, while the **foreign equity** market **is falling**.

奇怪的是，外國股市在下跌之際，現在國內資本市場竟然在走高。

✏️ 填填看

請從「搭配詞表」中選出適當的字，完成下面句子。例解請見第333~353頁。

☐ Cheap goods from overseas have (1)_____ the (2)_____ market. (3)_____ make it difficult for us to sell our products here.

☐ This is usually a very (4)_____ market, but now (5)_____ shows that the market is (6)_____ because the economy is bad, so it's even more difficult to sell our products.

☐ We (7)_____ the market 10 years ago and now we (8)_____ it. We are the (9)_____.

☐ The (10)_____ market is a(n) (11)_____ market for us. Nearly all of our products are exported.

☐ The (12)_____ market is too (13)_____. There are too many rules and laws which make business difficult.

☐ The government should (14)_____ an (15)_____ market, so that everyone has the same chances. This market is too (16)_____. There is no room for growth.

☐ (17)_____ markets are more profitable for us, as our margins are so small. We need sales volume.

☐ (18)_____ markets are more profitable for us, as our margins are so huge. We need high end customers. (19)_____ is important in order to make sure our products match customers' needs.

☐ The market (20)_____. Sales have almost stopped. We have lost (21)_____. I recommend that we (22)_____ the market immediately and try to reduce our losses.

☐ We need to look for new markets and (23)_____ them as soon as possible.

進階造句

請嘗試利用「搭配詞表」中的字彙，造出想要表達的句子。

_____

_____

_____

_____

_____

_____

_____

marketing
[ˋmɑrkɪtɪŋ]

不可數名詞 行銷

搭配在前面的動詞	搭配的形容詞	關鍵字
do undertake	successful effective	**marketing (for sth.)**
come up with	good imaginative	marketing activity marketing agency
improve	aggressive	marketing campaign
see ★ as	direct	marketing department
handle manage	global international worldwide	marketing plan marketing strategy marketing tool

★為關鍵字

 好搭例句

 MP3-56

☐ The marketing department has **come up with** some really **imaginative** marketing for this product. The marketing activities are really fun and exciting.
行銷部針對這樣產品提出了一些極富創意的行銷方式。行銷活動極為好玩又刺激。

☐ We are **doing** some very **effective** marketing at the moment. It's really having an impact on sales.
我們目前在做一些非常有效的行銷。它對於業績極具影響力。

☐ We need to **undertake** some more **aggressive** marketing. Sales are too slow. We should change to another marketing agency, and start a new marketing campaign.
我們需要從事一些更積極的行銷。業績太差了。我們應該改換另一個行銷機構，並展開新的行銷宣傳。

☐ Is there any way we can **improve** our **direct** marketing? What about using DMs? Or do you have any other ideas for marketing tools?
我們有沒有什麼方法可以改善我們的直效行銷？用直接郵寄怎麼樣？還是你們對於行銷工具有什麼其他的想法？

☐ Our senior management **sees good** marketing **as** the key to successful growth. That's why we have a large marketing department.
我們的管理高層認為好的行銷是順利成長的關鍵。那就是為什麼我們有個龐大的行銷部。

☐ We need a bigger team to **handle global** marketing. Our current team is too small.
我們需要一個更大的團隊來處理全球行銷。我們目前的團隊太小了。

☐ You did a fantastic job of **managing** the marketing **for** this product. Your marketing strategy was excellent. Sales have been fantastic.
在管理這項產品的行銷上，你表現得十分優異。你的行銷策略很出色。業績很優異。

☐ I'm presenting my new marketing plan for this product next week.
我下星期要針對這項產品提報我的行銷計畫。

填填看

請從「搭配詞表」中選出適當的字，完成下面句子。例解請見第333~353頁。

☐ We (1)_____ some (2)_____ marketing for that product. It was so exciting to work on it, and to see the results. The (3)_____ was excellent, and we used some very innovative (4)_____ .

☐ We need to (5)_____ our marketing efforts. So far our (6)_____ are not really having an impact on consumers.

☐ I think we should let the (7)_____ (8)_____ the marketing for this product. They have more experience.

☐ (9)_____ marketing will help us to keep ahead of our competitors. We need a new (10)_____. We must fight to win!

☐ Many companies (11)_____ (12)_____ marketing (13)_____ being too difficult. They don't understand how you can create markets in many different countries at the same time with the same (14)_____.

進階造句

請嘗試利用「搭配詞表」中的字彙，造出想要表達的句子。

---

meeting
[ˈmitɪŋ]

可數名詞 會議

搭配在前面的動詞		搭配的形容詞	關鍵字
have have got arrange schedule call hold go to attend take part in	call off cancel postpone chair open miss	breakfast lunchtime afternoon all-day brief regular departmental team urgent emergency board	**meeting (with sb.) (about sth.)**

 好搭例句

◎ MP3-57

☐ I've just **had** an **all-day** meeting **with** our partners **about** the merger. I'm exhausted.
我剛為了合併的事跟合夥人開了整天的會。我累死了。

☐ I**'ve got** a **lunchtime** meeting **with** my manager tomorrow **about** the project progress.
我明天要跟經理開個午餐會談案子的進度。

☐ Can you **arrange** an **afternoon** meeting **with** the supplier for me?
你能不能幫我安排下午跟供應商開個會？

☐ Let's **schedule** a **breakfast** meeting for Friday.
我們在星期五排個早餐會吧。

☐ They have **called** an **emergency board** meeting for this afternoon at 3:00.

他們今天下午三點要召開緊急董事會。

☐ I would like to **hold** a **brief team** meeting in 30 minutes. Can you get everyone together?

我想在三十分鐘後舉行簡短的小組會議。你能不能把大家都找來？

☐ Are you **going to** the meeting **with** Mike tomorrow? He was asking about you.

你明天要跟麥克開會嗎？他問到了你。

☐ I'm afraid that due to reasons beyond my control I will be unable to **attend** the **departmental** meeting.

基於我不可抗力的原因，恐怕我沒辦法出席部門會議了。

☐ I hate **taking part in finance** meetings. They are really boring.

我討厭參加財務會議。無聊得不得了。

☐ Hey, did you know the **regular** meeting has been **called off**? Yes, they **cancelled** it.

嘿，你知道例行會議取消了嗎？沒錯，他們把它取消了。

☐ We will have to **postpone** the meeting until next week.

我們必須把會議延到下星期。

☐ I would like to ask you to **chair** the meeting, since you know most of the issues.

我想請你主持會議，因為你熟知大部分的議題。

☐ I'd like to **open** this meeting by thanking everyone for coming.

在這場會議的一開始，我想謝謝大家的光臨。

☐ Why did you **miss** the meeting? Everyone noticed you were absent. The boss was asking for you.

你為什麼沒去開會？大家都注意到你缺席了。老闆也要找你。

填填看

請從「搭配詞表」中選出適當的字，完成下面句子。例解請見第333~353頁。

☐ I (1)_____ a meeting tomorrow at 9:00. Can we talk after the meeting?

☐ Can you please (2)_____ a (3)_____ meeting (4)_____ all the team members for this afternoon at 3:00? Tell them the meeting will be very short, but it is very important everyone is there.

☐ Why does she always (5)_____ the meetings at lunchtime? I would like to eat my lunch in peace!

☐ I'm (6)_____ a (7)_____ meeting (8)_____ new developments in the software industry at the Hyatt. I hope the food is good!

☐ Why didn't you (9)_____ the last (10)_____ meeting? The new manager was asking about you.

☐ We will need to (11)_____ the (12)_____ meeting until after the merger begins. The board members will want to be briefed on how the merger is going.

☐ I'm sorry I (13)_____ the (14)_____ meeting. I had to collect my little girl from school.

☐ I've just been (15)_____ an (16)_____ meeting (17)_____ the specs for the new products. I am very exhausted from talking all day and trying to moderate the meeting.

☐ I'd like to (18)_____ this (19)_____ meeting by asking
Mike to brief us quickly on the project status, as usual.

進階造句

請嘗試利用「搭配詞表」中的字彙，造出想要表達的句子。

---

merger
[mɝdʒɚ]

可數名詞 合併

搭配在前面的動詞	搭配的形容詞	關鍵字
propose		
consider	proposed	**merger**
approve	planned	**(between sth. and sth.)**
oppose	possible	**(of sth.)**
announce	company	**(with sb.)**
complete	department	
cancel		

 好搭例句

◎ **MP3-58**

☐ I would like to **propose** a merger **of** the two departments. This will help us to reduce costs.
我想提議合併兩個部門。這將有助於我們降低成本。

☐ We are **considering** a **possible** merger **between** us **and** our main competitor.
我們正在考慮，我們和主要的競爭對手有沒有可能合併。

☐ We are **considering** a merger **with** them.
我們正在考慮跟他們合併。

☐ Regarding your **proposed department** merger, we **approve** of this.
關於你所提議的部門合併，我們贊成這麼做。

☐ The shareholders **opposed** the **planned company** merger, so it was **cancelled**.
股東反對所規劃的公司合併，所以它被撤銷了。

☐ They **announced** the **company** merger yesterday, and the share prices of both companies shot up.

他們昨天一宣布公司合併，兩家公司的股價都暴漲。

☐ We should be able to **complete** the merger in six months.

我們應該有辦法在六個月內完成合併。

🖊 填填看

請從「搭配詞表」中選出適當的字，完成下面句子。例解請見第333~353頁。

☐ I (1)_____ a merger (2)_____ these two departments a year ago, and it was (3)_____. Now I am not surprised that these problems have occurred. They should have (4)_____ the merger.

☐ Your (5)_____ merger (6)_____ the training and the personnel departments has been (7)_____.

☐ I think we can (8)_____ the (9)_____ merger in a few weeks. They are not big departments.

☐ We are (10)_____ a (11)_____ merger (12)_____ the subsidiaries.

☐ The CEO (13)_____ the (14)_____ merger, and the news was very well received by the market.

☐ We have decided to (15)_____ the (16)_____ merger. It will be too expensive and not benefit the companies that much.

☐ What about if we (17)_____ a merger (18)_____ them? I mean, it's just a suggestion.

進階造句

請嘗試利用「搭配詞表」中的字彙，造出想要表達的句子。

59	**minutes** [ˋmɪnɪts]	可數名詞 會議記錄

搭配在前面的動詞		搭配的形容詞	關鍵字
take keep circulate read through	accept sign reject	accurate meeting	**minutes (of sth.)**

 好搭例句　　　　　　　　　　◎ MP3-59

☐ My job is to **take meeting** minutes for my boss.
我的工作是幫老闆做會議記錄。

☐ Tracy, can you **keep** the minutes for the team?
翠西，你能幫小組做一下記錄嗎？

☐ I have **circulated** the minutes for the last project status meeting. Everyone, please **read through** them carefully, and let me know if you want to make any changes.
我把上次專案進度會議的記錄發下去了。每個人請仔細看一遍，如果想要修改任何地方，就跟我說一聲。

☐ You **read through** the minutes **of** the meeting, if you think they are **accurate** minutes, you **sign** the minutes at the bottom, to show that you **accept** the minutes as a true record of the meeting.
各位把會議記錄看一遍。假如各位認為記錄準確，就在記錄底下簽名，以證明各位認定這些記錄是會議的確實記錄。

☐ I'm afraid I will have to **reject** these minutes. They are not accurate.
恐怕我必須否決這些記錄。它們並不準確。

✎ 填填看

請從「搭配詞表」中選出適當的字，完成下面句子。例解請見第333~353頁。

☐ I'm going to chair the meeting, but I'd like someone else to

(1)_____ the minutes.

☐ I'm sorry I forget to (2)_____ the minutes (3)_____ the

last meeting. Here they are, everyone. Can you quickly (4)_____

them now, and (5)_____ the minutes at the bottom if you

(6)_____ them, then we can get started on this meeting.

☐ They (7)_____ the (8)_____ minutes. They say the

minutes do not reflect the terms reached during the negotiation.

However, I (9)_____ them carefully, and checked with Mike and

Tina who were also at the meeting, and they say they are

(10)_____ minutes of the negotiation. I don't know what to do.

✎ 進階造句

請嘗試利用「搭配詞表」中的字彙，造出想要表達的句子。

_____

_____

_____

_____

_____

_____

60 negotiation

[nɪ.goʃɪ`eʃən]

可數名詞 談判；協商

搭配在前面的動詞		搭配的形容詞	關鍵字	搭配在後面的動詞
conduct hold enter into open begin start	complete conclude handle resume	ongoing protracted lengthy prolonged intensive detailed delicate	**negotiation (with sb.) (about sth.) (to V)**	take place go well go badly continue involve break down

 好搭例句·

◉ MP3-60

☐ We are currently **conducting delicate** negotiations **with** their top management.
我們目前在跟他們的管理高層做密切的協商。

☐ We are **holding detailed** negotiations **to** work out the terms of the deal.
我們在舉行詳細的協商，以訂出買賣的條件。

☐ I don't want to **enter into protracted** negotiations **with** you **about** this. Take it or leave it.
我在這件事上不想跟你陷入冗長的協商。不要就拉倒。

☐ I would like to **open** the negotiation by thanking you all for coming.
我想在協商的一開始謝謝大家的光臨。

☐ Let's **begin** the negotiations by stating our positions.
我們就以表明我們的立場來展開協商吧。

☐ We **start intensive** negotiations **with** them on Monday. It will be very tough.

我們星期一要跟他們展開密集的協商。那將會非常辛苦。

☐ We need to **complete** the negotiations by the end of the day.

我們要在下班前完成協商才行。

☐ We eventually **concluded** the negotiations with a deal that was satisfactory to both parties.

我們終於以令雙方都滿意的條件敲定了協商。

☐ You are doing an excellent job of **handling** the negotiations.

你在處理協商方面表現得很出色。

☐ After a break to reconsider our positions, we **resumed** the negotiation.

經過休息並重新考慮我們的處境後，我們恢復了協商。

☐ The **ongoing** negotiation **involves** the terms of the deal.

進行中的協商是在談買賣的條件。

☐ These **lengthy** negotiations **are** not **going well**.

這些耗時的協商進行得並不順利。

☐ The **prolonged** negotiations **are going well**. Both sides are finding plenty to agree about.

漫長的協商進行得很順利。雙方獲得了很多共識。

☐ The negotiations **are** still **taking place**.

協商還在進行。

☐ The negotiations **with** the union **about** wage increases **are going badly**.

跟工會的調薪協商陷入了僵局。

☐ Although both sides are not happy, the negotiation **is** still **continuing**.

雖然雙方都不滿意，但協商還在繼續。

☐ The negotiations have now **broken down**. No deal has been reached.

協商現在破裂了，並沒有達成協議。

填填看

請從「搭配詞表」中選出適當的字，完成下面句子。例解請見第333~353頁。

☐ We are (1)_____ negotiations (2)_____ see if we can make an alliance with them.

☐ Let's (3)_____ the negotiations by stating our objectives first, shall we?

☐ My job is to (4)_____ negotiations (5)_____ major customers (6)_____ the terms of the deal.

☐ These negotiations are very difficult and (7)_____. I hope we can (8)_____ them soon.

☐ After a break for lunch, we (9)_____ the negotiations, and now they are (10)_____. Stopping for food was a good idea.

☐ The negotiation is (11)_____ in a hotel over a one-week period and (12)_____ the terms of the deal. It's taking so long because both sides cannot agree. The negotiation is (13)_____.

☐ Because the other side was not able to be flexible, the negotiation has (14)_____. I'm very disappointed.

☐ We still have not been able to reach a deal. The negotiation is (15)_____.

進階造句

請嘗試利用「搭配詞表」中的字彙，造出想要表達的句子。

network
[ˈnɛt,wɜk]

可數名詞 網路

搭配在前面的動詞	搭配的形容詞	關鍵字	搭配在後面的動詞
develop build install		**network** **(of sth.)**	link connect
upgrade improve	peer-to-peer client-server local area (LAN) wireless local area (WLAN) wide area (WAN)	network protocol network topology	support provide
expand extend			allow
manage run maintain			be down be up be slow be fast

 好搭例句

◉ **MP3-61**

☐ I am currently **developing** a **client-server** network for my company.
我目前正在為公司開發主從式網路。

☐ It's quite easy to **build** a simple **peer-to-peer** network. You just connect two computers together.
建立簡單的對等網路相當容易。你只要把兩台電腦連在一起就行了。

☐ They are **installing** a **local area** network.
他們在安裝區域網路。

☐ We want to **upgrade** our **LAN** to a **wireless LAN**.
我們想要把我們的區域網路升級成無線區域網路。

☐ Our LAN uses the Ethernet network protocol.
我們的區域網路是採用乙太網路的網路協定。

☐ We are going to **expand** our **WLAN**.
我們要擴充我們的無線區域網路。

☐ Can you **extend** our **wide area** network to cover the whole region?
你能不能擴大我們的廣域網路，以涵蓋整個範圍？

☐ My job is to **manage** the network. **Running** the network is very easy.
我的工作是管理網路。掌管網路非常簡單。

☐ Your job will be to **maintain** the network and make sure it works all the time.
你的工作是要維護網路，並確保它隨時暢通。

☐ How much will it cost to **improve** the network?
改善網路要花多少錢？

☐ This kind of network will **link** your computer to everyone else's in the office.
這種網路可以把你的電腦連結到辦公室裡其他每個人的電腦。

☐ This network **connects** everyone's computers together.
這種網路是在把每個人的電腦串連在一起。

☐ The network **supports** all kinds of applications.
這個網路支援各式各樣的應用程式。

☐ The network **provides** an easy way to contact our suppliers.
這個網路提供了便捷的方式來聯絡供應商。

☐ The network doesn't **allow** peer-to-peer. The network **topology** is client-server, so all messages have to go through the server.
這個網路不允許對等式。網路拓樸是主從式，所以一切的訊息都必須經過伺服器。

☐ The network **is down**. Can you call the IT department and ask them when the network will **be up**?
網路掛了。你能不能打電話問一下資訊科技部，網路什麼時候才能用？

☐ The network **is slow**. Must be lots of traffic on it.

網路很慢。一定是流量很大。

☐ The network **is** always really **fast** in the morning.

網路在早上總是快得很。

填填看

請從「搭配詞表」中選出適當的字，完成下面句子。例解請見第333~353頁。

☐ The network (1)_____. I think they are (2)_____ it. Don't worry, just wait a few moments. It will (3)_____ again soon.

☐ We are very busy at the moment (4)_____ a new network for the company. It's difficult because they want a (5)_____ network. This (6)_____ is more complex than a (7)_____ network, which you can make easily by just connecting two computers together.

☐ We are currently (8)_____ our (9)_____ network to include the office upstairs. We have to put the cables through the wall.

☐ The network (10)_____ all the computers in the company. It (11)_____ most major applications, and also (12)_____ visitors to plug in their computers and access the network with a password.

☐ A (13)_____ network (WLAN) is a little more difficult to (14)_____ because sometimes external factors can effect the signal. Of course, a (15)_____ network (WAN) is even more difficult to (16)_____ because the problem might be in a different country.

☐ What (17)_____ do you use? Is it Ethernet, like ours?

☐ The network (18)_____ a secure and convenient working

environment. You can connect to anyone in the company.

進階造句

請嘗試利用「搭配詞表」中的字彙，造出想要表達的句子。

_____

_____

_____

_____

_____

_____

_____

offer
[ˋɔfə]

可數名詞 供應；出價

搭配在前面的動詞	搭配的形容詞	關鍵字
have	special	
	generous	
make	better	
	best	
consider		
accept	conditional	**offer**
		(to/for sth.)
reject	initial	
refuse	final	
receive	formal	
increase	firm	

 好搭例句

◎ **MP3-62**

☐ This month we **have** a **special** offer to first time buyers.
本月我們對首次購買的人有特別優惠。

☐ We **made** a **generous** offer **for** the factory, but the seller **rejected** it.
Now we will have to find another location.
我們針對工廠提出了高額的報價，可是賣方拒絕了。現在我們必須去找別的地點。

☐ They are **considering** our **initial** offer, but my feeling is that it's too low and that they will **refuse** it.
他們在考慮我們的最初報價，但我覺得太低了，他們會把它否決。

☐ If this is your **final** offer, then we will be happy to **accept** it.
假如這是你們的最終報價，那我們樂於接受。

☐ We have **received** your **formal** offer. Please give us some time to **consider** it.

我們收到了你們的正式報價。請給我們一點時間考慮。

☐ We would like to **increase** our **initial** offer by 3%. However, that is our budget limit.

我們想要把最初報價提高3%。但那是我們的預算上限了。

☐ This is a **conditional** offer only; it's not a **firm** offer. We still need to work out the details.

這只是有條件的報價，而不是確切的報價。我們還需要訂出細節。

☐ Let's look around for a **better** offer before we **accept** this one.

在接受這個之前，我們先四處看看更好的報價。

☐ Is that really your **best** offer?

那真的是你們最好的報價嗎？

填填看

請從「搭配詞表」中選出適當的字，完成下面句子。例解請見第333~353頁。

☐ They (1)_____ a (2)_____ offer for the products, so I sold everything to them. Now I have met my sales target!

☐ The suppliers (3)_____ many (4)_____ offers this month. Now is a good time to buy extra stock.

☐ We are (5)_____ your (6)_____ offer. We will let you know our decision in a few days.

☐ Further to our conversation last week, we have (7)_____ your (8)_____ offer and would like to (9)_____ it. Our lawyers will be in touch to draw up the contract.

☐ If that's your (10)_____ offer, I'm afraid we will have to

 (11)_____ it. I hope we can do business some other time.

☐ Your (12)_____ offer is simply too low for us. Can you

 (13)_____ us a (14)_____ offer?

進階造句

請嘗試利用「搭配詞表」中的字彙，造出想要表達的句子。

opportunity
[ˌɑpɚˋtjunətɪ]

可數名詞 機會

搭配在前面的動詞	搭配的形容詞	關鍵字
be on the look out for wait for		
be find come across get have	good great excellent golden perfect	**opportunity (for sth.) (to V)**
grasp seize take ~ to V	unique rare unexpected	
take advantage of exploit	wasted missed	
lose waste		

 好搭例句　　　　　　　　　　　　◎ **MP3-63**

☐ We **are** always **on the look out for** a **rare** opportunity.
我們一直在尋找難得的機會。

☐ I don't want to **wait for** another opportunity. Let's **seize** this one.
我不想等別的機會了。我們就把握這個機會吧。

☐ It's difficult to **find good** opportunities **for** the company in this market.
在這個市場上很難替公司找到好機會。

☐ He **came across** an **unexpected** opportunity while he was on a business trip in Holland. He quickly **took advantage of** it. Now one of our main customers is located there.

他去荷蘭出差時，碰到了一個意想不到的機會。他趕緊善加利用。現在我們的一個主顧就在那裡。

We **get** lots of **excellent** opportunities **to** do business with them.
我們要抓住很多絕佳的機會跟他們做生意。

I don't **have** many opportunities **to** speak Korean. I am forgetting what I learned.
我沒有什麼機會說韓語。我學過的都快忘了。

If you don't know how to **grasp** an **unexpected** opportunity, you will **lose** it.
假如你不曉得要怎麼掌握意想不到的機會，你就會失去它。

I'd like to **take** this opportunity **to** welcome you all to the factory.
我想藉這個機會歡迎大家蒞臨工廠。

His great skill as a manager is his ability to **exploit rare** opportunities.
他擔任經理的優異技巧在於，他懂得利用難得的機會。

It's a shame we didn't get that new customer. **It's** a **missed** opportunity **to** break into a new market.
可惜我們沒有爭取到那個新顧客，錯失了一個機會去打入新市場。

I was too shy to speak to him. It**'s** a **wasted** opportunity!
我太過害羞而不敢跟他說話，浪費了一個機會！

填填看

請從「搭配詞表」中選出適當的字，完成下面句子。例解請見第333~353頁。

It's no good sitting around (1)＿＿＿＿＿ (2)＿＿＿＿＿ opportunities to arrive. You have to go out and (3)＿＿＿＿＿ them.

We (4)＿＿＿＿＿ (5)＿＿＿＿＿ opportunities (6)＿＿＿＿＿ increase our market share. However, they are difficult to find.

☐ We were too slow to (7)_____ the opportunity. We may not get another chance.

☐ It's a (8)_____ opportunity. We should have been faster.

☐ Can I (9)_____ this opportunity (10)_____ say how happy we are that you have decided to join our company.

☐ I have never (11)_____ such a (12)_____ opportunity in my whole career. What amazing luck!

☐ It's a (13)_____ opportunity which we must (14)_____. These things happen maybe only once every few years.

☐ Let's not (15)_____ this opportunity. We should move quickly before we lose the chance.

進階造句

請嘗試利用「搭配詞表」中的字彙，造出想要表達的句子。

_____

_____

_____

_____

_____

_____

_____

option
[`ɑpʃən]

可數名詞 選擇方案

搭配在前面的動詞	搭配的形容詞	關鍵字
have consider explore look at discuss choose take give limit	number of ★ +s various ★ +s viable best alternative easy realistic	**option (to V)**

★為關鍵字

 好搭例句

◎ MP3-64

☐ At this point we **have** a **number of** options.
眼下我們有一些選項。

☐ We are **considering** all the **various** options. I'll let you know when we decide.
我們在考慮所有不同的選項。等我們決定後，我就會告訴你。

☐ Let's **explore** a few **alternative** options.
我們來探討幾個替代選項。

☐ At this stage I'd like to **discuss** the **realistic** options we have.
在這個階段，我想要討論我們既有的現實選項。

☐ Even though we did not succeed, I still think we **chose the best** option. We didn't **have** that many to choose from!
即使我們沒成功，我還是認為我們挑了最好的選項。我們能挑的並沒有那麼多！

☐ It's a mistake to always **take** the **easy** option.

老是採取簡單的選項是個錯誤。

☐ That is not a **viable** option. We don't have the resources to do that.

那並不是個可行的選項。我們沒有資源可以做這件事。

☐ I don't want to **limit** our options here. I think we should **look at** all the options available to us.

我不想把我們的選項侷限在此。我認為我們應該檢視手邊所有的選項。

☐ Let's **give** them the option, and let them choose.

我們給他們選項，讓他們來挑。

填填看

請從「搭配詞表」中選出適當的字，完成下面句子。例解請見第333~353頁。

☐ We (1)＿＿＿＿＿ a (2)＿＿＿＿＿ options (3)＿＿＿＿＿ discuss. You can see them on the slide here.

☐ We (4)＿＿＿＿＿ you an option. You made your choice.

☐ At this point we are still (5)＿＿＿＿＿ (6)＿＿＿＿＿ options. We will let you know what we decide.

☐ I (7)＿＿＿＿＿ what I thought was the (8)＿＿＿＿＿ option. I did not realize that it was actually the most difficult option!

☐ I think this is the (9)＿＿＿＿＿ option. It's cheapest and easiest to implement, and will give the best results.

☐ I don't think that's a good idea. Do you have any (10)＿＿＿＿＿ options for me to (11)＿＿＿＿＿?

☐ That's not a (12)＿＿＿＿＿ option. Try to be more practical.

☐ If we do that, that will **(13)**_____ our options, and may cause
problems for us in the future.

進階造句

請嘗試利用「搭配詞表」中的字彙，造出想要表達的句子。

_____

_____

_____

_____

_____

_____

_____

_____

order
[`ɔrdə]

可數名詞 訂單

搭配在前面的動詞		搭配的形容詞	關鍵字
place			**order (for sth.)**
fax	win	big	
phone		large	
email	receive	bulk	order book
send	confirm		order form
dispatch		urgent	order number
ship	process		
		minimum	
increase	chase up		
		purchase	
cancel			

 好搭例句

◉ MP3-65

☐ If you **send** your order before lunch today, we can **process** it immediately.
假如你在今天中午以前把訂單寄來，我們就能立刻處理。

☐ You can **fax**, **phone**, or **email** your order. As soon as we **receive** it, we'll start **processing** it.
你可以用傳真、電話或電子郵件訂貨。我們一收到就會開始處理。

☐ We **shipped** your order yesterday. Yes, I know it's **urgent**; I **dispatched** it immediately.
我們昨天把你們的訂貨運送出去了。對，我知道很急；我立刻就快遞了。

☐ Please remember to include your order number on the order form.
請記得註明訂單上的訂貨號碼。

☐ Due to unforeseen circumstances, we need to **cancel** our order.
由於碰到出乎預料的情況，我們要取消訂貨。

☐ I'd like to **place** an order **for** product number B-15-50-G.

我想訂購產品編號B-15-50-G。

☐ If we **win** this **big** order, we will increase our revenue by millions.

假如我們拿到這筆大訂單，我們的營收就會增加好幾百萬。

☐ I have **received** your **purchase** order. Unfortunately, your order is below the **minimum** order. Would you like to **increase** it?

我收到了你們的採購訂單。遺憾的是，你們的訂單低於最小訂購量。你們要不要增加？

☐ Can I just **confirm** your order? You would like to purchase 300 units of the G-16-60-B. Is that correct?

我能不能確認一下你們的訂單？你們要買300件G-16-60-B。這樣正確嗎？

☐ I forgot to enter your last order into the order book. Can you send the order number again please?

我忘了把你們上次的訂單輸入訂貨冊裡。能不能麻煩你把訂貨號碼再傳一次？

☐ It's a very **large** order. I hope you will be able to give me a discount.

這是非常大的訂單。希望你們能給我折扣。

☐ I still haven't **received** my order. Can you **chase** it **up** for me please — find out where it is?

我還沒收到我的訂貨。能不能麻煩你幫我查一查，找出它在哪裡？

✎ 填填看

請從「搭配詞表」中選出適當的字，完成下面句子。例解請見第333~353頁。

☐ I have just (1)＿＿＿＿＿＿ you a (2)＿＿＿＿＿＿ order. Can you please (3)＿＿＿＿＿＿ it immediately? The (4)＿＿＿＿＿＿ is C-17-70-Q.

☐ Due to the delay, I'm afraid I have to (5)＿＿＿＿＿＿ this order. I hope in future you can (6)＿＿＿＿＿＿ our orders faster.

☐ We (7)_____ a (8)_____ order today, worth millions. Looks like I might get my bonus this year after all!

☐ We have just (9)_____ an order from you (10)_____ 1 million units, but there is no (11)_____ attached. Can you please (12)_____ it? Is the quantity correct?

☐ I understand that I can only (13)_____ a (14)_____ order for 100 units. Is that right?

☐ Who's got the (15)_____? I need to enter my order into it.

☐ If you don't (16)_____ your order within 10 days, please let me know, and I'll (17)_____ the order for you.

進階造句

請嘗試利用「搭配詞表」中的字彙，造出想要表達的句子。

_____

_____

_____

_____

_____

_____

_____

payment
[ˈpemənt]

可數名詞 付款

搭配在前面的動詞		搭配的形容詞		關鍵字
make		monthly		
remit				
receive	reduce	interest	advance	
accept	meet	cash	prompt	payment (to sb.) (for sth.) (of #)
withhold	require	one off	overtime	
delay		lump		
suspend	spread	sum down	late	
collect		bonus		

為數字

 好搭例句

◎ MP3-66

☐ We have not yet **received** your payment. Please **make prompt** payment.
我們還沒收到你們的付款。請即刻付款。

☐ If we do not receive our order in the next 7 days, we shall **withhold** payment.
假如我們在未來七天內沒有收到訂貨，我們就會保留付款。

☐ We do not **accept cash** payments **for** orders over $1,000.
對於超過1000美元的訂單，我們不接受現金付款。

☐ It seems our payment has been **delayed** because of new interbanking regulations.
由於新的銀行同業規定，看來我們的付款受到了延誤。

☐ Please **remit** payment directly to our bank account.
請把付款直接匯到我們的銀行帳戶。

☐ We have no choice but to **suspend** all **overtime** payments. We simply have no money, due to the **late** payments of many of our customers.
我們別無選擇，只能凍結所有的加班費。我們根本沒有錢了，因為我們有許多顧客都延遲付款。

☐ The bank is not willing to **reduce** the **interest** payments. If our current revenue levels continue, we cannot **meet** our **monthly interest** payments.
銀行不願意調降利息款項。假如我們目前的營收水準持續下去，我們就付不起每個月的利息款項。

☐ For large orders, we **require advance down** payment **of** 10%.
對於大筆的訂單，我們有規定10%的預付頭期款。

☐ This is a **one off bonus** payment. Please do not expect it next year.
這是一次性的獎金款項。請不要指望明年還有。

☐ You can **make** one **lump sum** payment, or **spread** the payments over 6 months.
你可以一次付清全額款項，也可以用六個月分期付款。

☐ I've been having problems **collecting** payment from this customer.
我一直沒辦法向這位顧客催收到款項。

✦ ✏️ 填填看

請從「搭配詞表」中選出適當的字，完成下面句子。例解請見第333~353頁。

☐ Usually my customers prefer to (1)_____ (2)_____ payments, rather than (3)_____ the payments over 6 months.

☐ If we (4)_____ (5)_____ payment, we can give you a discount.

☐ It is not the custom in this company to (6)_____ (7)_____ payments to employees.

☐ Please (8)_____ (9)_____ payment (10)_____

$169,834 (11)_____ 21 units (12)_____ account

number 123-45-6789-0. (13)_____ payment is not acceptable.

☐ We have to make sure we make enough money so that we can continue

to (14)_____ our (15)_____ (16)_____

payments.

☐ We have decided to (17)_____ payment until your service

improves.

☐ Please make sure you (18)_____ all payments on time. Don't let

our customers keep us waiting for our money.

進階造句

請嘗試利用「搭配詞表」中的字彙，造出想要表達的句子。

_____

_____

_____

_____

_____

_____

_____

_____

67	**personnel** [ˌpɝsn̩ˋɛl]	不可數名詞 職員、人事 同義字：staff、employee

搭配在前面的動詞	搭配的形容詞		關鍵字
recruit hire	skilled senior	administrative clerical	**personnel**
employ have train retain manage	junior authorized existing key new	technical engineering service sales executive legal	personnel department personnel management personnel file personnel administration

 好搭例句　◎ MP3-67

☐ It's quite difficult to **recruit skilled technical** personnel at the moment.
熟練的技術人員目前相當難招募。

☐ Every company needs **skilled engineering** personnel.
每家公司都需要熟練的工程人員。

☐ We **have** 3000 personnel worldwide.
我們在全世界有3,000個職員。

☐ We are currently **hiring senior administrative** personnel. We also need some **junior clerical** personnel.
我們目前在找高級行政人員。我們也需要一些初級辦事人員。

☐ We need to **employ** 30 **new junior sales** personnel.
我們需要雇用30位新的初級業務人員。

☐ It's the responsibility of the personnel department to **train existing** personnel.
訓練現任職員是人事部的責任。

☐ One of the main difficulties of personnel administration is **retaining key** personnel.

人事行政的一個主要難題在於留住重要職員。

☐ Only **authorized** personnel are allowed to see the personnel files.

只有獲得授權的人員才能調閱人事檔案。

☐ I studied personnel management at college. Now I **manage** the **service** personnel for a large insurance company.

我在大學讀的是人事管理。現在我在一家大型保險公司管理服務人員。

☐ We **employ** a lot of **legal** personnel, as we have contracts in four different countries.

我們請了很多法務人員,因為我們在四個不同的國家簽有合約。

☐ Most of our **executive** personnel have been with the company for years.

我們的主管人員大部分都在公司待了很多年。

✎ 填填看

請從「搭配詞表」中選出適當的字,完成下面句子。例解請見第333~353頁。

☐ I work in the (1)＿＿＿＿＿＿ of a large technology company. My job is to (2)＿＿＿＿＿＿ (3)＿＿＿＿＿＿ personnel for the R& D team.

☐ (4)＿＿＿＿＿＿ is a very interesting job. It involves (5)＿＿＿＿＿＿ personnel so that they know how to do their jobs. I also have to try to (6)＿＿＿＿＿＿ personnel so that they don't leave the company.

☐ We are trying to (7)＿＿＿＿＿＿ (8)＿＿＿＿＿＿ (9)＿＿＿＿＿＿ personnel for the customer service centre. They need to be young and don't need a lot of experience, as we will train them.

☐ Finding (10)_____ (11)_____ personnel can be difficult. You have to offer them lots of money to match their management experience and their age.

☐ As the manager of the sales department, you will have to (12)_____ the (13)_____ personnel.

☐ I'm afraid only (14)_____ personnel have access to this office. This is where we keep the (15)_____.

☐ We (16)_____ the largest number of personnel in the industry in this country. It's a huge company.

☐ Our (17)_____ personnel are the best in the business. They know how to use every kind of computer.

☐ We don't (18)_____ enough (19)_____ personnel. Lots of routine jobs are not getting done, you know, filing and stuff like that. I can't do it all.

☐ Now that we don't have so many new contracts, I think we don't need so many (20)_____ personnel.

☐ We need three more (21)_____ personnel. It will be difficult to fill these high level positions.

進階造句

請嘗試利用「搭配詞表」中的字彙，造出想要表達的句子。

_____

_____

_____

point
[pɔɪnt]

可數名詞 觀點、論點

搭配在前面的動詞		搭配的形容詞		關鍵字
have make raise	get to stick to	crucial essential		
develop clarify	agree with	fundamental	similar	point (about sth.)
emphasize	appreciate	general	controversial	
consider discuss	miss	important main key	difficult	
agree to differ on				

 好搭例句

◎ MP3-68

☐ I **have** a few points to **make** here.
我在這裡有幾點要說明。

☐ I'd like to **make** a few **important** points now **about** our market position.
我現在想針對我們的市場定位說明幾個重點。

☐ I'd like to **raise** a **crucial** point here.
我想在這裡提個要點。

☐ I think you need to **develop** this **general** point a bit.
我認為你需要稍微引申一下這個概括的論點。

☐ Can you **clarify** this **difficult** point please?
能不能麻煩你釐清這個困難點？

☐ I'd like to **emphasize** the **fundamental** point. Time is money.
我想強調基本論點。時間就是金錢。

☐ We need to **consider** this **essential** point first.
我們需要先考慮到這個要點。

☐ I hope at the end of my presentation we will have time to **discuss** some of the **key** points.

我希望在我提報結束後，我們還有時間討論一些關鍵點。

☐ Sorry, but time is running out. Can you **get to** the **main** point?

抱歉，時間不夠了。你能不能切入主要的論點？

☐ What you're saying is very interesting, but can you **stick to** the point?

你所說的非常有趣，但你能不能緊扣論點？

☐ I **made** a **similar** point last week. I **agree with** your point here.

我上星期提過類似的論點。我同意你在這裡的論點。

☐ Well, it seems we will just have to **agree to differ on** this **controversial** point.

嗯，看來我們在這個爭議點上只好求同存異了。

☐ I **appreciate** your point. Let me think about it some more and then get back to you.

我很欣賞你的論點。我再考慮看看，然後回覆你。

☐ No, that's not what I meant. I think you **missed** my point.

不，我不是那個意思。我想你誤會我的論點了。

填填看

請從「搭配詞表」中選出適當的字，完成下面句子。例解請見第333~353頁。

☐ Let's (1)＿＿＿＿＿ this point in more detail. John. What do you think?

☐ This is a very (2)＿＿＿＿＿ point, so I want to (3)＿＿＿＿＿ it. It's really the key issue confronting us.

☐ I just want to (4)＿＿＿＿＿ this (5)＿＿＿＿＿ point, so that we all understand it in greater depth.

☐ I've got a clear idea of the background situation, but can you (6)_____ your (7)_____ point? Otherwise we will not have enough time for discussion.

☐ I'd like to (8)_____ a (9)_____ point now, and I know that many of you are not going to (10)_____ this point, but I hope at least we can talk about why we have different views on this issue.

☐ It's such a/an (11)_____ point that we need to talk about it some more.

☐ Can we (12)_____ the point? Otherwise we will not be able to get through the agenda.

☐ Yes, I agree. I (13)_____ a (14)_____ point. John and I often think the same way on these issues.

☐ I (15)_____ your point, but I think we will have to (16)_____ this point. We will never agree with each other.

☐ No, that's not what I said. I think you (17)_____ my point.

☐ I'd like to (18)_____ a (19)_____ point (20)_____ wage increases for the coming year — a very tricky topic!

![pen icon] 進階造句

請嘗試利用「搭配詞表」中的字彙，造出想要表達的句子。

_____

_____

_____

position
[pə`zɪʃən]

可數名詞 見解；立場；處境

搭配在前面的動詞	搭配的形容詞	關鍵字
explain outline state assess clarify discuss accept be aware of find oneself in be in put sb. in	earlier previous present current awkward delicate difficult embarrassing	**position (on sth.)**

 好搭例句

◎ **MP3-69**

☐ Let me just briefly **explain** our **earlier** position **on** this.
且讓我針對這點簡短解釋一下我們之前的立場。

☐ I have **outlined** our **previous** position. Now let me talk you through the strategy.
我大致描述了我們原本的處境。現在我來跟各位談談策略。

☐ Well, you have **stated** your **present** position very clearly. Thanks.
嗯，你把你目前的立場說得非常清楚，謝謝。

☐ We need to **assess** our **current** position before we can make a decision about how to proceed.
我們要先評估目前的處境，才能決定要怎麼進行下去。

☐ Can you **clarify** your position **on** the interest rate hike?
你能釐清一下你們在調升利率上的立場嗎？

☐ We need to **discuss** our position in the market.
我們需要討論一下我們在市場上的處境。

☐ I **am aware of** your **awkward** position and will try to find a way out of the dilemma for you.
我明白你的尷尬處境，並且會努力幫你設法擺脫困境。

☐ I **accept** your position, but I'm afraid I cannot help you.
我接受你的立場，但恐怕我幫不了你。

☐ I **find myself in** a very **delicate** position.
我發現自己處境十分微妙。

☐ I**'m in** a **difficult** position here.
我在這裡陷入了困難的處境。

☐ Your request **puts me in** a very **embarrassing** position.
你的要求會使我面臨非常為難的處境。

✦ ✎ 填填看

請從「搭配詞表」中選出適當的字，完成下面句子。例解請見第333~353頁。

☐ Can you **(1)**＿＿＿＿＿＿ your position **(2)**＿＿＿＿＿＿ this issue? What are your views?

☐ Let me **(3)**＿＿＿＿＿＿ our **(4)**＿＿＿＿＿＿ position and get back to you with a report on how things stand at the moment.

☐ I **(5)**＿＿＿＿＿＿ your **(6)**＿＿＿＿＿＿ position, but I need your reply as soon as possible. Are you going to come and work for us or not? Remember, your current company is loosing market share and will probably go bust. I know the boss is your high-school classmate, but you need to decide on your future. I don't want to (7)_____ you (8)_____ an (9)_____ position, but we can promise you a great future.

☐ I'd like to begin by (10)_____ our (11)_____ position and then show how things have changed.

☐ I (12)_____ a very (13)_____ position, as I have to show loyalty to two companies who are competitors now.

進階造句

請嘗試利用「搭配詞表」中的字彙，造出想要表達的句子。

_____

_____

_____

_____

_____

_____

_____

_____

presentation
[ˌprizɛnˋteʃən]

可數名詞 簡報

搭配在前面的動詞	搭配的形容詞		關鍵字
make give deliver	excellent effective		**presentation (on sth.)**
prepare practice attended see	formal informal short	product	presentation skill presentation handout presentation slide presentation package

 好搭例句

🎵 MP3-70

☐ I have to **make** a **formal** presentation **on** my company tomorrow.
我明天必須針對我們公司做一場正式的提報。

☐ I hate **giving** presentations in English. I get so nervous.
我討厭用英文提報。我會搞得緊張兮兮。

☐ She **delivered** an **excellent product** presentation. Her presentation skills are really professional.
她發表了一場出色的產品提報。她的提報技巧十分專業。

☐ I'm **preparing** my presentation at the moment. I'm working on the presentation slides and presentation handouts.
我目前正在準備我的提報。我在做提報投影片和提報大綱。

☐ I didn't **practice** my presentation enough.
我在練習提報上做得不夠。

☐ I **attended** a very **effective** presentation yesterday. It was an **informal** presentation, but the presentation package was very high quality.
我昨天出席了一場非常精彩的提報。那是一場非正式提報，但提報配套有非常高的品質。

☐ I would like to **see** a **short** presentation **on** your project status tomorrow.

我明天想針對你們的案件進度看個簡短的提報。

✦ 🖊 填填看

請從「搭配詞表」中選出適當的字，完成下面句子。例解請見第333~353頁。

☐ I quite like (1)_____ presentations. I can show off my

(2)_____. I had a lot of training in college, and I get to usc it.

☐ When you (3)_____ your presentation, don't forget to work on

the (4)_____ and the (5)_____ handouts. The whole

(6)_____ must look really good.

☐ It was a (7)_____ presentation — it only took about 10 minutes,

but it was really (8)_____. Everyone loved it.

☐ I have to (9)_____ a (10)_____ presentation

(11)_____ my company to the new shareholders and board of

directors on Monday. I'm very nervous, so I guess I need to

(12)_____ again and again until I feel confident.

☐ I will be out all afternoon. I'm (13)_____ a (14)_____

presentation by a new manufacturer. If I like the product, we'll sell it for them.

📝 進階造句

請嘗試利用「搭配詞表」中的字彙，造出想要表達的句子。

_____

_____

_____

price
[praɪs]

可數名詞 價錢

搭配在前面的動詞	搭配的形容詞	關鍵字	搭配在後面的動詞
pay	good	**price**	
raise	fair	**(for sth.)**	
increase	special		
	half		rise
cut		price list	go up
reduce	wholesale	price hike	
lower	retail	price freeze	fall
	unit	price war	go down
set		price sensitive	
quote sb.	high		include n.p.
give sb.	low		
agree on	list		

 好搭例句

◎ MP3-71

☐ I've seen your price list, but I don't want to **pay** the **list** price for this. Can you **give me** a **special** price?

我看了你們的價目表，但我不想付表訂價格來買這個。你能不能給我個特價？

☐ We need to **raise** our prices if we want to maintain our margins. How about a price hike?

假如我們想維持毛利，我們就需要漲價。調高價格怎麼樣？

☐ The **retail** price is much higher than the **wholesale** price. The retailer is making a huge profit!

零售價比批發價高得多。零售商賺翻了！

☐ That's a **high** price. I don't think people will buy it if we **set** the price too high.

那算是高價。假如我們訂價過高，我不認為大家會去買。

☐ But if we **set** a **low** price, then we won't be able to make a profit.
但假如我們訂出低價，那我們就沒辦法賺錢了。

☐ Can you please **quote me** a **good** price for this?
能不能麻煩你在這樣東西上給我個好價錢？

☐ That's a **fair** price. I'm happy to **pay** that kind of price.
那算是公道價。我樂意付那種價錢。

☐ You always have to **pay** a price **for** every opportunity. We call this "opportunity cost."
你永遠必須為每個機會付出代價。我們稱之為「機會成本」。

☐ If we **reduce** our prices too much, we might start a price war.
假如我們降價太多，我們可能會掀起價格戰。

☐ We should **lower** our prices. This is a very price sensitive market. People don't like to pay too much.
我們應該調降價格。這是個價格敏度感極高的市場，大家不喜歡付太多錢。

☐ We **agreed on** a price. Don't change your mind now.
我們談好了價格。現在可別改變心意。

☐ Commodity prices are **rising**. That makes our raw materials more expensive.
商品價格在上漲。那會使我們的原料變得更貴。

☐ But the oil price is **falling** again. That should help to reduce costs.
可是油價又跌了。那應該有助於降低成本。

☐ The **unit** price **includes** all the extras and a two-year service warranty.
單位價格包含了一切附加費用和兩年的服務保固。

☐ House prices have been **going up** for ages.
房價上漲了好久。

☐ It's about time prices **for** this type of product **went down**. The price freeze has gone on too long.
這種產品的價格差不多要下跌了。價格凍結維持得太久了。

請從「搭配詞表」中選出適當的字，完成下面句子。例解請見第333~353頁。

☐ I (1)_____ a very (2)_____ price for that ticket. It was a 60% discount!

☐ If we (3)_____ our (4)_____ price, we can give people a better discount. That might encourage them to buy more units.

☐ I don't want to (5)_____ our (6)_____ price. It might start a (7)_____. Each unit is already quite cheap.

☐ We must (8)_____ our prices at a reasonable level. This is a (9)_____ market. If our prices are too high, we will not meet our sales target.

☐ I can (10)_____ you the lot for (11)_____ price. How's that?

☐ There's a big gap between (12)_____ and (13)_____ prices here. The distributor buys low and sells high.

☐ They (14)_____ me a very (15)_____ price, so I went to another supplier and got a much lower one.

☐ The price (16)_____ this kind of consultancy service (17)_____ a full report.

☐ Because there is a (18)_____, prices have not (19)_____ for a long time.

☐ We need to (20)_____ a price before we can finish this negotiation.

☐ I've looked at our **(21)**_____ and I think we need a

(22)_____ if we are going to increase profit margins.

進階造句

請嘗試利用「搭配詞表」中的字彙，造出想要表達的句子。

_____

_____

_____

_____

_____

_____

_____

_____

problem
[ˈprɑbləm]

可數名詞 問題
同義字：issue、question

搭配在前面的動詞		搭配的形容詞		關鍵字
solve	detect	main	recurring	
deal with	come across	real	common	
address	come up against	basic	familiar	
overcome	encounter		related	**problem**
sort out	run into	underlying	minor	**(with sth.)**
tackle		fundamental		**(Ving)**
	cause		unexpected	
examine	pose	serious	unforeseen	
identify	present	tricky		
		complex	pressing	
		difficult		
			potential	

 好搭例句

◎ MP3-72

☐ We need to **solve** the **main** problem before we can move on to the next stage of the project.
我們要先解決主要問題，才能往案子的下一個階段邁進。

☐ Any ideas about how to **deal with** this **tricky** problem?
關於要怎麼應付這個棘手的問題，有任何想法嗎？

☐ We need to **address** two **pressing** problems here.
我們在這裡需要解決兩個迫切的問題。

☐ Once we can **overcome** the **minor** problems **with** the distribution network, we should be able to gain market share.
只要我們能克服經銷網的小問題，我們應該就能提高市占率。

☐ Did you **sort out** the **underlying** problem **with** the software?
你有沒有針對軟體找出根本的問題？

☐ Let's ask Brad. He's very good at **tackling** these **complex** problems.
我們去請教布雷德。他非常善於應付這些複雜的問題。

☐ Once you **examine** the **basic** problem carefully, it should be easy to **solve**.
等你仔細檢查了基本問題，應該就很好解決了。

☐ There is a **serious** problem **with** the system. We need to **identify** it and **solve** it.
系統出了嚴重的問題。我們需要加以查明並解決。

☐ We have **detected** a problem **with** the plant.
我們偵測到廠房有問題。

☐ We have **come across** a **common** problem: Our margins are too small. Another **related** problem is that our costs are too high. These are **familiar** problems for small businesses like ours.
我們碰到了一個常見的問題：我們的毛利太低了。另一個相關問題是，我們的成本太高了。這是像我們這種小企業很熟悉的問題。

☐ We've **come up against** an **unforeseen** problem **with** the parts you sent us. They are the wrong size.
在你們寄給我們的零件上，我們碰到了一個出乎預料的問題。它的尺寸不對。

☐ We've **encountered** an **unexpected** problem **with** the system.
我們在系統上遇到了一個意想不到的問題。

☐ If you **run into** any problems **opening** the file, please let me know.
假如你在開啟檔案方面遇到任何問題，請通知我一聲。

☐ This is a **difficult** and **recurring** problem which we need to **address**.
這是個麻煩的老問題，我們需要解決才行。

☐ It's a **real** problem. How should we **resolve** it?
這是個實實在在的問題。我們該怎麼化解才好？

☐ The new machinery is **causing** all sorts of problems.
新機器引發了各種問題。

☐ This situation **poses** a **fundamental** problem. We must **solve** it.
這個情形點出了根本問題。我們必須加以解決。

☐ The payment procedure **presents** a **potential** problem for new customers. We need to simplify it.
付款程序會對新顧客造成潛在的問題。我們需要簡化才行。

填填看

請從「搭配詞表」中選出適當的字，完成下面句子。例解請見第333~353頁。

☐ The (1)_____ problem is that our products are useless and nobody wants to buy them. When we (2)_____ this problem, everything else will probably be okay as well.

☐ I have not been able to (3)_____ the problem. I need to do that before I can (4)_____ it.

☐ I have (5)_____ an (6)_____ problem. I didn't foresee that this would be a (7)_____ problem.

☐ In addition to the problem (8)_____ the server, I have also (9)_____ a (10)_____ problem with the printer. Do you want me to fix that as well?

☐ The machine breakdown could (11)_____ a (12)_____ problem with the production schedule. You need to be prepared for that.

☐ Don't worry. It's a (13)_____ problem with this type of product. Easy to fix.

請嘗試利用「搭配詞表」中的字彙,造出想要表達的句子。

搭配在前面的動詞	搭配的形容詞	關鍵字
follow use carry out introduce adopt repeat simplify streamline develop establish	correct proper normal simple straightforward standard operational standard complaints documentation emergency	**procedure (for sth.)**

 好搭例句　　　　　◎ MP3-73

☐ What's the **correct** procedure **for** claiming expenses?
報銷費用的正確程序是什麼？

☐ Please make sure you **follow standard** procedure at all times.
請各位一定要隨時遵守標準程序。

☐ We are **carrying out** the last phase of our **standard operationing** procedure now.
我們現在要實施最後一階段的標準作業程序。

☐ The head office has **introduced** some **simple documentation** procedures.
總部訂出了簡單的文書程序。

☐ We have recently **adopted** a more **straightforward complaints** procedure.
我們最近採用了更簡明的投訴程序。

☐ If it doesn't work, shut down your computer and **repeat** the **normal** procedure.
假如它不動的話，就把電腦關機，並重複正常程序。

☐ We need to **simplify** our **emergency** procedures.
我們需要簡化我們的緊急程序。

☐ Did you **use** the **proper** procedure?
你有採用適當的程序嗎？

☐ I'm **developing** a new procedure **for** dealing with data.
我在為處理資料制訂新的程序。

☐ Last year I **established** a procedure **for** dealing with incoming mail.
去年我為處理來信建立了一套程序。

填填看

請從「搭配詞表」中選出適當的字，完成下面句子。例解請見第333~353頁。

☐ There is a very (1)_____ procedure (2)_____ claiming expenses. It's easy, so please make sure you (3)_____ the procedure.

☐ We are currently (4)_____ the last part of the procedure. This is a tricky part of the procedure.

☐ Hmm. I don't know what is causing the problem. Did you (5)_____ the (6)_____ procedure? You didn't make the same mistake as last time, did you?

☐ On Monday we are going to (7)_____ the same

(8)_____ procedure as the other branches in the region. Then

all our procedures will be the same globally.

☐ If it doesn't work, just (9)_____ the procedure. It sometimes

works better the second time.

☐ I have recently had lots of calls from customers asking us to

(10)_____ the (11)_____ procedure. They say it's very

difficult to make a complaint and nothing ever gets done about it.

☐ If we could (12)_____ a (13)_____ procedure, then

reports and other documents wouldn't get lost all the time.

☐ In the event of a fire or other emergency, please (14)_____ the

(15)_____ procedure.

進階造句

請嘗試利用「搭配詞表」中的字彙，造出想要表達的句子。

_____

_____

_____

_____

_____

_____

_____

product
[ˈprɑdəkt]

可數名詞 產品

搭配在前面的動詞		搭配的形容詞		關鍵字
distribute sell buy advertise market promote create demand for	endorse use develop produce manufacture launch introduce	finished innovative branded defective range of the company's	consumer skincare agricultural natural household software	**product** product range product category product line product information product development

好搭例句

◎ MP3-74

☐ We **produce** a full **range of innovative software** products.
我們是在生產全套的創新軟體產品。

☐ We need to find a reliable partner to **distribute** our **consumer** products.
我們需要找個可靠的夥伴來經銷我們的消費產品。

☐ We **sell skincare** products. Our products are the best in that product category.
我們是在賣護膚產品。我們的產品是那類產品中最棒的。

☐ No one will **buy** these **defective** products.
沒有人會買這些瑕疵品。

☐ We are **advertising** our **branded** products in all the key magazines.
The ads include a lot of product information.
我們要在所有的重要雜誌上替我們的品牌產品打廣告。廣告中會包含許多產品資訊。

☐ The marketing department's job is to **market** the product by **creating demand for** the **company's** product and **promoting** it.
行銷部的工作是行銷產品，一方面為公司的產品創造需求，一方面促銷它。

☐ Sometimes we get a celebrity to **endorse** the product.
有時候我們會請名人來為產品代言。

☐ Most of the people who **use** this kind of **household** product are women.
使用這種家用產品的人大部分是女性。

☐ We are **developing** a new product range under a new brand name. It's still in the product development stage.
我們要以新的商標開發新的產品類別。它還在產品開發階段。

☐ We **manufacture agricultural** products and **sell** them in developing countries.
我們是在製造農產品，並把它賣到開發中國家。

☐ We **launched** the **finished** product last month. It's the first in the new product line.
我們上個月推出了成品。它是新產品線的第一批。

☐ We are trying to **introduce natural** products to the market.
我們嘗試要引進天然產品到市場上。

填填看

請從「搭配詞表」中選出適當的字，完成下面句子。例解請見第333~353頁。

☐ The marketing department (1)＿＿＿＿＿＿ our products by (2)＿＿＿＿＿＿ them on TV and in the media.

☐ The sales department (3)＿＿＿＿＿＿ the products and finds partners to (4)＿＿＿＿＿＿ them.

☐ Our (5)＿＿＿＿＿＿ products are very popular. Mostly women (6)＿＿＿＿＿＿ them.

☐ We (7)_____ the product last year. It has been very successful.

☐ If we (8)_____ (9)_____ products, the consumer will not buy them and we will damage our market share.

☐ We only (10)_____ (11)_____ products. We care about the environment, and we know our customers do too.

☐ We have (12)_____ some (13)_____ (14)_____ products recently. Computer users around the world are very excited about the new possibilities.

☐ The factory (15)_____ (16)_____ products. It causes lots of pollution and is not pleasant for the people who live near it.

☐ If we can get a celebrity to (17)_____ our new product. it will help to boost sales.

☐ In this (18)_____ we have two (19)_____, each with several (20)_____.

☐ We have a great new product in the (21)_____ stage at the moment. It will be launched in a few months.

☐ If the (22)_____ is not clear, people will not know how to use it.

進階造句

請嘗試利用「搭配詞表」中的字彙，造出想要表達的句子。

_____

_____

_____

_____

production
[prə`dʌkʃən]

不可數名詞 生產

搭配在前面的動詞		搭配的形容詞	關鍵字
			production (of sth.)
begin commence increase boost stimulate double triple/treble reduce	maintain delay cut stop cease discontinue outsource	full smooth	production capability production capacity production cost production line production manager production process production schedule production team production unit

 好搭例句

◎ MP3-75

☐ We **begin** production **of** the new product on Monday. The production line is all ready.

我們在星期一要開始生產新產品。生產線已全部就緒。

☐ We should be able to **commence full** production next week. If we work at **full** production capacity for three days, we should be able to produce the whole batch in that time.

我們下星期應該就能展開全面生產。假如我們以最大產能運轉三天,我們應該就能在那個時間把整批生產出來。

☐ The accident damaged our production capacity, so we will need to **reduce** production for a few days.

意外事故損及了我們的產能,所以我們需要減產幾天。

☐ The new production manager has managed to **increase** production by 2%.

新的生產經理好不容易增產了2%。

☐ Will we be able to **maintain smooth** production for another four days?

我們能不能再撐四天維持順利的生產？

☐ The production team has been working really hard to try to **boost** production.

生產團隊十分拚命地想要提高產量。

☐ Last quarter we **tripled** production, but managed to keep our production costs the same.

上一季我們把產量提高了兩倍，但生產成本還能維持原狀。

☐ This new production process will allow us to **double** production.

這套新的生產流程可以讓我們提高一倍的產量。

☐ We need to **stimulate** production. Demand is increasing.

我們需要刺激生產。需求正在擴大。

☐ Let's **delay** production a bit until we can find out what the problem with the product is.

我們不妨稍微延後生產，直到我們找出產品有什麼問題為止。

☐ Please let the production unit know that we have decided to **stop** production **of** the unit.

請通知生產單位，我們決定把裝置停產。

☐ Please try to **cut** production by 20%. Demand for this product is slowing down.

請設法減產20%。這項產品的需求正在減弱。

☐ The production schedule is too tight. I don't think we can meet the target.

生產時程太緊了。我不認為我們能達到目標。

☐ I'm sorry that we have no choice but to **cease** production until we can fix the machine.

很抱歉我們別無選擇，只能停產到我們有辦法把機器修好為止。

☐ The production line is experiencing problems. We will need to **discontinue** production for a few hours.

生產線出了問題。我們需要中斷生產幾小時。

☐ If we buy more machinery, we will be able to **increase** our production capability by producing a wider variety of products.

假如我們購買更多機器，我們就能擴大產能，並生產更多種類的產品。

填填看

請從「搭配詞表」中選出適當的字，完成下面句子。例解請見第333~353頁。

☐ I work in the (1)_____. I am a member of the (2)_____. We are responsible for production. The (3)_____ is very good at keeping the (4)_____ running smoothly. He is a very good manager.

☐ The new product line will (5)_____ production next month.

☐ Our boss wants us to (6)_____ production because there is a big increase in demand for this product. The new (7)_____ is very tight. I don't know if we can make it.

☐ We need to (8)_____ (9)_____. The factory is not producing enough.

☐ The new machinery will allow us to (10)_____ our (11)_____. We will be able to make a wider range of products.

☐ Because demand for this product is falling, we are going to

(12)_____ production for a while.

☐ We had some problems getting hold of raw materials. That's why we had

to (13)_____ production (14)_____ the product for a

few days.

☐ As long as we don't have any more problems, we will be able to

(15)_____ (16)_____ production for a few weeks.

☐ (17)_____ are rising all the time. It's getting more expensive to

produce the products.

進階造句

請嘗試利用「搭配詞表」中的字彙，造出想要表達的句子。

_____

_____

_____

_____

_____

_____

_____

76 profit ['prɑfɪt]		可數名詞 獲利 同義字：return	

搭配在前面的動詞	搭配的形容詞		關鍵字	搭配在後面的動詞
make earn generate produce	half year quarterly interim	operating pre-tax net taxable	**profit (of #)**	rise increase grow
report announce	annual		profit margin profit forecast profit growth profit share	fall decrease shrink
increase maximize	great good better than expected			remained steady
see show	low lower than expected			stabilized

為數字

 好搭例句　　　　　　　　　　　　　　◎ MP3-76

☐ Last year we **made** a **pre-tax** profit **of** 19 million. It was a good year.
去年我們達到了 1,900 萬的稅前盈餘，是不錯的一年。

☐ We **earned low quarterly** profits **of** 1 million.
我們賺進了偏低的季度獲利 100 萬元。

☐ This product **generates good** profits. The profit margin is very high on this product.
這樣產品帶來了不錯的獲利。這樣產品的毛利非常高。

☐ This market **produces good** profits for us.
這個市場使我們產生了不錯的獲利。

☐ I have to **report lower than expected** profits **of** 90 million.
我必須指出還不到預期的獲利 9,000 萬。

☐ They **announced better than expected half year** profits **of** 70 million, up 3% from the profit forecast.
他們宣布優於預期的半年期獲利7000萬，比獲利預估高了3%。

☐ We need to **increase** our profits.
我們需要增加獲利。

☐ How can we **maximize** profits?
我們要怎麼樣才能衝高獲利？

☐ Last year we **saw** profits **of** 317 million in all markets, only up 0.5% from the previous year. Profit growth is quite slow.
去年我們在各個市場上所呈現的獲利是3億1700萬，只比前年多了0.5%。獲利成長相當慢。

☐ This quarter **shows great** profits **of** 2 million. We are going to get a big bonus this year as this company operates a profit share system for its employees.
本季所達到的獲利是200萬。我們今年會拿到高額的獎金，因為本公司為員工推出了利潤分享制度。

☐ **Interim operating** profits have **increased**.
期中的營業利益提高了。

☐ **Taxable** profits have **increased**.
應稅利潤提高了。

☐ **Annual** profits have **grown** year on year for the last 5 years.
過去五年來，同年期的年度獲利都有所成長。

☐ **Net** profits have **fallen** this half.
這半年的淨利有所下跌。

☐ **Operating** profits **have been** steadily **decreasing** as costs rise.
隨著成本提高，營業利益正持續下滑。

☐ The shrinking market means profits **have** also **shrunk**.
市場萎縮意謂著獲利也萎縮了。

☐ Profits so far this year have **remained steady**.

到目前為止，今年的獲利都保持平穩。

☐ This month, profits have **stabilized**. We hope they will start to go up again next month.

本月獲利穩定。我們希望下個月會開始上升。

填填看

請從「搭配詞表」中選出適當的字，完成下面句子。例解請見第333~353頁。

☐ Last year we (1)＿＿＿＿＿＿ (2)＿＿＿＿＿＿ profits of 100 billion in all our markets. That's up 6% from the year before. (3)＿＿＿＿＿＿ is really good.

☐ The company (4)＿＿＿＿＿＿ (5)＿＿＿＿＿＿ (6)＿＿＿＿＿＿ profits of 5 billion — that's before tax and for the whole year. That's 5% more than the (7)＿＿＿＿＿＿, and was totally unexpected. The market went wild and the company shares increased in value.

☐ Is there any way we can (8)＿＿＿＿＿＿ our profits on this product? I know the current (9)＿＿＿＿＿＿ is very low, so how can we increase it? Can we cut costs?

☐ This market is (10)＿＿＿＿＿＿ profits of 100 million. It's our most profitable market.

☐ Last year, we (11)＿＿＿＿＿＿ profits (12)＿＿＿＿＿＿ 20%. This year we are (13)＿＿＿＿＿＿ (14)＿＿＿＿＿＿ profits. What's going wrong?

☐ (15)_____ profits are (16)_____. I was expecting something better. I know these are not the final figures, but can you explain the reason for the fall?

☐ (17)_____ (18)_____ profits are up from the same half the year before. However, once we deduct the tax, those figures will not look good at all.

☐ What were our (19)_____ (20)_____ profits for the same quarter the year before last? After we paid tax? Oh good! Profits are (21)_____. The shareholders will be happy with their (22)_____!

☐ After a rapid fall last quarter, profits (23)_____. We hope that the downward trend is now over and profits will start to rise again.

☐ There was not much movement in profits last quarter. They (24)_____.

進階造句

請嘗試利用「搭配詞表」中的字彙，造出想要表達的句子。

_____

_____

_____

_____

_____

program
[ˋprogræm]

可數名詞 程式

搭配在前面的動詞	搭配的形容詞	關鍵字	搭配在後面的動詞
write	word processing	**program**	run
	spreadsheet		run on
design			allow
develop	computer		enable
	software	program designer	
run	antivirus	program documentation	provide
	anti-spyware	program code	offer
install	email		
test	shareware		work

 好搭例句

◉ MP3-77

☐ I am a program designer. It's my job to **write computer** programs for the company.
我是個程式設計師。我的工作是替公司撰寫電腦程式。

☐ I am **designing** a new **shareware** program.
我在設計新的共享軟體程式。

☐ There's no point in **developing** a **word processing** program. Why don't we just use Word?
開發文書處理程式毫無道理。我們為什麼不用 Word 就好？

☐ When I **run** the **spreadsheet** program, my computer crashes.
我在執行試算表程式時，電腦會當掉。

☐ Can you please **install** the **antivirus** program for me?
能不能麻煩你幫我安裝防毒程式？

☐ We are **testing** the **software** program right now. We think there is a problem with the program code.
我們現在正在測試軟體程式。我們認為程式碼有問題。

☐ There's a problem with the **email** program. Let's check the program documentation.
電子郵件程式出了問題。我們來查查程式文件。

☐ The program **runs** perfectly.
這套程式跑得很順。

☐ The program **runs on** the Posix subsystem only.
這套程式只能在可攜式作業系統界面的子系統上跑。

☐ The program **allows** you to find your customer information quickly and easily.
這套程式可以讓你快速又輕鬆地找到顧客資料。

☐ Will the program **enable** file sharing?
這套程式可以分享檔案嗎？

☐ The program **provides** easy access to the database.
這套程式可輕鬆讀取資料庫。

☐ The program will **offer** all kinds of great functions.
這套程式提供了各種優異的功能。

☐ The program **works** just great now!
這套程式目前運作得好極了！

填填看

請從「搭配詞表」中選出適當的字，完成下面句子。例解請見第333~353頁。

☐ I'm (1)＿＿＿＿＿＿ a (2)＿＿＿＿＿＿ program which is going to be better than Word!

☐ I can't (3)＿＿＿＿＿＿ the (4)＿＿＿＿＿＿ program on my computer, but I really need to bring my sales figures up to date. Please help me.

☐ The new (5)_____ program (6)_____ much faster than the old one. And it (7)_____ more functionality. It even (8)_____ me to play games and work at the same time! It's really cool!

☐ We're (9)_____ the new (10)_____ program on Monday, then we are going to (11)_____ it for a few days. You should be able to write emails again by the end of the week.

☐ I'm a (12)_____. I design (13)_____ programs which customers can initially use for free.

☐ I have found the problem. There is an error in the (14)_____. I'm rewriting it now.

☐ The program (15)_____ Unix.

☐ If we don't have the (16)_____, it will be difficult to fix the program.

☐ I think someone forgot to (17)_____ the (18)_____ program. My computer has so many strange pop-ups this morning!

進階造句

請嘗試利用「搭配詞表」中的字彙，造出想要表達的句子。

_____

_____

_____

_____

project
[ˈprɑdʒɛkt]

可數名詞 專案

搭配在前面的動詞	搭配的形容詞	關鍵字
		project
plan		
implement		project coordinator
launch	pilot	project finance
complete	new	project leader
	major	project management
manage		project manager
run	R&D	project proposal
coordinate	joint	project team
		project status
approve		project status report
support		

 好搭例句

◎ MP3-78

☐ As project leader, my job is to **manage** the whole project from start to finish.
身為專案領導人，我的工作是從頭到尾管理整件案子。

☐ I **planned** the project last year, but since my boss only now **approved** the project, I can finally start to **implement** it. My first task is to assemble a good project team, and then get some project finance.
我去年就規劃了這個案子，但由於老闆直到現在才批准案子，所以我總算能開始實行了。我的首要之務是組一支理想的專案團隊，然後申請一些專案經費。

☐ He's an excellent project manager. He knows how to **coordinate** the project.
他是傑出的專案管理師。他知道要怎麼協調案子。

☐ We are going to **launch** several **new major R&D** projects this year.
我們今年將推出幾件新的重大研發案。

☐ Project management includes **running** all aspects of the project.
專案管理包含了推動專案的各個層面。

☐ I have just **completed** this **pilot** project. My boss **supported** the whole project. He was fantastic.
我剛完成了這件試辦案。我老闆支持整件案子，他很了不起。

☐ This will be a **joint** project involving several departments. We need a really good project coordinator to **run** the project.
這將是牽涉到好幾個部門的聯合專案。我們需要相當好的專案主持人來執行這件案子。

☐ My boss has **approved** my project proposal!
我老闆批准了我的專案企畫！

☐ How can I know your project status if you never give me a project status report?
假如你從來不交案件進度報告給我，我怎麼會知道你的案件進度？

✏️ 填填看

請從「搭配詞表」中選出適當的字，完成下面句子。例解請見第333~353頁。

☐ I am currently (1)_____ a (2)_____ project. When the (3)_____ is ready, I will present it to my boss. I hope he (4)_____ it!

☐ Although we (5)_____ the project, it was delayed by 6 months. The (6)_____ worked very hard to complete it on time, but the (7)_____ did not give very good (8)_____, so we were plagued by lots of problems.

☐ I'm (9)_____ several (10)_____ projects at the moment. Each one is very important, so I'm really busy!

☐ We will (11)_____ this (12)_____ project on Monday, and (13)_____ it over the next few weeks. It's very important that we develop a new product for the company.

☐ It's difficult to get (14)_____ for (15)_____ projects in this company. It seems they are not really willing to spend money on testing new IT procedures.

☐ The senior management just (16)_____ this (17)_____ project. They think working with another team from another department is a good idea.

☐ Please keep me informed about your (18)_____. I have not seen a (19)_____ for a long time, so I don't know how the project is going.

進階造句

請嘗試利用「搭配詞表」中的字彙，造出想要表達的句子。

_____

_____

_____

_____

_____

_____

_____

| | | 79 | **proposal** [prə`pozl] | | 可數名詞 提案 同義字：recommendation、suggestion | |

搭配在前面的動詞		搭配的形容詞	關鍵字	搭配在後面的動詞
make submit outline put forward write draft put together come up with read	consider discuss support approve back block oppose reject	concrete detailed preliminary excellent controversial a set of ★ +s a number of ★ +s viable practical	**proposal (concerning sth.) (for sth.)**	involve n.p. involve Ving include n.p.

★爲關鍵字

 好搭例句　　　　　　　　　　　　　◎ MP3-79

☐ At this stage I would like to **make** a **preliminary** proposal **concerning** the implementation of this project.

在這個階段，我想針對這個案件的實施做個初步的提案。

☐ I **submitted** my proposal on Monday, they **discussed** the proposal, and then they **approved** it on Tuesday. They said it was an **excellent** proposal and they would **support** it.

我在星期一遞出提案，他們討論了提案，接著在星期二就批准了。他們說這是個出色的提案，他們會支持。

☐ After **considering** my proposal, they **rejected** it. They said it was too **controversial**.

在考慮我的提案後，他們否決了。他們說它太具爭議性。

☐ I would like to quickly **outline a set of** proposals **for** the project.
我想趕緊為案子勾勒出一套提案。

☐ I am currently **writing** a **detailed** proposal.
我目前在寫一份詳細的提案。

☐ I **put forward** a **practical** proposal **for** this problem, but someone **blocked** it in the final stage.
我為這個問題提出了實用的提案，但有人在最後階段把它擋了下來。

☐ I'm sorry but I **oppose** this proposal. I don't think it's **viable**.
很抱歉，我反對這個提案。我認為它並不可行。

☐ I've **come up with a number of** proposals **for** the design. Do you want to hear them?
我為設計構思了一些提案。你想要聽聽看嗎？

☐ If you can **put together** a **concrete** proposal, I'll **back** it.
假如你能拿出具體的提案，我就支持。

☐ They are **reading** my proposal at the moment. I hope they accept it.
他們現在正在看我的提案。希望他們會接受。

☐ This **practical** proposal **includes** revenue projections and cost estimates.
這個實用的提案包含了營收推算和成本估計。

☐ I **drafted** a proposal which **involved** restructuring the project team.
我擬了一個提案要求重組專案團隊。

☐ The proposal **involves** an entire rethink of the project.
這個提案要求把案子整個重新考慮一遍。

✏ 填填看

請從「搭配詞表」中選出適當的字，完成下面句子。例解請見第333~353頁。

☐ I am currently (1)＿＿＿＿＿＿ a (2)＿＿＿＿＿＿ proposal

(3)_____ this. It's taking me a long time to finish because of all the figures.

☐ Last week I (4)_____ (5)_____ proposals. Have you had time to (6)_____ them yet?

☐ I don't think this is a (7)_____ proposal. It's too (8)_____ and will (9)_____ firing too many of our people. I don't think we should (10)_____ it.

☐ John in my team has (11)_____ an (12)_____ proposal. It's so good I think you should hear it.

☐ Look, this is just a (13)_____ proposal. I don't think we should (14)_ _____ the proposal until it's more complete. It might be just what we are looking for.

☐ The proposal needs to (15)_____ more figures in it.

☐ My proposal doesn't (16)_____ a lot of extra expense.

☐ Did you actually (17)_____ my proposal?

進階造句

請嘗試利用「搭配詞表」中的字彙，造出想要表達的句子。

_____

_____

_____

_____

_____

prospects
[ˈprɑspɛkts]

可數名詞 前景

搭配在前面的動詞	搭配的形容詞		關鍵字	搭配在後面的動詞
have improve enhance damage assess	good excellent exciting brighter better poor gloomy limited long-term short-term	growth financial economic market	**prospects (for sth.)**	be look

 好搭例句

◎ MP3-80

☐ Is there any way we can **improve** our **gloomy market** prospects? We are losing market share all the time.
我們有沒有什麼方法可以改善低迷的市場前景？我們一直在流失市占率。

☐ We **have excellent short-term** prospects.
我們有絕佳的短期前景。

☐ The rise in interest rates might **damage** our **financial** prospects. We might need to revise our projections.
利息上升可能會損及我們的財務前景。我們可能需要修正我們的推估。

☐ At the moment, we **have limited growth** prospects. We must come up with some new business ideas soon.
目前我們具備有限的成長前景。我們必須快點提出一些新的經營理念。

☐ The country **has exciting economic** prospects. I think we will see rapid and sustainable growth.

該國擁有令人振奮的經濟前景。我想我們會看到迅速又持久的成長。

☐ In order to **enhance** our prospects, we are going to look for further investment.

為了提升我們的前景，我們將尋求進一步的投資。

☐ I am in the process of **assessing** our **short-term** prospects to see whether it's worth continuing to operate.

我正在評估我們的短期前景，以了解是否值得繼續營運下去。

☐ A more secure financial base will give the company **brighter** prospects **for** the future.

更穩固的財務基礎將使公司未來具有更光明的前景。

☐ She is an excellent manager, she **has good** prospects.

她是個出色的經理，擁有美好的前景。

☐ The **long-term financial** prospects of the company are **looking** excellent.

公司的長期財務前景看起來很棒。

☐ The **economic** prospects **are** rather **poor**.

經濟前景相當差。

☐ The **financial** prospects **are looking better** now that we have this new major customer.

既然我們有了這個重量級的新顧客，財務前景看起來就更好了。

✏️ 填填看

請從「搭配詞表」中選出適當的字，完成下面句子。例解請見第333~353頁。

☐ We had a bad year last year, but the prospects (1)_____ next year (2)_____ much (3)_____.

☐ According to my financial projections, we (4)_____

(5)_____ (6)_____ prospects.

☐ Because of the political uncertainty, the (7)_____ prospects are

(8)_____ quite (9)_____.

☐ If the new customers place very large orders quickly, this will

(10)_____ our (11)_____ prospects; our situation will

improve quickly.

☐ The lack of investment in machinery under the previous management

(12)_____ our (13)_____ prospects. It will be very

difficult for us to grow without direct investment.

☐ Part of my job as a strategic planner is to (14)_____ the

(15)_____ prospects. I have to work out how I think the market

is going to change, and plan strategy accordingly.

進階造句

請嘗試利用「搭配詞表」中的字彙，造出想要表達的句子。

_____

_____

_____

_____

_____

_____

question ①
[ˈkwɛstʃən]

可數名詞 詢問；問題

搭配在前面的動詞		搭配的形容詞		關鍵字
be have ask put ★ to sb. answer respond to reply to	avoid evade ignore	good relevant pointed probing searching direct difficult tricky embarrassing	simple stupid personal	**question (about sth.)**

★爲關鍵字

 好搭例句

⊚ **MP3-81**

☐ Can I **ask** a **stupid** question?
我能問個笨問題嗎？

☐ They **had** so many **pointed** questions, I had difficulty **evading** them.
他們有一大堆尖銳的問題。我閃不了。

☐ That journalist always **asks** a lot of **searching** questions. Take care how you **reply to** his questions.
那個記者老是問許多追根究底的問題。對於要怎麼答覆他的問題，你要小心處理。

☐ That's a **good** question. Can I **respond to** that question at the end of my presentation? Thanks.
那是個好問題。我能等我提報完再回答那個問題嗎？謝謝。

☐ If I think the question is not **relevant**, I usually don't **answer** it.
假如我認為問題不相干，我通常就不會回答。

☐ Can I **ask** you a **personal** question?

我能問你一個私人問題嗎？

☐ Sometimes it's just too difficult to **avoid probing** questions. You just have to lie.

有時候要避開窮追猛打的問題真是難上加難。你就是非說謊不可。

☐ I'd like to **put** a very **simple** question **to** the speaker.

我想向發言人提個非常簡單的問題。

☐ He **asks** very **direct** questions which are impossible to **ignore**.

他會問非常直接而令人無法忽略的問題。

☐ That **was** a very **embarrassing** question!

那是個非常尷尬的問題！

☐ Hmm, yes, that's a **tricky** question. Thanks for **asking** it.

姆，對，那是個吊詭的問題。謝謝發問。

☐ Oh, what a **difficult** question. Can I get back to you later with an answer?

噢，真是個困難的問題。我能晚點再回覆你答案嗎？

🖊 填填看

請從「搭配詞表」中選出適當的字，完成下面句子。例解請見第333~353頁。

☐ I would like to (1)_____ a question (2)_____ the speaker (3)_____ the figures he presented.

☐ That journalist (4)_____ some very (5)_____ questions. It was very difficult to (6)_____ them. I hope I (7)_____ the questions without revealing too much of our strategy.

☐ The best way to deal with (8)_____ questions is to

(9)_____ them, you know, don't really answer them directly. If they are very difficult, then just pretend you didn't hear the questioner and (10)_____ the question.

☐ That (11)_____ a very (12)_____ question. Let me think.

☐ It's a very (13)_____ question. Just give me a simple answer.

☐ Well, that's a (14)_____ question, so I'm not going to answer it. My private life is my own business.

☐ This is a kind of (15)_____ question, but, do you like me? Do you think we have a future?

☐ That's a (16)_____ question! Of course I like you!

進階造句

請嘗試利用「搭配詞表」中的字彙，造出想要表達的句子。

_____

_____

_____

_____

_____

_____

_____

| 82 | **question** ② [ˋkwɛstʃən] | 可數名詞 問題 同義字：problem、issue |

搭配在前面的動詞		搭配的形容詞	關鍵字
raise avoid ignore consider discuss examine deal with go into look at	tackle settle	complex difficult crucial fundamental immediate real	**question (of sth.)**

 好搭例句

◎ **MP3-82**

☐ That **raises** the question **of** tax settlement.
那點出了完稅的問題。

☐ We simply can't **avoid** the **immediate** question **of** low staff moral. How do you intend to **tackle** this question?
我們根本避不開人員士氣低落這個眼前的問題。你打算怎麼因應這個問題？

☐ Up to now we have simply **ignored** the **crucial** question **of** capital investment in new machinery. We need to **consider** this **fundamental** question now.
到目前為止，我們完全忽略了對新機器投資這個重要的問題。我們現在需要考慮一下這個根本的問題。

☐ I'd like to **discuss** the **complex** question **of** market strategy now.
我現在想討論一下市場策略這個複雜的問題。

☐ Let's **examine** this **difficult** question in more detail.
我們來更詳細地研究一下這個困難的問題。

272

☐ Can we **deal with** the question **of** overtime at the next meeting? We haven't got time to **go into** this question now.
我們下次開會時能不能談談加班的問題？我們到現在都沒時間提到這個問題。

☐ The **real** question here is what are we going to do about falling revenues?
此處的真正問題在於，我們要如何因應營收的下滑？

☐ I think we have at long last been able to **settle** the question **of** foreign competition.
我想我們總算可解決國外競爭的問題了。

☐ Let's **look at** the question in more detail.
我們來更詳細地探討這個問題。

填填看

請從「搭配詞表」中選出適當的字，完成下面句子。例解請見第333~353頁。

☐ In this meeting I want to (1)_____ the (2)_____ question (3)_____ falling revenues. This is the most important issue facing us today.

☐ His management style is very strange. He has the habit of (4)_____ (5)_____ questions, instead of (6)_____ them, so important things never get done.

☐ I'd like to (7)_____ the (8)_____ question of bonuses. Chinese New Year is two weeks away, so we really need to (9)_____ this now.

☐ In my last talk I (10)_____ the question (11)_____ interest rates and how they affect the economy. I'd like to develop this a bit now.

The (12)_____ question is not how we persuade the customer to accept these changes, but whether we should even try. Maybe we should just drop the project and start from scratch.

進階造句

請嘗試利用「搭配詞表」中的字彙，造出想要表達的句子。

_____

_____

_____

_____

_____

_____

_____

_____

83	**recommendation** [ˌrɛkəmɛnˋdeʃən]	可數名詞 推薦；建言 同義字：proposal、suggestion

搭配在前面的動詞	搭配的形容詞	關鍵字	搭配在後面的動詞
make submit put forward offer come up with consider adopt accept follow carry out implement review oppose reject be in line with	clear detailed draft far-reaching firm strong general important main official	**recommendation (for sth.) (to V)**	be involve Ving involve n.p. include n.p. include Ving

好搭例句　　　　　　　　　　　　　◎ **MP3-83**

☐ I would like to **make** a **firm** recommendation **for** more lead time.
我想就延長前置時間提出懇切的建言。

☐ I'll be **submitting** my recommendation tomorrow morning.
我明天早上會提出我的建言。

☐ The consultant we hired has **put forward** some **far-reaching**
recommendations.
我們所請的顧問提出了一些廣泛的建言。

☐ The report **offers clear** and **detailed** recommendations.
報告中提供了明確而詳盡的建言。

☐ So far I've only managed to **come up with** a **draft** recommendation. I will need more time.
到目前為止，我只勉強想出了建言的草案。我需要更多的時間。

☐ We are **considering** your recommendation now, and we will let you know whether we have decided to **adopt** your recommendations by the end of the week.
我們現在在考慮你的建言，而且我們會在週末前讓你知道，我們是否決定採用你的建言。

☐ We have decided to **accept** your **general** recommendations. We will be **implementing** them over the next few months.
我們決定接受你的概括建言。我們會在未來幾個月實施。

☐ We are **reviewing** your recommendations now.
我們現在在審查你的建言。

☐ I think we should **follow** the recommendations in the report. It might be difficult to **carry out** the recommendations, but I think they will improve the work flow.
我想我們應該聽從報告中的建言。落實這些建言可能很困難，但我想它可以改善工作流程。

☐ We **oppose** your recommendation **to** increase the team and we **reject** your recommendation **for** a longer lead time.
我們反對你所建言的擴大編組，我們也否決了你所建言的延長前置時間。

☐ Our quality controls **are in line with official** recommendations.
我們的品管符合官方的建言。

☐ The most **important** recommendation **involves** changing the specs of the product.
最重要的建言涉及修改產品的規格。

- [ ] This is a **strong** recommendation **for** cancelling the project.
這是對於撤銷案件的強烈建言。

- [ ] The recommendation **includes** examples from other companies and **involves** companies from different markets as well.
建言中包含了其他公司的實例，也提到了不同市場的公司。

- [ ] The **main** recommendation **is for** greater quality control.
主要的建言在於加強品管。

填填看

請從「搭配詞表」中選出適當的字，完成下面句子。例解請見第333~353頁。

- [ ] The consultant has (1)_____ some (2)_____
recommendations (3)_____ . changing our working practices.
Although they are pretty strong, I think we should (4)_____
them. They may help us to increase our performance.

- [ ] If we (5)_____ these recommendations, what will they
(6)_____?

- [ ] I'm (7)_____ your (8)_____ recommendations now. Of
course you need more figures, but I think it's a good start.

- [ ] This is a very (9)_____ recommendation (10)_____
restructure our project teams, and it won't (11)_____ firing
anyone, so I really think we should not (12)_____ the
recommendations.

- [ ] The (13)_____ recommendation from the team
(14)_____ more emphasis on marketing strategy.

☐ This new working practice guide (15)_____ the

(16)_____ recommendations from the government.

☐ The recommendation (17)_____ a good one, I think, as it

(18)_____ an overhaul of our systems, which will benefit us in

the long run.

進階造句

請嘗試利用「搭配詞表」中的字彙，造出想要表達的句子。

_____

_____

_____

_____

_____

_____

_____

84	**report** [rɪˋport]		可數名詞 報告	

搭配在前面的動詞	搭配的形容詞		關鍵字	搭配在後面的動詞
prepare write read receive present give (sb.) submit issue	annual quarterly complete comprehensive full detailed interim initial final	status progress press audit credit	**report (on sth.)**	recommend that v.p. recommend n.p. suggest that v.p. suggest n.p. say that v.p. state that v.p. show that v.p. show n.p. conclude that v.p.

 好搭例句

◎ MP3-84

☐ I am **preparing** my **annual status** report now.
我現在在準備我的年度概況報告。

☐ I'm in the middle of **writing** a **quarterly progress** report.
我正在寫季進度報告。

☐ I have just **read** the **press** report. It's interesting.
我剛看了這則新聞報導，很有趣。

☐ I still haven't **received** your **audit** report.
我還沒有收到你的稽核報告。

☐ I'll be **presenting** a **complete credit** report at the next financial meeting.
我在下次的財務會議上會提出完整的徵信報告。

☐ Can you **give** me a **comprehensive** report **on** your team's efforts to produce a new product?
你能不能針對貴團隊在生產新產品上的作為交一份綜合報告給我？

☐ I'll be **submitting** a **full** report on Monday.

我會在星期一提出完整的報告。

☐ The company has just **issued** a **detailed** report **on** their current
financial status.

該公司剛剛針對他們的財務現況發布了詳細的報告。

☐ My **interim** report **recommends that** we give the team a bigger budget.
It also **recommends** more lead time.

我的臨時報告建議，我們要給團隊更多的預算。其中還建議要延長前置時間。

☐ The **initial** report **suggested that** we increase our staff. It also
suggested a wage increase.

初步的報告建議，我們應該擴編人員。其中還建議要加薪。

☐ The report **says that** the coming year will be more difficult. It **states
that** a recession is likely.

報告上說，來年會更困難。它表示可能會出現衰退。

☐ The **final** report **shows that** the year before last was a peak. It **shows**
a drop in revenue after the end of the year, and then **concludes that** a
recession is likely.

總結報告顯示，前年是高峰。其中顯示了營收會在年底後下滑，接著又推斷可
能會出現衰退。

填填看

請從「搭配詞表」中選出適當的字，完成下面句子。例解請見第333~353頁。

☐ I have to (1)_____ (2)_____ (3)_____ reports
every three months (4)_____ the results and activities of my
team. It's the worst part of my job.

☐ I'm going to (5)_____ the (6)_____ report. I want to
know what information the company is giving to the press.

280

☐ I'll be (7)_____ a (8)_____ report (9)_____ the situation at the next meeting. I'll explain everything then.

☐ They have just (10)_____ an (11)_____ report on the situation. It's not complete, but it's still useful to read.

☐ Have you (12)_____ our (13)_____ (14)_____ report yet? It (15)_____ that our financial status for the whole of last year was really strong.

☐ He made lots of good recommendations in his first few reports, but his (16)_____ report (17)_____ that there were problems with our work flow practices, and the report also (18)_____ that we change our team structure.

☐ The report (19)_____ a change of personnel.

進階造句

請嘗試利用「搭配詞表」中的字彙，造出想要表達的句子。

_____

_____

_____

_____

_____

_____

_____

85	**research** [risɜtʃ]	不可數名詞 研究 同義字: analysis、assessment

搭配在前面 的動詞	搭配的形容詞		關鍵字	搭配在後面的動詞
do conduct undertake carry out study	previous recent further detailed extensive	market background quantitative qualitative consumer	**research (into sth.)**	show n.p./v.p. suggest n.p./v.p. indicate n.p./v.p. demonstrate n.p./v.p.

好搭例句

MP3-85

☐ We are **conducting extensive market** research **into** the size and scope of the market.

我們正針對市場的規模和範疇舉辦廣泛的市場研究。

☐ We **did** lots of **consumer** research before we built the product, so that we could understand consumers' needs.

我們在製作產品前做了很多消費者研究，以藉此了解消費者的需求。

☐ We are **undertaking** research **into** the fault. When we find the cause, we'll let you know.

我們正針對缺失展開研究。等我們找到成因時，我們就會通知你。

☐ We **carried out** months of **quantitative** research **into** our P&L. Now our financials are in much better shape.

我們針對損益從事了幾個月的量化研究。現在我們的財務狀況健全多了。

☐ I **studied** the **background** research carefully, so I think I have a good understanding of the situation.

我仔細研讀了背景研究，所以我想我相當了解情況。

☐ Our **market** research **shows** that this product is very popular with the youth segment.

我們的市場研究顯示，這樣產品非常受年輕客層歡迎。

☐ The **quantitative** research **suggests** that we cannot expect to break even in the next three years.

量化研究呈現出，我們無法指望在未來三年內打平。

☐ All the research **indicates** that our product is indeed bad for consumers' health.

所有的研究都指出，我們的產品的確有害消費者的健康。

☐ **Recent** research **demonstrates** that this kind of direct marketing is very effective.

近來的研究證明，這種直效行銷非常有效。

填填看

請從「搭配詞表」中選出適當的字，完成下面句子。例解請見第333~353頁。

☐ We usually **(1)**_____ lots of **(2)**_____ research before we launch a new product. That helps us to plan the marketing campaign.

☐ **(3)**_____ research is very important for understanding the mind of the consumer.

☐ We **(4)**_____ lots of **(5)**_____ research before we entered the market. We knew what to expect.

☐ **(6)**_____ research helps us to estimate the direction of the financial markets. We use computer models to work this out.

☐ **(7)**_____ research helps us to understand the purchasing decisions the buyer makes. We use focus groups for this.

☐ Our **(8)**_____ **(9)**_____ research **(10)**_____

that woman are an important segment in the market. We know everything

about their needs in detail.

☐ **(11)**_____ research **(12)**_____ this topic might

(13)_____ clearer results. These results are too unclear to be

useful.

進階造句

請嘗試利用「搭配詞表」中的字彙，造出想要表達的句子。

_____

_____

_____

_____

_____

_____

_____

86	**return** [rɪˋtɜn]	可數名詞 報酬 同義字：profit

搭配在前面的動詞	搭配的形容詞		關鍵字
yield achieve produce earn get maximize	expected better high maximum guaranteed	annual tax free financial	**return** **(on sth.)** **(of #)**

 好搭例句

◎ **MP3-86**

☐ This fund **yields annual** returns **of** 13%. It's very successful.
這筆基金所產生的年報酬是13%，非常成功。

☐ Let's see if we can **get high** returns **on** our investment.
我們來看看能不能從投資上獲得高報酬。

☐ Last year we **achieved tax free** returns **of** 15%. Let's see if this year we can **achieve better** returns.
去年我們所達到的免稅報酬率是15%。我們來看看今年我們能不能達到更好的報酬。

☐ This investment will **produce expected** returns **of** 11%.
這筆投資可帶來的預期報酬是11%。

☐ Our shares should **earn** investors a **maximum** return **of** 9%. It's not really enough, is it?
我們的股票應該要幫投資人賺到9%的最大報酬。它其實不夠，對吧？

☐ If we want to **maximize** our return **on** this investment, we need to cut costs and focus on generating revenue.
假如我們想要從這筆投資中獲得最大的報酬，我們就要削減成本，並全力創造營收。

☐ There are no **guaranteed financial** returns **on** this. There is a risk to everything.

這並不保證財務報酬。凡事皆有風險。

✏️ 填填看

請從「搭配詞表」中選出適當的字，完成下面句子。例解請見第333~353頁。

☐ We need to choose a fund which will (1)_____

(2)_____ returns (3)_____ 13% or more. This is what my boss expects.

☐ What's the return (4)_____ investment for this fund?

☐ I would like to (5)_____ a (6)_____ return

(7)_____ investment. So far, returns have not really been good enough.

☐ (8)_____ returns are 20%. This is the yearly figure, and of course, it's (9)_____, so there are no deductions.

☐ We need to (10)_____ our (11)_____ returns. We need to get as much money as possible from them, so that we can reinvest back into the company.

☐ There are (12)_____ returns (13)_____ 7%. We can probably get more, but this is what we can guarantee.

進階造句

請嘗試利用「搭配詞表」中的字彙，造出想要表達的句子。

risk
[rɪsk]

可數名詞 風險

搭配在前面的動詞		搭配的形容詞	關鍵字
		high great minimal low	**risk (of sth.) (to sth.)**
be (not) worth the	reduce		
take	pose		
run	involve	calculated	risk factor
increase	avoid	potential	risk rating
minimise	assess	serious real unnecessary	risk assessment risk management

 好搭例句

◎ MP3-87

☐ This project **is not worth the** risk. Let's drop it.
這件案子不值得冒險。我們放棄吧。

☐ I don't want to **take** this risk. It's too **high**. My job as company manager is to **reduce** our exposure to risk, not **increase** it.
我不想冒這個險,它太拚了。我身為公司經理,工作是要減少曝險,而不是增加。

☐ If we don't keep bringing out new products, we **run** the risk **of** losing market share to the competition.
假如我們不持續推出新產品,我們就會面臨把市占率拱手讓人的風險。

☐ Lack of security **poses** a **great** risk **to** our plans for this new product. We must increase security at the factory.
缺乏安全性會為這樣新產品的計畫帶來很大的風險。我們必須提高廠內的安全性。

☐ This project **involves minimal** risk. I think we should go ahead with it.
這件案子所冒的風險最低。我想我們應該採用。

☐ Part of my job is risk management. My job is to **assess** risk when we invest capital. In this case, I think the risk factor is low.
我的部分工作在於風險管理。我的工作是在投入資金時評估風險。在本案中，我認為風險係數不高。

☐ It's impossible to **avoid** any kind of risk, but in this case the risk **is minimal**. I think we should **take** it.
要避開任何一種風險是不可能的事，但本案的風險最低，我想我們應該去做。

☐ We **took a calculated** risk, and it paid off! Well done!
我們去冒計算過的風險，結果成功了！幹得好！

☐ The **potential** risk in this case is quite high. Are you sure you want to go ahead?
本案的潛在風險相當高。你確定你要採用嗎？

☐ If we go ahead with this investment we **run** the **real** risk **of** losing quite a lot of money.
假如我們從事這項投資，我們就會面臨鉅額虧損的實質風險。

☐ The risk rating on this fund is very low, but so is the return.
這支基金的風險評等非常低，但報酬也是。

☐ According to the risk assessment carried out by the consultant, there is an **unnecessary** risk here. Why do you want to continue?
根據顧問所做的風險評估，此處有不必要的風險。你們為什麼想要繼續？

☐ There is a **serious** risk that we could lose everything, and there is no way we can **minimize** this risk.
有個嚴重的風險是，我們可能會失去一切，而且我們沒辦法把這層風險降到最低。

填填看

請從「搭配詞表」中選出適當的字，完成下面句子。例解請見第333~353頁。

☐ He (1)_____ a (2)_____ risk when he started the company, but his decision was right.

☐ We (3)_____ the risk (4)_____ losing money if we go into the market now.

☐ It (5)_____ risk (6)_____ invest now. The (7)_____ is too high and we could lose everything.

☐ If we open more factories, we (8)_____ the risk of growing too fast.

☐ We need to (9)_____ the (10)_____ risk. Let's be very careful so that we are safe if something bad happens.

☐ It should be safe, the risk is (11)_____, if my (12)_____ is correct.

☐ We need to (13)_____ the risk of injury to our workers. We don't want them to get hurt.

☐ The current economic environment (14)_____ a (15)_____ risk to the future of our company.

☐ Doing business in emerging markets always (16)_____ risk.

☐ We run a (17)_____ risk of going bankrupt if we cannot get more capital. This is pretty certain.

☐ We need to (18)_____ (19)_____ risks. Please don't be careless.

☐ Our company has a low (20)_____, so it's easy to find investors.

☐ Strategic management is often the same as (21)_____: you
have to make decisions based on how you (22)_____ risks.

進階造句

請嘗試利用「搭配詞表」中的字彙，造出想要表達的句子。

salary
[ˈsælərɪ]

可數名詞 薪資

搭配在前面的動詞	搭配的形容詞		關鍵字	搭配在後面的動詞
get receive earn pay offer draw increase cut review	annual monthly basic average starting good	gross net current	**salary** **(of #)** salary raise salary scale salary review salary cut	be start at # include n.p. be commensurate with

＃為數字

好搭例句

MP3-88

☐ Most people at my level **get** an **annual** salary **of** 3.5 million.
我這個層級的人大部分拿到的年薪都是350萬。

☐ I **received** a **basic gross monthly** salary **of** 15,000 at my previous job, but I got a lot of benefits as well.
我前一份工作所領的每月總底薪是1萬5千元，但我還享有許多福利。

☐ I **earn** a **good** salary, but I hope they will **increase** it.
我所賺的薪水還不錯，但我希望他們能把它調高。

☐ We **pay** a **starting net** salary **of** 1 million, but after your first year there will be a salary review, and possibly a salary raise.
我們給的淨起薪是100萬，但過了第一年後，你會經過薪資考核，並可能把薪資提高。

☐ We can only **offer** a **basic** salary, but we will **review** your salary at the end of the first year.

我們只能提供底薪，但等到第一年結束，我們就會檢討你的薪資。

☐ You can **draw** your salary at the local bank.

你可以去本地的銀行提領薪水。

☐ I'm afraid that due to current circumstances, we are going to have to **cut** your salary by 5%.

恐怕在當前的環境下，我們不得不把你的薪資縮減5%。

☐ The **average** salary in this industry **is** quite low by global standards.

依全球的標準來看，這行的平均薪資相當低。

☐ We will need to ask our staff to take a salary cut.

我們得要求員工接受減薪才行。

☐ According to our salary scale, a salary for someone at your level **starts at** 13,000 per month.

根據我們的薪級，你那級人員的薪資是從每個月1萬3千元起跳。

☐ **Current** salary **includes** tax.

現有的薪資含稅。

☐ Most salaries in Taiwan **are commensurate with** regional standards.

台灣的薪資大部分都符合地區標準。

填填看

請從「搭配詞表」中選出適當的字，完成下面句子。例解請見第333~353頁。

☐ In my previous job I (1)_____ an (2)_____

(3)_____ salary (4)_____ 3.5 million. That's for the

year, and after tax. I hope my salary for this job can (5)_____

the same level, because I'm not really prepared to take a

(6)_____.

☐ According to our (7)_____ we can (8)_____ a

(9)_____ (10)_____ salary (11)_____ 1,000

per month, but there will also be benefits.

☐ Your salary (12)_____ an annual bonus, and you can

(13)_____ it at your local bank.

☐ (14)_____ salaries (15)_____ industry standards. If we

want to retain staff, we will need to conduct a (16)_____, and

preferably (17)_____ salaries.

☐ Hey, I just found out that they are going to (18)_____ our

salaries, and we might even get a (19)_____!

☐ I (20)_____ quite a (21)_____ (22)_____

salary, but then they increased the tax I have to pay, and now I get less

money than before. It feels like they (23)_____ my salary.

進階造句

請嘗試利用「搭配詞表」中的字彙，造出想要表達的句子。

89	**sale** [sel]		可數名詞 特價；業績

搭配在前面的動詞	搭配的形容詞	關鍵字	搭配在後面的動詞
boost ★ +s increase ★ +s handle ★ +s achieve ★ +s make close have	retail ★ +s annual (★ +s) direct ★ +s overseas ★ +s domestic ★ +s	**sale** sales rep sales promotion sales pitch sales volume sales tax sales forecast	★ +s rise ★ +s grow ★ +s increase ★ +s soar ★ +s fall ★ +s decrease ★ +s total # ★ +s reach # go ahead go through

★為關鍵字、#為數字

 好搭例句　　　　　　　　　　　◎ MP3-89

☐ We must try to **boost** sales this quarter. The sales volume is too low.
我們必須設法在本季提升業績，銷量太低了。

☐ If we had more sales reps, and did more sales promotions, we could **increase** sales.
假如我們有更多的業務代表，並做更多的促銷，我們就有可能提高業績。

☐ My job is to **handle** sales in the northern region. I have to **achieve annual** sales of 3 million. However, I think the sales forecast is too high, and I won't be able to make it.
我的工作是掌管北區的業務。我必須達到的年業績是300萬。不過我認為銷量預測太高了，我沒辦法做到。

☐ I **handle direct** sales, selling to the customer direct, rather than through a distributor.
我掌管的是直銷，也就是直接對顧客銷售，而不透過經銷商。

☐ He's on the verge of **making** a huge sale. I know he can **close** it. His sales pitch was very effective.
他即將做成一筆大生意。我知道他有辦法搞定，他的推銷話術非常有效。

☐ We are **having** a sale right now. 20% off everything.
我們目前在拍賣。每樣東西都打八折。

☐ **Annual** sales **rose** by 3% last year, and they **grew** by 4% in the previous year. Now they are **falling**. As a result of the sales promotions, sales **soared**.
年度業績去年增加了3%，前年成長了4%，如今則在下滑。由於促銷的關係，業績突飛猛進。

☐ There are too many foreign goods on the market, and sales **are decreasing**.
市面上外國貨太多了，使業績下滑。

☐ **Retail** sales last quarter **reached** 5 million, and the quarter before that they **totalled** 5.1 million.
上一季的零售額達到了500萬，而前一季總共是510萬。

☐ **Overseas** sales **increased**, while **domestic** sales didn't.
海外業績提高了，國內業績則不然。

☐ I really hope this sale **goes ahead**. It will increase my bonus!
我衷心希望這筆生意能拿下來。它可以提高我的獎金！

☐ If the sale **goes through**, my boss has promised me a big raise!
假如生意做成了，老闆答應要幫我大幅加薪。

☐ Sales tax is so high in this country!
這個國家的營業稅還真高！

填填看

請從「搭配詞表」中選出適當的字，完成下面句子。例解請見第333~353頁。

☐ This year, (1)_____ sales have (2)_____ to 5 million. This is better than last year, when sales only (3)_____ 3 million.

☐ We must have a (4)_____ to try to (5)_____ sales, otherwise we will not be able to reach our target.

☐ My job is to (6)_____ the (7)_____. The tax office is very picky.

☐ During our (8)_____ sale, we had 2 million customers in the store, and (9)_____ was enormous. We made a lot of money!

☐ He is the best (10)_____ in the company. You should hear his (11)_____. It's amazing!

☐ Due to the credit crunch, the (12)_____ for next year is (13)_____.

☐ The sale (14)_____ and I got a huge bonus!

進階造句

請嘗試利用「搭配詞表」中的字彙，造出想要表達的句子。

_____

_____

_____

_____

service
[ˋsɝvɪs]

可數名詞 服務

搭配在前面的動詞	搭配的形容詞		關鍵字
provide offer	free limited	advisory consultation	**service**
deliver	online confidential	delivery maintenance	service charge
improve	professional efficient	support	service agreement
use	regular excellent	after sales	service center
require	great	customer client	service contract
be of	# year	financial	service representative

為數字

 好搭例句

MP3-90

☐ We also **provide** a **regular 1-year maintenance** service as well as **a free delivery** service for this product. There is no service charge.
我們還會給予這項產品一年定期的維修服務，以及免費運送服務。服務費則免收。

☐ We **deliver** a completely **confidential advisory** service in addition to a **professional financial** service to all our clients. Just check the service agreement for details.
我們對所有的客戶都會履行完全保密的諮詢服務，外帶專業的金融服務。詳情請參閱服務協定。

☐ We **offer excellent customer** service in our brand new service center.
我們嶄新的服務中心提供了一流的顧客服務。

☐ Our **client** service is the best in the market.
我們的客服是市場上最棒的。

☐ We need to **improve** our **online consultation** service. It's not very **efficient** at the moment.

我們需要改進我們的線上諮詢服務。目前它並不是非常有效率。

☐ If you would like to **use** our **great support** service, you will need to sign a service contract.

假如你想使用我們良好的支援服務，你就要簽署服務契約。

☐ Most of our customers only **require** a **limited after sales** service, so we only have a very small team of service representatives here.

我們的顧客大部分只需要有限的售後服務，所以我們這裡只有一組人數非常少的服務代表。

☐ How may I **be of** service?

我可以幫什麼忙？

填填看

請從「搭配詞表」中選出適當的字，完成下面句子。例解請見第333~353頁。

☐ How may I (1)_____ service? Or would you like to see one of our other (2)_____?

☐ We (3)_____ a 1-(4)_____ (5)_____ (6)_____ service to all our clients. If you would like to extend this service after the first year, you will need to sign another (7)_____ to continue receiving advice.

☐ If you live locally, there is no (8)_____ if you require (9)_____ or (10)_____ service. However, if you live far away, you will need to pay to have the product delivered and maintained regularly.

☐ Have you (11)_____ our (12)_____ (13)_____
service? It's really easy to use. You just need a laptop and an Internet
connection, and then you can get all kinds of advice, and it's a
(14)_____ service too, so you don't need to worry about your
family finding out.

☐ They provide really (15)_____ (16)_____
(17)_____ service, and they have a great new
(18)_____, with all the latest equipment. That's why they are the
market leader.

☐ I think we will only (19)_____ a (20)_____
(21)_____ service from you, as we already have our own
financial consultants.

進階造句

請嘗試利用「搭配詞表」中的字彙，造出想要表達的句子。

_____

_____

_____

_____

_____

_____

_____

situation
[ˌsɪtʃʊˈeʃən]

可數名詞 情況

搭配在前面 的動詞	搭配的形容詞		關鍵字	搭配在後面 的動詞
improve resolve	complicated difficult			arise occur
handle	present current	economic financial political market		change develop become adj.
assess	similar different		**situation**	
review describe clarify	particular			worsen deteriorate
be in a brief sb. on	ideal background			improve be

 好搭例句

◉ **MP3-91**

☐ We are trying to **improve** the situation. It's a **difficult** situation to **resolve**, however.

我們正設法改善情況。但這是個有待解決的棘手情況。

☐ Sandra is **handling** this **particular** situation and she will report to us later.

桑德拉正在處理這個特殊情況，等一下他會向我們報告。

☐ I'd just like to **review** the **current economic** situation before we go any further.

在我們有任何進一步的行動前，我想先審視一下目前的經濟情況。

☐ We've **assessed** the **present financial** situation of the company carefully and we think it's in pretty good shape.

我們仔細評估了該公司目前的財務狀況，我們認為情況相當不錯。

☐ I would **describe** the **market** situation as favorable.
我會說市場情況堪稱有利。

☐ It's quite a **different market** situation from 20 years ago when we started doing business.
市場情況跟20年前我們開始做生意時相去甚遠。

☐ I don't want to go any further until we can **clarify** the **political** situation.
我不想有任何進一步的行動，直到我們有辦法釐清政治情況為止。

☐ It's not an **ideal** situation by any means. I have never **been in a similar** situation.
這絕對不是理想的情況。我從來沒碰過類似的情況。

☐ Can you **brief me on** the **background** situation?
你能不能跟我說明一下背景情況？

☐ A situation has **arisen** where we need your expertise. Can you help us?
有個情況出現了，我們需要你的專長。你能不能幫幫我們？

☐ A **complicated** situation has **occurred** in our factory.
我們的工廠發生了複雜的情況。

☐ The **economic** situation has **changed** over the last few years.
過去幾年來，經濟情況有所轉變。

☐ The **political** situation is **becoming** more stable.
政治情況變得更加穩定。

☐ An **interesting** situation has **developed**.
有趣的情況產生了。

☐ The **market** situation has **worsened**. It's really difficult to sell our products in this market now.
市場情況變差了。我們的產品現在在這個市場上非常難賣。

☐ The situation has **deteriorated** since we last spoke about it.
自從我們上次談過以後，情況就惡化了。

☐ I hope the situation **improves** soon.
我希望情況能快快好轉。

☐ The situation **is** pretty bad, to be honest.
情況相當糟，老實說。

📝 填填看

請從「搭配詞表」中選出適當的字，完成下面句子。例解請見第333~353頁。

☐ Because you were very successful at (1)_____ a

(2)_____ situation before, I would like you to (3)_____

this one. You have the right experience.

☐ I'd like to begin by (4)_____ the (5)_____

(6)_____ situation. Generally speaking, the economy is in better

shape now than it was 5 years ago.

☐ Could you (7)_____ the situation for us? What's going on there?

☐ This is a very (8)_____ situation. I'm sending you over there to

(9)_____ it. Please find out what's going on and let us know

what we need to do to (10)_____ it.

☐ There is a very (11)_____ (12)_____ situation

happening here. Our usual marketing strategies probably won't work here.

☐ Our (13)_____ situation is far from (14)_____. It's

terrible, in fact.

☐ The (15)_____ situation is (16)_____. It's very unstable.

You never know what the government will do next.

☐ Our (17)_____ situation can only (18)_____. Our cash flow has never been so bad.

☐ A (19)_____ situation has (20)_____ in our overseas market. We are being sued by our competitors for copyright infringement.

☐ You will need to (21)_____ the (22)_____ situation carefully, so that she understands it.

進階造句

請嘗試利用「搭配詞表」中的字彙，造出想要表達的句子。

skills
[`skɪlz]

可數名詞 技能

搭配在前面的動詞	搭配的形容詞	關鍵字
have develop work on learn use exercise require lack	necessary considerable advanced new basic set of	presentation communication interpersonal people leadership administrative management organizational technical negotiating time management
		skills

 好搭例句

◎ MP3-92

☐ This candidate does not **have** the **necessary presentation** and **communication** skills for this job.
這位人選並不具備這份工作所必需的提報與溝通技巧。

☐ I hope I will be able to **develop** my **interpersonal** skills in this position.
我希望我能在這個職位上培養好我的人際技巧。

☐ I want to **learn** a **new set of** skills.
我想要學一套新技術。

☐ You need to **work on** your **time management** skills.
你需要精進你的時間管理技巧。

☐ I love my job because I get to **use** my **people** skills!
我熱愛我的工作，因為我可以施展我的待人技巧！

☐ You will need to **exercise** some **leadership** skills in this job.
你在這份工作上需要發揮一些領導技巧。

☐ The position **requires considerable administrative** skills.
這個職位需要相當好的行政技巧。

☐ He **lacks basic management** and **organizational** skills.
他缺乏基本的管理與組織技巧。

☐ We need someone with **advanced technical** skills to lead this department.
我們需要一個專門技術高超的人來領導這個部門。

☐ She **has considerable negotiating** skills. She always wins the deal.
她擁有相當好的談判技巧。她總是能贏得交易。

填填看

請從「搭配詞表」中選出適當的字，完成下面句子。例解請見第333~353頁。

☐ I (1)_____ all the (2)_____ skills to do the job well.

☐ I know I am often late and that my projects are often delayed. I think I need to (3)_____ my (4)_____ skills.

☐ In my previous job I (5)_____ (6)_____ skills, so I'm confident I can run this department.

☐ He's very efficient, but he's not very popular with his team. I think he needs to (7)_____ his (8)_____ skills.

☐ I want a job where I can (9)_____ my (10)_____ (11)_____ skills. From a technical point of view, this job is simply too easy for me.

☐ In this training session we will be showing you (12)_____

(13)_____ skills which will help you to persuade your audience to

accept your ideas.

☐ My new job (14)_____ a completely (15)_____

(16)_____ skills. I have never done anything like this before!

☐ The deal didn't go through because he (17)_____

(18)_____ skills. They couldn't agree on terms.

進階造句

請嘗試利用「搭配詞表」中的字彙，造出想要表達的句子。

| 93 | **solution** [sə`luʃən] | 可數名詞 解決方法 |

搭配在前面的動詞		搭配的形容詞		關鍵字
propose provide put forward	work out look for produce	obvious possible	drastic easy effective	
adopt agree on	reject rule out	clever neat simple	feasible viable	**solution (to sth.)**
arrive at come up with find hit upon	implement	concrete realistic sensible acceptable practical	immediate prompt quick lasting permanent temporary	

 好搭例句　　　　　　　　　　　　　◉ **MP3-93**

☐ I'd like to **propose** a number of **possible** solutions **to** this problem.
我想針對這個問題提出一些可能的辦法。

☐ Can you **provide** a **temporary** solution for now, and then **come up with** a more **lasting** solution later?
你能不能暫且提供一個臨時的辦法，等事後再想個比較長遠的辦法？

☐ The consultant has **put forward** a **neat** solution **to** the problem. Before we **reject** it, I think we should **look at** it carefully to see whether it's a **viable** solution.
顧問針對問題提出了一個巧妙的辦法。在我們否決前，我想我們應該仔細看一看，以了解它是不是可行的辦法。

☐ This is not really an **acceptable** solution. I don't think we should **adopt** it.
這其實不是個可令人接受的辦法。我認為我們不應該採用。

☐ We need to **agree on** a **realistic** solution, otherwise we will continue to have this problem.
我們需要共謀一個務實的辦法,否則我們就會不斷碰到這個問題。

☐ The production team have **arrived at** a **simple** solution **to** the problem.
生產團隊針對問題想出了一個簡單的辦法。

☐ The marketing department have **come up with** a **clever** solution — **easy** and **effective**.
行銷部想了個聰明的辦法,既簡單又有效。

☐ One **obvious** solution is to stop production, but that might be a bit **drastic**. Can we **find** another more **feasible** solution?
有一個顯而易見的辦法是停產,但那可能有點極端。我們能不能找到其他更合用的辦法?

☐ I still haven't managed to **hit upon** a **sensible** solution. Any ideas?
我想破了頭還是想不到明智的辦法。有什麼想法嗎?

☐ We need to **work out** an **immediate practical** solution before the problem gets worse.
在問題惡化前,我們需要找出一個立即可用的辦法。

☐ **Look for** a **concrete**, **permanent** solution, but don't **rule out** a **quick** solution either.
找個具體且一勞永逸的辦法,但也不要排除立竿見影的辦法。

☐ It's difficult to **produce** a **prompt** solution **to** every problem. Please give me some time to **work out** a solution, okay?
要對每個問題都拿出即時的辦法很困難。請給我一點時間去找出辦法,好嗎?

☐ If we **implement** this solution, how much will it cost?
假如我們實行這個辦法,要花多少錢?

填填看

請從「搭配詞表」中選出適當的字，完成下面句子。例解請見第333~353頁。

☐ Although I have been thinking for a long time about this problem, I still haven't been able to (1)_____ a (2)_____ solution — one which will not be too difficult or expensive to implement.

☐ During the meeting, the board decided to (3)_____ a (4)_____ _____ solution first, and then (5)_____ a more (6)_____ solution later.

☐ This solution is simply not (7)_____. We will lose too much money if we (8)_____ it.

☐ The market is too competitive for our products. One (9)_____ solution is to withdraw from the market.

☐ There is no (10)_____ solution. Whatever we decide is going to be hard to (11)_____.

☐ This solution is simply too (12)_____. We are going to (13)_____ it. It will cost too much money in lost revenue if we (14)_____ it. Can you (15)_____ another solution?

進階造句

請嘗試利用「搭配詞表」中的字彙，造出想要表達的句子。

_____

_____

_____

staff
[stæf]

不可數名詞 職員
同義字：personnel、employees

搭配在前面的動詞		搭配的形容詞		關鍵字
have recruit hire employ appoint train	encourage motivate enable support retain	senior junior full-time permanent part-time temporary additional experienced member of small	administrative clerical engineering technical executive legal sales support	**staff** **(a ★ of #)**
				staff member staff recruitment staff management staff training

★為關鍵字、#為數字

好搭例句

 MP3-94

☐ We only **have a** staff **of 5** in this department, so it's very busy.
我們這個部門只有5名職員，所以非常忙。

☐ Due to the company expansion, we will need to **recruit** 700 **full-time technical** and **engineering** staff over the next 3 months. Staff recruitment is the main part of my job.
由於公司擴張，我們在未來三個月需要招募700位全職的技術與工程職員。職員招募是我主要的工作內容。

☐ I heard that they are currently **hiring administrative** and **clerical** staff. Why don't you apply?
我聽說他們目前在徵聘行政與庶務職員。你為什麼不去應徵？

☐ We **employ** over 3,000 **permanent** staff worldwide. Staff management is a big issue for HR.

我們在世界各地雇用了超過3,000位的正式職員。職員管理是人力資源上的一大課題。

☐ We will need to **appoint additional senior executive** staff Oh, and some **junior part-time** staff as well.

我們需要任命額外的高階主管職員。噢，還有一些低階兼職人員。

☐ We **train** all our **sales** and **support** staff. Staff training is a big part of our work in this department.

我們要訓練所有的銷售與後勤職員。職員訓練占了我們這個部門一大部分的工作。

☐ We are **encouraging** our staff to take their leave before the end of the year.

我們正鼓勵職員在年底前把假休掉。

☐ How can we **motivate** our staff to work harder?

我們要如何激勵職員更努力工作？

☐ Our systems **enable** a **small** staff to work very efficiently.

我們的制度使不多的職員能工作得非常有效率。

☐ Your job is to **support** every **member of** staff who needs it.

你的工作是支援每位有需要的職員。

☐ We are having problems **retaining experienced legal** staff.

我們在留住老經驗的法務職員上遇到了問題。

☐ Would all staff members please report to their supervisors immediately. This does not apply to **temporary** staff.

全體職員請立刻向所屬主管報到。其中不含臨時職員。

✎ 填填看

請從「搭配詞表」中選出適當的字，完成下面句子。例解請見第333~353頁。

☐ The company, which is one of the biggest in the world, (1)_____ over 5,000 staff worldwide. Many of those are (2)_____, but some are also part-time.

☐ He is a (3)_____ (4)_____. He has been with the company for many years, and he started at the bottom and worked his way up to the top.

☐ We are currently (5)_____ (6)_____ staff, as we don't really have enough headcount. My job is (7)_____, so I am really busy.

☐ It's very difficult to (8)_____ (9)_____ staff. They all want to go to China, where they can make more money in the booming Chinese IT industry.

☐ We have (10)_____ ten in this department. Most of those (11)_____ have been with the company for a long time.

☐ We need to (12)_____ the (13)_____ staff in how to use the new office management systems. Shall we ask a (14)_____ the IT staff to conduct the (15)_____?

☐ We will need to (16)_____ an (17)_____ (18)_____ staff to this post. It needs to be someone who knows the company very well.

☐ What can we do to (19)_____ the (20)_____ staff to make more sales?

☐ The new system will (21)_____ the (22)_____ staff to do their job more efficiently. All the information they need about the products is online now.

☐ The main job of (23)_____ is to (24)_____ staff. We only have a (25)_____ staff, so in this company the job is really easy, as there are not so many people to manage.

☐ We currently (26)_____ enough (27)_____ and (28)_____ staff. Our legal department is always asking us to get more staff, and the top management level of the company has some vacancies.

☐ We (29)_____ too many (30)_____ (31)_____ staff. We would actually save costs in the long run if we made them permanent and full time.

進階造句

請嘗試利用「搭配詞表」中的字彙，造出想要表達的句子。

_____

_____

_____

_____

_____

_____

_____

| 95 | **strategy**
[ˈstrætədʒɪ] | | 可數名詞 策略 | |

搭配在前面 的動詞	搭配的形容詞		關鍵字	搭配在後面 的動詞
develop devise prepare map out plan outline propose suggest recommend implement execute use employ	right viable innovative new long-term short-term regional global overall broad detailed	marketing sales financial PR investment business corporate	**strategy (for Ving/n.p.) (to V)**	involve n.p.

 好搭例句 ◎ MP3-95

☐ We have **developed** a **short-term** strategy **for** this problem.
我們為這個問題擬訂了短期策略。

☐ My job involves **devising long-term business** strategy **to** achieve growth.
我的工作是在訂定長期的營業策略,以達到成長。

☐ I **prepared** a **detailed marketing** strategy **for** this new product, but the marketing director didn't like it.
我為這項新產品研擬了詳細的行銷策略,但行銷總監不喜歡。

☐ Can you **map out** a **broad** strategy **for** the new market?
你能不能針對新市場規劃出廣泛的策略？

☐ We are **planning** an **innovative corporate** strategy **to** help the new business grow fast.
我們正在籌畫創新的公司策略，以協助新事業快速成長。

☐ Let me **outline** the **broad** strategy for you.
我來替你們勾勒廣泛的策略。

☐ At this stage I'd like to **propose** a **detailed investment** strategy.
在這個階段，我想提出詳細的投資策略。

☐ The consultant **suggested** a **global marketing** strategy **for** the new product.
顧問為新產品建議了一套全球行銷策略。

☐ I don't think this is a **viable** strategy. It will be difficult to **implement**.
我不認為這是可行的策略。它會難以執行。

☐ We achieved such great targets because we **employed** the **right sales** strategy.
我們達成了這麼重大的目標是因為，我們採取了正確的銷售策略。

☐ We have decided to **execute** a **regional PR** strategy.
我們決定實行區域性的公關策略。

☐ We need to **use** a **new** strategy. This one isn't working.
我們需要採用新策略。這個沒有效。

☐ This new **corporate** strategy **involves** three departments: PR, marketing, and sales.
這項新的公司策略牽涉到三個部門：公關、行銷、業務。

*✎ 填填看

請從「搭配詞表」中選出適當的字，完成下面句子。例解請見第333~353頁。

☐ I work in the marketing department. My job is to (1)_____ and then (2)_____ (3)_____ strategy for new products.

☐ Let me very briefly (4)_____ the new (5)_____ strategy for you. We hope it will help to increase sales volume.

☐ I would like to (6)_____ a new (7)_____ strategy (8)_____ the company's revenues. We need to make more use of the money we already have.

☐ At regional level they are (9)_____ a (10)_____ (11)_____ strategy. This means that all branches of the business will have to follow it, including us.

☐ We have (12)_____ a (13)_____ strategy for the next 5 years (14)_____ make sure our current growth rate continues.

☐ I don't think this is a (15)_____ (16)_____ strategy for this market. The media here are very heavily controlled by the government.

☐ This (17)_____ strategy (18)_____ all levels of the company, all departments, and all personnel. We must all work together.

☐ I don't think that's the (19)_____ (20)_____ strategy (21)_____ (22)_____ with this problem. It will be okay for now, but we need something more long-term.

進階造句

請嘗試利用「搭配詞表」中的字彙，造出想要表達的句子。

_____

_____

_____

suggestion
[sə`dʒɛstʃən]

可數名詞 建議
同義字：recommendation、proposal

搭配在前面的動詞		搭配的形容詞	關鍵字	搭配在後面的動詞
have come up with make offer put forward	take (★) up act on take sb. up on welcome consider look at dismiss	constructive practical sensible excellent impractical tentative	**suggestion** **(regarding sth.)** **(for sth.)**	involve Ving involve n.p. include n.p. include Ving

★為關鍵字

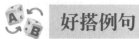 好搭例句

◉ **MP3-96**

☐ I **have** a suggestion.
我有個建議。

☐ John on my team has **come up with** an **excellent** suggestion **for** improving our systems.
我這組的約翰針對改善我們的制度提出了絕佳的建議。

☐ I'd like to **make** a **practical** suggestion, if I may.
我想提個實際的建議，假如可以的話。

☐ Can I **offer** a **tentative** suggestion at this point?
我能不能在這個時候提供一個初步的建議？

☐ I'd like to **put forward** a suggestion **regarding** this issue.
我想針對這個問題提出建議。

☐ We have decided to **take up** your **sensible** suggestion.
我們決定採用你的明智建議。

☐ If we **act on** this suggestion, what will the consequences be?
假如我們照這個建議來做，結果會怎麼樣？

☐ Let's **take Julie up on** her suggestion. Julie, tell us more about your idea.
我們就採納茱莉的建議吧。茱莉，跟我們多說一下你的想法。

☐ At this stage of the project, I **welcome constructive** suggestions from everybody.
在案子的這個階段，我歡迎大家發表有建設性的建議。

☐ This suggestion is completely **impractical**. Do we even need to **consider** it?
這項建議完全不切實際。我們還需要考慮嗎？

☐ I never **dismiss** suggestions, but **look at** all of them.
我絕對不會對建議置之不理，而會全部看過。

☐ Will this suggestion **involve** delaying the project?
這項建議會耽誤到案子嗎？

☐ This suggestion **involves** a complete rewrite of the underlying code. That will take ages to complete.
這項建議會關係到完全重寫基本程式碼。那要花很長的時間才能完成。

☐ This suggestion **for** more input **includes** everybody. Please give me your ideas.
這項廣納雅言的建議包含了每個人。請把各位的想法告訴我。

☐ The suggestion **includes** paying more attention to customer needs.
建議中包含了要更加留意顧客的需求。

✏ 填填看

請從「搭配詞表」中選出適當的字，完成下面句子。例解請見第333~353頁。

☐ Does anybody (1)_____ suggestions (2)_____ how to deal with this problem?

☐ I'd like to (3)_____ a suggestion at this point. My suggestion (4)_____ looking at the specs of the product again. I think there is a problem with the specs.

☐ Julie's suggestion is (5)_____. I think it will solve the problem efficiently and easily, and I think we should (6)_____ it.

☐ Let's (7)_____ some other suggestions before we (8)_____ Julie's suggestion.

☐ Julie, I'd like to (9)_____ your suggestion. Can you tell us again in more detail. Does it (10)_____ any cost?

☐ I was at that meeting, and I (11)_____ a (12)_____ suggestion. You know I was very polite and respectful, but they (13)_____ my suggestion. They said my suggestion was (14)_____, but they didn't really give me a chance to explain it in more detail.

☐ I (15)_____ any suggestions (16)_____ the new system, as long as they don't (17)_____ rewriting the underlying code. We don't have time for that. Come on, guys, ideas please!

進階造句

請嘗試利用「搭配詞表」中的字彙，造出想要表達的句子。

_____

_____

_____

_____

97	**supplier** [sə`plaɪə]	可數名詞 供應商	

搭配在前面的動詞	搭配的形容詞		關鍵字
pay find use switch change choose	largest leading major local main current new	alternative service dependable reliable	**supplier** **(of sth.)**

 好搭例句

◎ **MP3-97**

☐ We have to **pay** our **main** supplier every month.
我們每個月都必須付款給我們的主要供應商。

☐ We need to **find** an **alternative** supplier. Our **current** supplier is simply too expensive.
我們需要找個替代供應商。我們目前的供應商真的太貴了。

☐ I think we should **choose** a **local** supplier. This will reduce costs and delivery times.
我想我們應該選個本地的供應商。這樣可以縮減成本與交貨時間。

☐ We use one of the **largest** suppliers **of** computer components.
我們為電腦零組件找了其中一家最大的供應商。

☐ We **switched** suppliers about three months ago. Our **new** supplier is more **dependable** than the old one.
我們大概在三個月前換了供應商。我們的新供應商比舊的可靠。

☐ Why don't we **change** suppliers and see if we can reduce our materials cost?

我們何不更換供應商,以看看我們能不能降低物料成本?

☐ We are the **leading** supplier **of** parts in this industry.

我們在這行中是零件的頭號供應商。

☐ Our **major** supplier is overseas, so all the raw materials have to be imported.

我們的大供應商在海外,所以一切的原料都必須進口。

☐ Our **service** supplier is not very **reliable**. It sometimes takes a few days for them to send a service agent out.

我們的服務供應商不是非常牢靠。要他們派個服務員過來有時候要好幾天。

✎ 填填看

請從「搭配詞表」中選出適當的字,完成下面句子。例解請見第333~353頁。

☐ Did you **(1)**_____ the supplier last month? I have an email from them saying they did not receive payment.

☐ If we have any more problems with the supplier, I recommend we **(2)**_____ to a more **(3)**_____ one.

☐ The problem is that it's difficult to **(4)**_____ a **(5)**_____ supplier. Most of them are overseas.

☐ At the moment we are using an **(6)**_____ supplier **(7)**_____ of raw materials, because our **(8)**_____ supplier is having distribution problems.

☐ The company is the **(9)**_____ supplier of gas to the region.

☐ We need to (10)_____ a (11)_____ (12)_____
supplier. Our (13)_____ one is too unreliable and sometimes
their service engineers don't have the right technical knowledge to fix the
problem!

進階造句

請嘗試利用「搭配詞表」中的字彙，造出想要表達的句子。

_____

_____

_____

_____

_____

_____

_____

system
[ˈsɪstəm]

可數名詞 制度

搭配在前面的動詞		搭配的 形容詞	關鍵字	搭配在後面 的動詞
install adopt create develop devise build introduce implement	establish upgrade improve manage enter sth. into maintain	operating filing ICT information control billing delivery inventory	**system (for sth.)** system utility system function system change system integration	work operate run allow enable provide offer use require support

好搭例句

MP3-98

☐ We are **installing** a new **operating** system, so the computers are down.
我們在安裝新的作業系統，所以電腦動不了。

☐ We have **adopted** an open source **operating** system.
我們採用了開放原始碼的作業系統。

☐ My assistant has **created** a new **filing** system. It has taken her three days to **develop** it and it is unstoppable!
我的助理建立了新的檔案系統。她花了三天把它開發出來，好用得不得了！

☐ I have **devised** a clever system **for** recording non-payments.
我設計了一套聰明的系統來記錄欠款。

☐ We are trying to **build** an **ICT** system using all the hardware in the company, but it's difficult to **implement** the system integration.
我們試圖要建立資通訊技術系統來運用公司內所有的硬體，但實施系統整合有困難。

☐ **Introducing** a new **control** system is difficult as everyone prefers to use the old one. No one likes a system change!
引進新的控制系統有困難，因為大家都偏好使用舊系統。沒有人喜歡變更系統！

☐ We need to **establish** a better **information** system. Many client details are getting lost.
我們需要建立更好的資訊系統。有許多客戶的詳細資料都不見了。

☐ We are going to **upgrade** our **billing** system next month.
我們下個月要把計費系統升級。

☐ If we **improve** our **inventory** system, I'm sure we can save money on inventory costs.
假如我們改善庫存系統，我相信我們就能在庫存成本上省到錢。

☐ Your job will be to **manage** the **delivery** system. You must make sure deliveries are on time.
你的工作是管理交貨系統。你必須確定交貨能準時。

☐ Don't forget to **enter** the new data **into** the system.
別忘了把新資料輸入系統。

☐ Many of the system functions are not working very well, and I can't find some of my system utilities and system extensions.
有很多系統功能運作得不是非常好，我找不到某些系統公用程式和系統延伸功能。

☐ Our computer system **runs** Linux. What does yours **operate**?
我們的電腦系統是跑Linux。你們的是用什麼？

☐ This system **allows** us to control the shipments 24 hours a day and also **enables** us to track lost shipments.
這套系統讓我們一天24小時都能控制貨運，還能讓我們追蹤遺失的貨運。

☐ The system **provides** easy access to the network.
此系統提供了簡便的網路連結。

☐ The system **uses** too much power.
系統耗了太多電。

☐ The system **requires** an experienced operator.
此系統需要有經驗的操作員。

☐ The system **supports** open source code.
此系統支援開放原始碼。

填填看

請從「搭配詞表」中選出適當的字，完成下面句子。例解請見第333~353頁。

☐ How much will it cost to (1)_____ a new (2)_____ system in the office, one which connects all the phones and all the computers together?

☐ There must be something wrong with my (3)_____ system. I can't find any of my (4)_____. All the icons have disappeared from my desktop and some of the (5)_____ are not working.

☐ I have spent the last month (6)_____ a new (7)_____ system. The system will (8)_____ us to manage our stocks better, so it should be easier to control our inventory costs now.

☐ The IT department is (9)_____ a new (10)_____ system. It will (11)_____ access to the company database from anywhere in the world.

☐ I forgot to (12)_____ the information into the (13)_____ system. That explains why the shipment went to the wrong address.

☐ I'm very junior here. My job is to (14)_____ the (15)_____ system. I basically just have to put things away. I hope they can give me something more challenging soon.

☐ If we (16)_____ our (17)_____ system, it will help us to collect payment from the customers better.

☐ What (18)_____ do you normally use? You know, what do you want your system to do?

☐ The (19)_____ system is not very good at keeping control! It doesn't (20)_____ smoothly.

☐ Don't forget Monday we are having a (21)_____. You need to turn off your computer by 5:00 p.m. so that they can change the system. It's an inconvenience, but all the computers will work better together after the change. (22)_____ will be enhanced.

☐ The system doesn't (23)_____ open source code.

☐ The system (24)_____ a better level of security.

進階造句

請嘗試利用「搭配詞表」中的字彙，造出想要表達的句子。

_____

_____

_____

_____

target
[ˈtɑrgɪt]

可數名詞 目標

搭配在前面的動詞	搭配的形容詞	關鍵字
set		
meet	annual	
achieve	monthly	
reach	quarterly	**target**
be below	sales	
be above	revenue	
exceed		

好搭例句

◎ **MP3-99**

☐ My **annual sales** target for next year has been **set** very high. I don't think I will be able to reach it.
我明年的年度銷售目標被訂得非常高。我不認為我有辦法達到。

☐ It will be easy to **meet** my **monthly** target if I can make this sale.
假如我能做成這筆生意，要達成當月目標就很容易。

☐ We have managed to **achieve** our **annual revenue** target in the third quarter. Congratulations!
我們在第三季就設法達到了年度營收目標。恭喜！

☐ I **am** still **below** my **monthly sales** target. I need to work harder.
我還是低於我的當月銷售目標，我要更加努力才行。

☐ John is already **above** his **monthly sales** target. How does he do it?
約翰已經高於他的當月銷售目標。他是怎麼做到的？

☐ Our **revenue** target for this month has already been **exceeded**.
我們這個月的營收目標已經超過了。

請從「搭配詞表」中選出適當的字，完成下面句子。例解請見第333~353頁。

☐ My department head usually (1)_____ my (2)_____
target. If I can't (3)_____ it, if I don't make enough sales, then I
don't get a bonus.

☐ I managed to (4)_____ my (5)_____ target. It was
even better than the same period last year!

☐ My cash inflow this month is still (6)_____ target. I need to
encourage my team to generate more income.

☐ Last year my team worked very hard, and our cash inflow was
(7)_____ target. I gave them all a big bonus.

☐ Sales volume is good, so we have (8)_____ our
(9)_____ target, but because the spending of each customer is
too low, we have not been able to (10)_____ our
(11)_____ target.

進階造句

請嘗試利用「搭配詞表」中的字彙，造出想要表達的句子。

_____

_____

_____

_____

100	**trip** [trɪp]	可數名詞 （因事）外出，旅程	

搭配在前面的動詞		搭配的形容詞		關鍵字
have go on take make arrange organize plan	postpone cancel be away on come back (from ★) return (from ★) cut short	disastrous enjoyable long good short successful unsuccessful tiring	weekend day foreign overseas business	**trip** **(to 地點)**

★為關鍵字

好搭例句

◎ **MP3-100**

☐ Did you **have** a **good** trip?
你的旅程愉快嗎？

☐ I **had** a **successful business** trip last week.
我上星期的出差很成功。

☐ I love my job because I get to **go on** lots of **foreign business** trips.
我熱愛我的工作，因為我要常常去外國出差。

☐ Shall we **take** a **weekend** trip next week?
我們下星期要不要來趟週末之旅？

☐ I **made** a very **enjoyable** trip **to** Hong Kong last week.
我上星期非常開心地去了一趟香港。

☐ I'm **arranging** a **short** trip **to** Macau.
我正在安排去澳門的短期之旅。

☐ The company is **organizing** a trip **to** Tokyo.
公司正在籌備東京之旅。

☐ I'm **planning** an **overseas** trip.

我正在規劃海外之旅。

☐ We will have to **postpone** the trip. The weather is too bad.

我們必須延後旅程。天氣太差了。

☐ They **cancelled** the trip.

他們取消了旅程。

☐ He**'s away on** a trip at the moment. Can I take a message?

他目前外出不在。我能為您留個話嗎？

☐ I've just **come back from** an **unsuccessful business** trip.

我剛結束了不成功的出差回來。

☐ When I **got back from** my **tiring** trip, I was just exhausted!

當我結束疲憊的旅程回到家時，我簡直累翻了！

☐ He **cut short** the **long** trip because of problems back in the office.

他縮短了長途旅程，因為辦公室裡出了問題。

☐ Last year we **had** a **disastrous day** trip **to** Hualian.

去年我們的花蓮一日遊真慘。

填填看

請從「搭配詞表」中選出適當的字，完成下面句子。例解請見第333~353頁。

☐ Because of the typhoon they had to (1)_____ the trip

(2)_____ Hong Kong.

☐ I (3)_____ a (4)_____ trip at the moment. Please leave

a message and I'll call you when I (5)_____.

☐ I (6)_____ a very (7)_____ (8)_____ trip last

week. I didn't get the deal I wanted.

☐ We (9)_____ an (10)_____ (11)_____ trip next week. Just for two days, to Okinawa!

☐ I hate (12)_____ (13)_____ (14)_____ trips. I don't like flying all that way for just one day.

☐ The HR department is (15)_____ a trip to Taichung for us. I haven't decided if I am going to go yet.

☐ I (16)_____ a (17)_____ trip. My flight was delayed, and then I lost my luggage, and customs confiscated my laptop.

☐ It was quite an (18)_____ trip. Then, because of some emergency at the office, I had to (19)_____ the trip and come home three days early. It's a shame because I was having fun.

☐ It was a (20)_____ but (21)_____ trip. Hard work, but good results.

☐ It's just a (22)_____ trip (23)_____ the airport, about 20 minutes by taxi.

☐ It's quite a (24)_____ trip. You'd better take something to read with you in case you get bored.

進階造句

請嘗試利用「搭配詞表」中的字彙，造出想要表達的句子。

_____

_____

_____

 **ANSWERS**

1.

(1) place/put/take out; (2) full-page/half-page; (3) newspaper/magazine/print;
(4) TV/television/radio; (5) run/show; (6) TV/television; (7) make/produce;
(8) series; (9) make/produce; (10) new/TV/television/radio; (11) went out;
(12) run; (13) TV/television/newspaper/magazine/print/new; (14) show;
(15) TV/television/newspaper/magazine/print/new; (16) feature; (17) new;
(18) good; (19) misleading

2.

(1) use; (2) media; (3) create; (4) great; (5) direct; (6) increase; (7) media;
(8) local; (9) national; (10) get; (11) free

3.

(1) draft / draw up; (2) for; (3) include on / put on; (4) turn to the next item / go
through / stick to; (5) removed; (6) conference; (7) approved; (8) meeting;
(9) have; (10) draft

4.

(1) form/make/forge/create/establish; (2) broke off; (3) seeking;
(4) strong / mutually beneficial; (5) strategic

5.

(1) did/performed/undertook/carried out/conducted; (2) financial;
(3) did/performed/undertook/carried out/conducted; (4) preliminary/brief;
(5) do/perform/undertake/carry out/conduct; (6) further/more;
(7) do/perform/undertake/carry out/conduct;
(8) careful/detailed/in-depth/thorough/extensive; (9) financial; (10) Market;
(11) shows/suggests/reveals/confirms/demonstrates/indicates;
(12) Careful/Detailed/In-depth/Thorough/Extensive; (13) cost-benefit;
(14) shows/suggests/reveals/confirms/demonstrates/indicates;
(15) do/perform/undertake/carry out/conduct; (16) strategic;
(17) do/perform/undertake/carry out/conduct; (18) of

6.

(1) made/arranged; (2) confirm; (3) cancel; (4) change;
(5) important/pressing/urgent; (6) have; (7) got; (8) urgent/important; (9) keep;
(10) missing; (11) failed to keep / failed to turn up for; (12) with; (13) to

7.

(1) do/make/carry out/undertake; (2) comprehensive/detailed/careful;
(3) environmental/impact; (4) initial/rough/general; (5) is; (6) provide; (7) self;
(8) doing / carrying out; (9) annual; (10) tax; (11) undertaken/made/carried
out/done; (12) comprehensive/detailed/careful; (13) risk; (14) accurate;
(15) initial; (16) of; (17) suggests/shows

8.

(1) instructed/authorized; (2) bank account; (3) bank statements; (4) borrowed;
(5) from; (6) bank loan; (7) commercial/savings;
(8) big/large/major/private/foreign/overseas/international; (9) investment;
(10) negotiate with; (11) clearing/issuing; (12) bank transfer; (13) bank balance;
(14) underwrite; (15) lend; (16) bank card; (17) bank charges

9.

(1) owns/sells; (2) leading/major/well-known/popular; (3) luxury/up-market;
(4) brands; (5) buy; (6) luxury/up-market;
(7) launched/created/developed/established; (8) particular/proprietary;
(9) launched/created/developed/established; (10) mass-market;
(11) develop/establish/promote; (12) brand image; (13) sell/own/produce;
(14) leading/major; (15) promote/develop/establish; (16) brand loyalty;
(17) promote/develop/establish; (18) brand awareness

10.

(1) am on / have; (2) tight/shoestring/limited; (3) training; (4) cut/reduced;
(5) entertainment; (6) setting/preparing/allocating; (7) annual/departmental/
advertising/marketing/training/entertainment/production/R&D/IT; (8) approve;
(9) prepare; (10) manage/control / keep within; (11) allocating;
(12) annual/quarterly/half-yearly; (13) overspent/exceeded/ran out of/went over;
(14) cut/reduced; (15) runs into; (16) run out

11.

(1) doing/conducting; (2) business associates; (3) do/conduct; (4) attract;
(5) business confidence; (6) affecting; (7) discussed; (8) business cycle;
(9) affects / is bad for; (10) affects / is good for; (11) business strategy;
(12) business administration; (13) conduct; (14) day-to-day

12.

(1) run/manage/operate; (2) good/thriving/profitable/lucrative;
(3) business manager; (4) medium-sized; (5) run/manage/operate;
(6) business plan; (7) develop/expand/build;
(8) started/established/formed/founded; (9) business community; (10) small;
(11) business unit; (12) large; (13) business enterprises; (14) affect/impact

13.

(1) planning/organizing/coordinating; (2) new; (3) advertising/promotional/media;
(4) launch: (5) nationwide/national; (6) marketing; (7) initiate/start/begin;
(8) sales; (9) direct mail; (10) target / focus on; (11) public relations;
(12) targeted / focused on; (13) marketing/advertising/media/promotional;
(14) lasted/ran

14.

(1) raise/attract; (2) have; (3) working; (4) raise/attract; (5) venture/private;
(6) invest; (7) raising/attracting; (8) additional/further; (9) borrow; (10) share;
(11) repay; (12) borrow; (13) capital investment / capital expenditure;
(14) capital investment / capital expenditure; (15) capital markets;
(16) capital gains / capital appreciation; (17) capital outflow; (18) private capital;
(19) capital inflow; (20) need

15.

(1) use/pay; (2) cash discount; (3) take; (4) get/withdraw; (5) cash dispenser;
(6) get; (7) petty; (8) spare/surplus/extra; (9) cash flow;
(10) cash inflow / cash outflow; (11) cash inflow / cash outflow; (12) cash flow;
(13) raise/generate; (14) cash reserve; (15) cash cow; (16) cash injection;
(17) cash limit; (18) cash card

16.

(1) greatest/biggest; (2) are facing / are meeting;
(3) serious/major/real/considerable; (4) poses/presents;
(5) serious/major/real/considerable; (6) to; (7) resist/overcome;
(8) relish/welcome; (9) exciting; (10) face/meet; (11) new

17.

(1) make/introduce/implement / bring about;
(2) fundamental/sweeping/significant/profound; (3) proposed;
(4) make/implement/introduce; (5) seen; (6) drastic/radical; (7) bring about;
(8) structural/organizational; (9) to; (10) implement/make/introduce; (11) recent;
(12) caused / brought about; (13) manage / deal with; (14) rapid/sudden;
(15) slow/gradual; (16) resisting; (17) necessary; (18) see; (19) major;
(20) possible

18.

(1) client base; (2) corporate clients; (3) private clients; (4) get; (5) new;
(6) have; (7) existing; (8) help/assist; (9) advise; (10) meeting/visiting;
(11) prospective/potential; (12) major; (13) client service; (14) regular;
(15) client profile; (16) tell/inform/notify; (17) client reports;
(18) client relationship; (19) client list

19.

(1) formed/founded/started/established; (2) run/manage; (3) runs/manages;
(4) own; (5) small; (6) trading; (7) sells; (8) listed; (9) controlled/owned;
(10) supplies; (11) sister/subsidiary; (12) financial; (13) sister/subsidiary;
(14) insurance; (15) manufacturing; (16) manufactures/produces; (17) shipping;
(18) consultancy; (19) company spokesperson; (20) company policy;
(21) company logo; (22) huge; (23) state-owned; (24) energy/oil (25) privatize;
(26) joined; (27) medium sized; (28) local; (29) IT; (30) company car;
(31) company director; (32) multinational/international;
(33) company headquarters; (34) private/family; (35) public;
(36) pharmaceutical; (37) operates; (38) employs; (39) buy/acquire

20.

(1) is; (2) key/primary/central/greatest/main; (3) address; (4) raised;
(5) legitimate; (6) shares; (7) about; (8) have; (9) initial; (10) expressed;
(11) vital/serious; (12) important; (13) is; (14) main; (15) is

21.

(1) deliver/despatch/send/ship; (2) accompany; (3) collect; (4) whole/entire;
(5) of; (6) valuable; (7) track; (8) send/ship/despatch; (9) single/small;
(10) collect; (11) whole/entire; (12) large/huge; (13) single/small;
(14) delivered/shipped/sent; (15) huge/large; (16) of; (17) delay; (18) particular

22.

(1) negotiate; (2) draw up; (3) signs; (4) written/new;
(5) stipulates/states/specifies; (6) follow/fulfil/honour; (7) terminating/cancelling;
(8) break; (9) enforce/cancel/terminate; (10) awarded; (11) year; (12) fixed term;
(13) renew/win/secure; (14) covers/stipulates/states/specifies; (15) sign;
(16) expires / runs out; (17) renew; (18) open ended; (19) runs;
(20) terminates/cancels; (21) terms of the

23.

(1) tight/strict; (2) financial/budgetary/cost; (3) exercise/maintain; (4) strict/tight;
(5) quality/production; (6) implement/put in place/establish; (7) effective;
(8) production; (9) security

24.

(1) had/incurred/bore; (2) high/heavy; (3) extra/additional;
(4) reduce/cut/minimize; (5) running/fixed; (6) cost efficiency;
(7) cost cutting/cost reduction; (8) estimate/calculate;
(9) operating/running/production; (10) rise / go up; (11) administrative/labor;
(12) administrative/labor; (13) recover/cover/meet; (14) development; (15) total;
(16) include

25.

(1) give/extend; (2) credit risk; (3) credit crunch; (4) extend/give; (5) interest-free;
(6) get/obtain; (7) interest-free/unsecured; (8) credit agreement; (9) credit rating;
(10) get/obtain; (11) credit limit; (12) credit card; (13) refused; (14) unsecured

26.

(1) have; (2) overseas; (3) get/attract; (4) new; (5) keep/retain; (6) existing;
(7) customer care/customer support/customer service; (8) have;
(9) satisfied/loyal; (10) valued/loyal; (11) serve/satisfy; (12) corporate;
(13) Prospective/Potential; (14) lost; (15) major/private/overseas;
(16) customer complaint; (17) approach; (18) Customer satisfaction;
(19) customer base

27.

(1) collect/get/look at/analyze/examine; (2) supporting/additional;
(3) data base / data bank; (4) access/retrieve; (5) a piece of; (6) data field;
(7) collect/get; (8) detailed/precise/clear/accurate/comprehensive;
(9) operational; (10) data collection/data gathering/data storage;
(11) collecting/storing/recording/analyzing; (12) detailed/precise/clear/accurate;
(13) market; (14) data storage capacity; (15) customer;
(16) shows/reveals/indicates; (17) supporting/additional; (18) supports;
(19) analyzing/examining/looking at/processing; (20) raw; (21) data processing;
(22) data entry

28.

(1) make/strike/sign; (2) negotiating/finalizing/signing/concluding/completing;
(3) the terms of the; (4) got/secured; (5) great; (6) offer; (7) better; (8) offer;
(9) fair; (10) on; (11) made/signed/negotiated/concluded/completed/struck/
secured; (12) good; (13) with

29.

(1) shipment; (2) was caused by; (3) production; (4) arose/occurred; (5) causing;
(6) production; (7) avoid; (8) experiencing; (9) considerable/long/unnecessary;
(10) was; (11) slight; (12) cost; (13) avoid; (14) to; (15) make up (for)

30.

(1) take/accept; (2) of; (3) delivery address; (4) guarantee/ensure;
(5) timely/prompt; (6) delivery charge; (7) quick/speedy/fast/next-day;
(8) arrange; (9) special/registered; (10) early/quick/speedy/fast/prompt;
(11) make; (12) delivery schedule/delivery date; (13) delivery form

31.

(1) working in; (2) advertising/marketing; (3) managing; (4) legal;

(5) sales/service; (6) work with / cooperate with; (7) sales/service;

(8) department manager/department head; (9) personnel;

(10) move to / transfer to / work in (11) finance; (12) department meeting;

(13) joined; (14) working with / cooperating with; (15) R&D

(16) cooperate with / work with; (17) IT

32.

(1) encourage/promote/stimulate; (2) industrial/technological/economic;

(3) development plan / development program; (4) facilitate/support/assist;

(5) product; (6) employee; (7) Sustainable; (8) business (9) rapid/uneven;

(10) rapid/uneven; (11) recent/latest/new; (12) development project; (13) await;

(14) future/further; (15) software

33.

(1) am; (2) managing/group/company; (3) acting as; (4) non-executive; (5) am;

(6) marketing; (7) acting as; (8) advertising; (9) appoint; (10) R&D; (11) IT;

(12) deputy; (13) was promoted to / got promoted to; (14) assistant;

(15) meeting; (16) legal/financial; (17) legal/financial; (18) ask; (19) become;

(20) R&D; (21) become; (22) HR; (23) of; (24) IT

34.

(1) gave/offered; (2) %; (3) on; (4) offer/give;

(5) substantial/special/generous/big; (6) discount card / discount voucher;

(7) get/receive; (8) discount price; (9) ask for; (10) asked for; (11) of;

(12) offered/gave

35.

(1) manage; (2) global/world; (3) becoming;

(4) stimulate/boost/strengthen/revitalize; (5) shrinking/sluggish/unstable;

(6) local/domestic; (7) transforming/affecting; (8) regional; (9) damaging;

(10) developing; (11) developing; (12) continued to; (13) weak;

(14) grow/expand; (15) mixed; (16) remain (17) shrank; (18) by

36.

(1) assess/examine; (2) of; (3) on; (4) likely/possible;
(5) go into /come into / be in / take; (6) have/produce;
(7) positive/beneficial/desired; (8) on; (9) minimize; (10) cumulative/knock-on;
(11) produced/had;
(12) negative/devastating/adverse/detrimental/damaging/harmful;
(13) significant/dramatic/noticeable/profound; (14) short-term; (15) long-term;
(16) opposite; (17) similar; (18) immediate/direct

37.

(1) recruiting; (2) new/full-time/part-time/salaried/temporary;
(3) employee benefits; (4) inform; (5) existing; (6) recruit;
(7) new/full-time/part-time/salaried/temporary; (8) receive; (9) give/pay;
(10) key/good; (11) leaving; (12) employee turnover;
(13) dismiss / lay off / make redundant; (14) bad; (15) employee training;
(16) retain; (17) employee satisfaction; (18) employee management;
(19) firing/sacking; (20) motivate/encourage; (21) work; (22) earn;
(23) are entitled to; (24) train; (25) be responsible for; (26) transfer

38.

(1) got/gained; (2) valuable/relevant/practical; (3) in/of; (4) Previous/Past;
(5) shows/suggests; (6) don't have / lack; (7) practical/work; (8) offer/provide;
(9) share; (10) broaden; (11) don't have; (12) teaches

39.

(1) examine/consider; (2) identify; (3) key/important/major/significant/critical;
(4) is; (5) common; (6) in; (7) take into account;
(8) key/important/major/significant/critical; (9) combination of / number of;
(10) contributed to / caused / led to; (11) contributory/contributing;
(12) affecting/influencing; (13) deciding; (14) explains / lead to; (15) external;
(16) various

40.

(1) standard; (2) additional; (3) unique/distinguishing/distinctive; (4) common;
(5) include; (6) main/important/key; (7) include/show; (8) product; (9) of

41.

(1) arrived at / calculated/prepared; (2) see; (3) latest / first quarter / second quarter / third quarter / fourth quarter / half year / year end; (4) sales; (5) adjust; (6) released; (7) official; (8) see; (9) financial; (10) for; (11) compare; (12) sales; (13) trading; (14) Key; (15) performance; (16) show/suggest/reveal/indicate; (17) put 關鍵字 at; (18) put 關鍵字 at; (19) productivity; (20) quoted; (21) suggest/show/reveal/indicate/represent; (22) include; (23) look at

42.

(1) raise/obtain; (2) raise/obtain; (3) additional; (4) private; (5) arrange; (6) private; (7) Corporate; (8) personal; (9) corporate; (10) short-term; (11) long-term; (12) provide; (13) need

43.

(1) extra; (2) perform; (3) has/performs/provides; (4) basic/useful/extra (5) serves/fulfils/has/performs; (6) administrative; (7) exercise/serve/perform/have/fulfil; (8) control; (9) search; (10) audit; (11) primary/main/basic; (12) of

44

(1) had/achieved/saw/experienced; (2) rapid/quick; (3) showed/experienced; (4) slow; (5) steady; (6) achieve; (7) sustainable; (8) shown; (9) steady/continued/sustained; (10) stimulate/promote; (11) growth targets; (12) growth rate; (13) control; (14) short-term; (15) sustain; (16) long-term; (17) Growth forecasts; (18) has been; (19) in; (20) expect; (21) of

45.

(1) provide/give; (2) personal; (3) input/enter; (4) correct/relevant; (5) information system; (6) require; (7) further; (8) get/obtain; (9) classified; (10) giving/providing; (11) confidential; (12) divulge; (13) have; (14) background; (15) on/about; (16) Information management; (17) gathering/collecting; (18) storing; (19) access/retrieve; (20) information service; (21) received; (22) useful; (23) information processing; (24) information technology; (25) accurate/necessary; (26) available; (27) gave; (28) detailed; (29) inside; (30) withhold

46.

(1) made; (2) substantial/massive/major; (3) in; (4) need/require (5) private;
(6) recouped; (7) long-term; (8) investment opportunity; (9) attract/encourage;
(10) foreign; (11) protected; (12) sound; (13) investment strategy; (14) minimum;
(15) capital; (16) of; (17) initial; (18) increase; (19) Total; (20) direct;
(21) investment fund; (22) short-term; (23) long-term; (24) additional

47.

(1) give/issue; (2) send; (3) tax; (4) sales; (5) receive/get; (6) for;
(7) submit/send/give; (8) original; (9) process; (10) tax/VAT; (11) check;
(12) submit/send; (13) completing

48.

(1) examine/explore/consider/discuss/address; (2) controversial/contentious;
(3) identified/highlighted; (4) important/major/specific/key/fundamental;
(5) settled/decided; (6) raised; (7) of; (8) arose; (9) have; (10) real; (11) with;
(12) clarify; (13) are related to / relate to; (14) tackle; (15) confuse;
(16) complicated/confusing; (17) raising; (18) don't relate to / aren't related to;
(19) recurring; (20) involves; (21) underlying; (22) is

49.

(1) looking for; (2) job vacancies / job opportunities; (3) get/find; (4) do;
(5) great/good; (6) involves; (7) job satisfaction; (8) have; (9) well-paying;
(10) full-time; (11) part-time/temporary; (12) job prospects; (13) new;
(14) involves; (15) previous/last; (16) lost; (17) previous/last; (18) find/get;
(19) job security; (20) changing / looking for / losing; (21) quit; (22) required;
(23) job description; (24) job interview; (25) offer

50

(1) reached/attained/achieved; (2) high; (3) raised/increased; (4) of;
(5) maintain; (6) current/present; (7) reduce/lower; (8) low; (9) certain;
(10) determine; (11) basic; (12) provides; (13) acceptable; (14) of; (15) entry

51.

(1) suffered/made/incurred; (2) heavy / worse than expected / big;

(3) report/announce; (4) annual; (5) net; (6) of; (7) reduce; (8) quarterly;
(9) half-year; (10) estimated; (11) of; (12) suffered/made/incurred; (13) financial;
(14) make up / cover;

52.

(1) management team; (2) provided; (3) effective/efficient; (4) of; (5) provide;
(6) day-to-day/operational; (7) delegate; (8) provide; (9) management strategy;
(10) improve; (11) financial/resource; (12) Poor; (13) waste; (14) Mid-level;
(15) oversees; (16) Top/Senior; (17) provides; (18) overall;
(19) management structure; (20) management consultant; (21) simplify;
(22) prudent/careful; (23) risk; (24) improve; (25) management style;
(26) requires; (27) prudent/careful; (28) project; (29) personnel;
(30) management buy-out, (31) report to, (32) inform/tell

53.

(1) was appointed to / got promoted to / was promoted to / became; (2) senior/
general/regional/accounts/advertising/finance/HR/IT/legal/marketing/R&D/sales;
(3) inform / tell / report to; (4) appoint; (5) project; (6) ask; (7) line; (8) sales;
(9) acting as; (10) marketing;
(11) become / be appointed to / be promoted to / get promoted to;
(12) assistant; (13) HR/personnel; (14) HR/personnel; (15) work with

54.

(1) forcing/encouraging; (2) of; (3) enable; (4) produce/make;
(5) leading/largest/major; (6) use; (7) give

55.

(1) cornered/flooded/dominated; (2) domestic/local; (3) Market conditions;
(4) competitive/tough; (5) market analysis / market research;
(6) depressed/shrinking/declining; (7) created/established; (8) dominate;
(9) market leader; (10) overseas/foreign/international/export;
(11) important/large/major; (12) domestic/local; (13) over-regulated;
(14) create/establish; (15) open; (16) saturated; (17) Mass; (18) Niche;
(19) Market segmentation; (20) has collapsed; (21) market share;
(22) withdraw from; (23) enter / break into

56

(1) did/undertook/came up with; (2) successful/effective/good/imaginative;
(3) marketing plan / marketing strategy; (4) marketing tools / marketing activities;
(5) improve; (6) marketing activities; (7) marketing agency / marketing department;
(8) handle/manage/do/undertake; (9) Aggressive;
(10) marketing campaign / marketing strategy; (11) see;
(12) global/international/worldwide; (13) as; (14) marketing strategy

57.

(1) have / 've got; (2) arrange/schedule/call; (3) brief/emergency/urgent; (4) with;
(5) hold/call; (6) going to / attending / taking part in; (7) lunchtime/breakfast;
(8) about; (9) attend / take part in / go to; (10) departmental/team;
(11) call off / cancel / postpone; (12) board; (13) missed; (14) afternoon;
(15) chairing; (16) all-day; (17) about; (18) open; (19) regular

58.

(1) proposed; (2) of; (3) opposed; (4) approved; (5) proposed; (6) between;
(7) approved; (8) complete; (9) department; (10) considering; (11) possible;
(12) of; (13) announced; (14) company; (15) cancel; (16) planned; (17) consider;
(18) with

59.

(1) keep/take; (2) circulate; (3) of; (4) read through; (5) sign; (6) accept;
(7) rejected; (8) meeting; (9) read through; (10) accurate

60.

(1) holding / conducting / entering into; (2) to; (3) open/begin/start;
(4) handle/conduct/hold; (5) with; (6) about;
(7) protracted/lengthy/prolonged/intensive/detailed; (8) conclude/complete;
(9) resumed; (10) going well; (11) taking place; (12) involves; (13) going badly;
(14) broken down; (15) continuing

61.

(1) is down/is slow; (2) upgrading/improving; (3) be fast/be up;
(4) developing/building/installing; (5) client-server; (6) network topology;

(7) peer-to-peer; (8) expanding/extending; (9) local area; (10) links/connects;
(11) supports; (12) allows; (13) wireless local area; (14) manage/run/maintain;
(15) wide area; (16) manage/run/maintain; (17) network protocol; (18) provides;

62

(1) made; (2) generous; (3) have; (4) special; (5) considering;
(6) generous/conditional/initial; (7) received; (8) formal/firm; (9) accept;
(10) final/best; (11) reject/refuse (12) initial; (13) make; (14) better

63

(1) waiting for; (2) good/great/excellent; (3) find/grasp/seize/get;
(4) are on the look out for; (5) unique/rare; (6) to;
(7) grasp / seize / take advantage of / exploit; (8) wasted/missed; (9) take;
(10) to; (11) come across / had / found; (12) golden/perfect/unique;
(13) rare/unique; (14) take advantage of /exploit / grasp / seize; (15) lose/waste

64

(1) have; (2) number of; (3) to; (4) gave;
(5) considering/exploring/looking at/discussing; (6) various; (7) chose/took;
(8) best; (9) best; (10) alternative; (11) consider/look at/explore;
(12) realistic/viable; (13) limit

65

(1) sent/faxed/email/phoned; (2) large/big/bulk/purchase/urgent;
(3) process/despatch/ship; (4) order number; (5) cancel; (6) process;
(7) won/received; (8) big/large; (9) received; (10) for; (11) order form; (12) confirm;
(13) place; (14) minimum; (15) order book; (16) receive; (17) chase up

66

(1) make; (2) one off / down / lump sum; (3) spread(ing); (4) receive;
(5) prompt/cash; (6) make; (7) overtime/bonus; (8) remit/make; (9) prompt;
(10) of; (11) for; (12) to; (13) Cash/Late; (14) meet; (15) monthly; (16) interest;
(17) suspend/withhold/delay; (18) collect

67

(1) personnel department; (2) recruit/hire/employ; (3) technical/skilled/engineering;
(4) Personnel management/Personnel administration; (5) training; (6) retain;
(7) recruit/hire/employ; (8) junior; (9) service; (10) senior;
(11) administrative/executive; (12) manage; (13) sales; (14) authorized;
(15) personnel files; (16) have; (17) engineering/technical; (18) have;
(19) clerical; (20) legal; (21) executive

68

(1) consider/discuss; (2) important; (3) emphasize; (4) develop/clarify;
(5) general; (6) get to; (7) main/key; (8) make/raise; (9) controversial;
(10) agree with; (11) crucial/essential/fundamental; (12) stick to; (13) have;
(14) similar; (15) appreciate; (16) agree to differ on; (17) missed;
(18) make/raise; (19) difficult; (20) about

69

(1) explain/outline/state/clarify; (2) on; (3) assess/clarify; (4) current/present;
(5) accept / am aware of; (6) awkward/delicate/difficult/embarrassing; (7) put;
(8) in; (9) awkward/delicate/difficult/embarrassing; (10) explaining/outlining/stating;
(11) earlier/previous; (12) am in / find myself in;
(13) awkward/delicate/difficult/embarrassing

70

(1) making/giving/delivering; (2) presentation skill(s); (3) prepare;
(4) presentation handouts / presentation slides; (5) presentation;
(6) presentation package; (7) short/informal; (8) excellent/effective;
(9) make/deliver/give; (10) formal; (11) on; (12) practice; (13) attending/seeing;
(14) product

71

(1) paid; (2) good/fair/special; (3) raise/increase; (4) list; (5) cut/reduce/lower;
(6) unit; (7) price war; (8) set; (9) price sensitive; (10) give; (11) half;
(12) wholesale/retail; (13) wholesale/retail; (14) quoted; (15) high; (16) for;
(17) includes; (18) price freeze; (19) gone up /gone down / risen / fallen;
(20) agree on; (21) price list; (22) price hike

72

(1) real/main/basic/underlying/fundamental;

(2) solve / deal with / address / overcome / sort out / tackle; (3) identify/examine;

(4) solve / deal with / address / overcome / tackle;

(5) detected / come across / come up against / encountered / run into;

(6) unexpected/unforeseen; (7) serious/tricky/complex; (8) with;

(9) detected / come across / come up against / encountered / run into;

(10) related/minor; (11) cause/pose/present; (12) potential;

(13) recurring/common/familiar

73

(1) simple/straightforward; (2) for; (3) follow/use; (4) carrying out; (5) follow/use;

(6) correct/proper/normal; (7) introduce/adopt; (8) standard / standard operational;

(9) repeat; (10) simplify/streamline; (11) complaints; (12) develop/establish;

(13) documentation; (14) follow/use; (15) emergency

74

(1) creates demand for / promotes / markets; (2) advertising; (3) sells;

(4) distribute; (5) skincare/household/consumer/branded; (6) buy/use;

(7) launched/introduced; (8) produce/manufacture/sell; (9) defective;

(10) sell/produce/manufacture; (11) natural; (12) developed/launched/introduced;

(13) innovative; (14) software; (15) produces/manufactures;

(16) industrial/agricultural; (17) endorse; (18) product category;

(19) product ranges; (20) product lines; (21) product development;

(22) product information

75

(1) production unit; (2) production team; (3) production manager;

(4) production line / production process; (5) begin/commence;

(6) increase/boost/double/triple/stimulate; (7) production schedule;

(8) boost/stimulate/ increase; (9) production capacity;

(10) boost/increase/stimulate/double/treble; (11) production capability;

(12) cut/stop/cease/discontinue; (13) delay; (14) of; (15) maintain;

(16) smooth/full; (17) Production costs

76

(1) made/earned/generated/produced/saw; (2) great / good / better than expected;
(3) Profit growth; (4) announced/reported; (5) annual; (6) pre-tax/operating;
(7) profit forecast; (8) increase/maximize; (9) profit margin; (10) showing;
(11) made/earned/generated/produced/saw; (12) of; (13) seeing;
(14) lower than expected; (15) Interim;
(16) lower than expected / falling / decreasing / shrinking; (17) Taxable;
(18) half year; (19) quarterly; (20) net; (21) rising/increasing/growing;
(22) profit share; (23) stabilized; (24) remained steady

77

(1) writing/developing/designing; (2) word processing; (3) run; (4) spreadsheet;
(5) software/computer (6) runs; (7) offers/provides; (8) allows; (9) installing;
(10) email; (11) test; (12) program designer; (13) shareware; (14) program code;
(15) runs on; (16) program documentation; (17) install; (18) anti-spyware

78

(1) planning; (2) new; (3) project proposal; (4) approves; (5) completed
(6) project team; (7) project coordinator / project leader / project manager;
(8) project management; (9) managing/running/coordinating; (10) major;
(11) launch; (12) R&D; (13) implement; (14) project finance; (15) pilot;
(16) approved; (17) joint; (18) project status; (19) project status report

79

(1) writing / drafting / putting together; (2) concrete/detailed; (3) concerning/for;
(4) made / submitted / outlined/ put forward; (5) a set of / a number of;
(6) consider/discuss; (7) viable/practical; (8) controversial; (9) involve;
(10) support/approve/back; (11) come up with; (12) excellent; (13) preliminary;
(14) block/oppose/reject; (15) include; (16) involve; (17) read

80

(1) for; (2) look/are; (3) better/brighter; (4) have; (5) excellent/good/exciting;
(6) financial; (7) economic; (8) looking; (9) poor/gloomy/limited;
(10) enhance/improve; (11) short-term; (12) damaged; (13) growth/long-term;
(14) assess; (15) market

81

(1) put; (2) to; (3) about; (4) had/asked;

(5) pointed/probing/searching/difficult/tricky/direct;

(6) answer / respond to / reply to; (7) answered / responded to / replied to;

(8) pointed/probing/searching/difficult/tricky/direct; (9) evade; (10) avoid/ignore;

(11) is; (12) relevant/good; (13) simple; (14) personal; (15) embarrassing;

(16) stupid;

82

(1) consider / discuss / examine / deal with / go into / look into;

(2) crucial/fundamental; (3) of; (4) avoiding/ignoring; (5) complex/difficult;

(6) tackling/settling; (7) consider / discuss / examine / deal with / go into / look into;

(8) immediate; (9) consider / discuss / examine / deal with / go into / look into / tackle / settle; (10) raised; (11) of; (12) real

83

(1) made / submitted / put forward / offered / come up with;

(2) strong/firm/far- reaching/important; (3) for; (4) consider;

(5) follow / carry out / implement / adopt / accept; (6) involve; (7) reviewing;

(8) draft; (9) clear/detailed; (10) to; (11) involve; (12) oppose/reject;

(13) general/main; (14) includes; (15) is in line with; (16) official; (17) is;

(18) involves/includes

84

(1) write/prepare; (2) quarterly; (3) status/progress; (4) showing; (5) read;

(6) press; (7) submitting/presenting/giving;

(8) complete/comprehensive/full/detailed; (9) on; (10) issued; (11) initial/interim;

(12) received/read; (13) annual; (14) credit/audit; (15) shows/says/states;

(16) final; (17) concluded; (18) recommended/suggested;

(19) recommends/suggests

85

(1) carry out / do / conduct / undertake; (2) background/market; (3) Consumer;

(4) carried out / did / conducted / undertook; (5) background/market;

(6) Quantitative; (7) Qualitative; (8) detailed/extensive/previous/recent;

(9) market/consumer; (10) shows/suggests/indicates/demonstrates;
(11) Further; (12) into; (13) show/suggest/indicate/demonstrate

86

(1) yield/produce/achieve/earn; (2) expected; (3) of; (4) on; (5) get/achieve;
(6) better/high; (7) on; (8) Annual/Maximum; (9) tax free; (10) maximize;
(11) financial; (12) guaranteed; (13) of

87

(1) ran; (2) high/great/serious/real; (3) increase/run; (4) of; (5) is not worth the;
(6) to; (7) risk factor; (8) increase/run; (9) minimize; (10) potential;
(11) low/minimal; (12) risk assessment; (13) reduce; (14) poses;
(15) serious/real/great/high; (16) involves; (17) real/serious; (18) avoid;
(19) unnecessary; (20) risk rating; (21) risk management; (22) assess

88

(1) got/received/earned; (2) annual; (3) net; (4) of; (5) start at / be at; (6) salary cut;
(7) salary scale; (8) offer/pay; (9) basic; (10) monthly; (11) of; (12) includes;
(13) draw; (14) Current/Average; (15) are not commensurate with;
(16) salary review; (17) increase; (18) review; (19) salary raise;
(20) got/received/earned; (21) good; (22) gross; (23) cut

89

(1) annual/retail/direct/overseas/domestic; (2) risen/grown/increased/soared;
(3) reached/totalled; (4) sales promotion; (5) boost/increase; (6) handle;
(7) sales tax; (8) annual; (9) sales volume; (10) sales rep; (11) sales pitch;
(12) sales forecast; (13) falling/decreasing; (14) went through / went ahead

90

(1) be of; (2) service representatives; (3) provide/offer/deliver; (4) year; (5) free;
(6) advisory/consultation; (7) service agreement / service contract;
(8) service charge; (9) delivery / maintenance / after sales / support;
(10) delivery / maintenance / after sales / support; (11) used; (12) online;
(13) advisory/consultancy; (14) confidential; (15) excellent/great;
(16) professional; (17) customer/client; (18) service center; (19) require;
(20) limited; (21) financial;

91

(1) improving/resolving; (2) similar; (3) handle; (4) reviewing/describing;
(5) current/present; (6) economic; (7) clarify/describe; (8) complicated/difficult;
(9) assess; (10) improve/resolve; (11) different; (12) market; (13) financial;
(14) ideal; (15) political; (16) changing/developing/worsening/deteriorating;
(17) financial; (18) improve; (19) complicated/difficult; (20) occurred/arisen;
(21) brief her on; (22) background

92

(1) have; (2) necessary/basic; (3) develop / work on; (4) time management;
(5) developed/learned; (6) administrative/management/organizational;
(7) develop / work on; (8) people/interpersonal/leadership; (9) use/exercise;
(10) considerable; (11) technical; (12) advanced; (13) presentation/communication;
(14) requires; (15) new; (16) set of; (17) lacks; (18) negotiating

93

(1) arrive at / come up with / find / hit upon; (2) clever/neat/simple/feasible/viable;
(3) agree on / adopt; (4) prompt/quick/temporary; (5) work out / look for / produce;
(6) lasting/permanent; (7) practical/feasible/realistic/sensible/viable/acceptable;
(8) adopt / agree on; (9) obvious/possible; (10) easy/effective; (11) implement;
(12) drastic; (13) reject; (14) implement / adopt / agree on;
(15) propose / put forward / provide / come up with

94

(1) has/employs; (2) full-time/permanent; (3) senior; (4) staff member;
(5) recruiting/hiring/employing/appointing; (6) additional; (7) staff recruitment;
(8) retain; (9) engineering/technical; (10) a staff of; (11) staff members;
(12) train; (13) administrative/clerical; (14) member of; (15) staff training;
(16) appoint; (17) experienced; (18) member of; (19) encourage/motivate/enable;
(20) sales; (21) enable; (22) support; (23) staff management; (24) support;
(25) small; (26) don't have; (27) legal/executive; (28) legal/executive;
(29) have/employ; (30) temporary/part- time; (31) temporary/part-time

95

(1) develop / devise / prepare / map out / plan; (2) implement/execute;
(3) marketing; (4) outline; (5) sales/marketing; (6) suggest/propose/recommend;
(7) financial/investment; (8) for;
(9) developing / devising / preparing / mapping out / planning; (10) regional;
(11) business/corporate; (12) developed / devised / prepared / mapped out / planned;
(13) long-term; (14) to; (15) viable; (16) PR; (17) detailed/new; (18) involves;
(19) right; (20) short-term; (21) to; (22) employ/use

96

(1) have; (2) for/regarding; (3) make / offer / put forward; (4) involves;
(5) excellent/ constructive/practical/sensible; (6) act on; (7) look at / consider;
(8) take up; (9) take you up on; (10) involve; (11) came up with; (12) tentative;
(13) dismissed; (14) impractical; (15) welcome; (16) for/regarding;
(17) include/involve

97

(1) pay; (2) switch/change; (3) reliable/dependable; (4) find; (5) local;
(6) alternative; (7) of; (8) main; (9) major/largest/leading; (10) choose/find;
(11) new; (12) service; (13) current

98

(1) install/adopt/introduce/implement/establish; (2) ICT; (3) operating;
(4) system utilities / system extensions; (5) system functions;
(6) creating/devising/developing/building/establishing; (7) inventory;
(8) allow/enable; (9) creating/devising/developing/building/establishing;
(10) information; (11) provide/offer; (12) enter; (13) delivery;
(14) manage/maintain; (15) filing; (16) upgrade/improve; (17) billing;
(18) system functions; (19) control; (20) work/operate/run; (21) system change;
(22) System integration; (23) use/support; (24) provides/offers

99

(1) sets; (2) sales; (3) meet/achieve/reach; (4) exceed;
(5) annual/monthly/quarterly; (6) below; (7) above; (8) achieved/reached/met;
(9) sales; (10) meet/achieve/reach; (11) revenue

100

(1) cancel/postpone; (2) to; (3) am away on; (4) business; (5) come back / return; (6) had; (7) unsuccessful; (8) business; (9) are going on / are making / are taking; (10) overseas; (11) weekend; (12) going on/making/taking; (13) foreign/overseas; (14) day; (15) organizing/planning/arranging; (16) had; (17) disastrous; (18) enjoyable; (19) cut short; (20) good/successful/tiring; (21) good/successful/tiring; (22) short; (23) to; (24) long

國家圖書館出版品預行編目資料

職場單字進化術 / Quentin Brand 作；戴至中譯. －－ 初版. －－
臺北市：貝塔出版: 智勝文化發行, 2010. 02
　　面； 公分
　ISBN 978-957-729-774-7（平裝附光碟片）

　1. 商業英文　2. 詞彙

805.12　　　　　　　　　　　　　　　　　　　99000547

職場單字進化術

作　　者 / Quentin Brand
翻　　譯 / 戴至中
執行編輯 / 朱慧瑛

出　　版 / 貝塔出版有限公司
地　　址 / 台北市 100 館前路 12 號 11 樓
電　　話 / (02) 2314-2525
傳　　真 / (02) 2312-3535
客服專線 / (02) 2314-3535
客服信箱 / btservice@betamedia.com.tw
郵撥帳號 / 19493777
帳戶名稱 / 貝塔出版有限公司

總 經 銷 / 時報文化出版企業股份有限公司
地　　址 / 桃園縣龜山鄉萬壽路二段 351 號
電　　話 / (02) 2306-6842

出版日期 / 2010 年 02 月初版一刷
定　　價 / 360 元
ISBN ： 978-957-729-774-7

職場單字進化術
Copyright 2010 by Quentin Brand
Published by Beta Multimedia Publishing

貝塔網址：www.betamedia.com.tw

喚醒你的英文語感 ！

對折後釘好，直接寄回即可！

| 廣　告　回　信 |
| 北區郵政管理局登記證 |
| 北 台 字 第 1 4 2 5 6 號 |
| 免　貼　郵　票 |

100 台北市中正區館前路12號11樓

貝塔語言出版 收
Beta Multimedia Publishing

寄件者住址

貝塔語言出版
Beta Multimedia Publishing

讀者服務專線（02）2314-3535　　讀者服務傳真（02）2312-353
客戶服務信箱　btservice@betamedia.com.tw

www.betamedia.com.tw

謝謝您購買本書！！

貝塔語言擁有最優良之英文學習書籍，為提供您最佳的英語學習資訊，您可填妥此表後寄回（免貼郵票）將可不定期收到本公司最新發行書訊及活動訊息！

姓名：_____　性別：□男 □女　生日：_____年_____月_____日

電話：(公)_____(宅)_____(手機)_____

電子信箱：_____

學歷：□高中職含以下 □專科 □大學 □研究所含以上

職業：□金融 □服務 □傳播 □製造 □資訊 □軍公教 □出版
　　　□自由 □教育 □學生 □其他

職級：□企業負責人 □高階主管 □中階主管 □職員 □專業人士

1. 您購買的書籍是？_____

2. 您從何處得知本產品？(可複選)

　　　□書店 □網路 □書展 □校園活動 □廣告信函 □他人推薦 □新聞報導 □其他

3. 您覺得本產品價格：

　　　□偏高 □合理 □偏低

4. 請問目前您每週花了多少時間學英語？

　　　□ 不到十分鐘 □ 十分鐘以上，但不到半小時 □ 半小時以上，但不到一小時

　　　□ 一小時以上，但不到兩小時 □ 兩個小時以上 □ 不一定

5. 通常在選擇語言學習書時，哪些因素是您會考慮的？

　　　□ 封面 □ 內容、實用性 □ 品牌 □ 媒體、朋友推薦 □ 價格 □ 其他_____

6. 市面上您最需要的語言書種類為？

　　　□ 聽力 □ 閱讀 □ 文法 □ 口說 □ 寫作 □ 其他_____

7. 通常您會透過何種方式選購語言學習書籍？

　　　□ 書店門市 □ 網路書店 □ 郵購 □ 直接找出版社 □ 學校或公司團購
　　　□ 其他_____

8. 給我們的建議：_____

_____

喚醒你的英文語感！

Get a Feel for English !